The

LAST TALE

of the

FLOWER
BRIDE

Also by Roshani Chokshi

THE GILDED WOLVES SERIES

The Gilded Wolves
The Silvered Serpents
The Bronzed Beasts

The

LAST TALE

of the

FLOWER
BRIDE

ROSHANI CHOKSHI

HODDER &
STOUGHTON

First published in Great Britain in 2023 by Hodder & Stoughton
An Hachette UK company

1

A CIP catalogue record for this title is
available from the British Library

Hardback ISBN 978 1 529 38404 8
Trade Paperback ISBN 978 1 529 38405 5
eBook ISBN 978 1 529 38406 2

Printed and bound in Great Britain by Clays Ltd, Elcograf S.p.A.

Hodder & Stoughton policy is to use papers that are
natural, renewable and recyclable products and made
from wood grown in sustainable forests. The logging and
manufacturing processes are expected to conform to the
environmental regulations of the country of origin.

Hodder & Stoughton Ltd
Carmelite House
50 Victoria Embankment
London EC4Y 0DZ

www.hodder.co.uk

For Aman, whom I would wear out iron shoes for, and for Niv,
whose friendship is the rarest form of magic

MYTHS ARE BUT LIES BREATHED THROUGH SILVER.

—C. S. Lewis

PROLOGUE

You warned me that knowing your secret would destroy us.

At first, it sat in our marriage like a blue-lipped ghost, hardly noticeable until a trick of the light drew it into focus. But you could always tell the days when it gnawed at my thoughts. You tried to comfort me. You stroked my face and curled my fingers to your heart.

You said: "If you pry, you'll destroy our marriage."

But oh, my love, you lied.

Chapter One

THE BRIDEGROOM

Once upon a time, Indigo Maxwell-Casteñada found me.

I had been lost a long time and had grown comfortable in the dark. I didn't imagine anyone could lure me from it. But Indigo was one of those creatures that can hunt by scent alone, and the reek of my desperate wanting must have left a tantalizing, fluorescent trail.

Before Indigo, I avoided places where money served as pageantry rather than payment. I clung to the opinion that they were loud and crass, the shabby but sturdy armor of a poor man. In those days, I was poor. But I had become rich in expertise, and it was in this capacity that I served as a visiting curator to *L'Éxposition Des Femmes Monstrueuses.* The exhibit had brought me to Paris on someone else's dime and, eventually, to the Hôtel de Casteñada.

Once one of the royal apartments of Louis XIV and Marie Antoinette, the Hôtel de Casteñada now ranked among the finest hotels in the world. The vaulted ceiling, a restoration of the original, I was told, still showed indifferent, muscular gods reclining amidst gold-bellied clouds. Ivy lined the walls, through which the snarling faces of stone satyrs peered and panted at the guests.

It was common knowledge that each of the Casteñada hotels centered on a fairy-tale motif. I gathered this one was an homage to Gabrielle-Suzanne Barbot de Villeneuve's *La Belle et la Bête*— Beauty and the Beast—and while I hated to admit it, something about it seemed not of this world. It was so lovely I could almost ignore the crowd of models and DJs, red-faced businessmen and whatever other brilliantly arrayed and ostensibly vapid creatures such beautiful places attracted.

"Sir?" A slim, dark-skinned waitress appeared at my side. This was the second time she'd stopped by my table. I had chosen one near the back of the room so I might keep an eye on the entrance. "Are you sure I cannot get you anything?"

I glanced at the menu beside the haphazard collection of notes I'd prepared for the evening. The cocktails started at fifty euros. I smiled at the waitress, raised my half-filled glass of water, and then tapped the empty dish of complimentary spiced nuts.

"Perhaps another of these?" I asked. "My guest must be running late."

The waitress managed a brittle smile and walked away without another word. She probably thought I was lying about meeting someone. Even I couldn't quite believe my intended guest would deign to meet with me.

After months of searching for the whereabouts of a thirteenth-century grimoire, I had traced it to the private collection of the Casteñada family. Initially, my requests to view the piece had gone unanswered. This was not surprising. I was well known only in academic circles as a Middle Ages historian with an interest in the preservation of incunabula. I had nothing to lose but time. So I wrote letter after letter, stood for hours as the fax machine spit them out into offices around the world. I lost a tiny fortune in long-distance phone calls until, finally, I received a message one week before I flew to Paris.

> *You may meet me at the hotel on the 7th of November.*
> *8 o'clock.*
>
> > *—I.M.C.*

I.M.C. Indigo Maxwell-Casteñada. The heir of the Casteñada fortune.

I knew nothing about him, and I preferred it that way. I have never understood this preoccupation with the rich and famous and how they spend their existence. All that naked yearning for their lives, the hushed surprise over the coincidence of a shared birthday . . . I preferred different fantasies.

I checked my watch: 8:45 P.M.

Perhaps he'd forgotten our meeting? Or maybe he was already here and simply wrapping up a previous engagement?

Across the room, I felt a pair of eyes on me. Twenty feet away sat a couple in an isolated booth that resembled a golden birdcage. The man caught me looking and grinned.

"A diamond martini for the lady!" he shouted, snapping his fingers.

The man had a mop of yellow hair, a head too heavy for his neck. He bore a distinct resemblance to a melting candle. Beside him sat a woman as voluptuous as a temple carving.

The bartender approached their booth, pushing a glass cart of cocktail accoutrements, and immediately set about measuring, pouring, shaking. He was followed close behind by a sharply dressed dark-skinned man carrying a velvet box. A jeweler. The man opened the box, revealing an assortment of diamonds.

"Pick," said the yellow-haired man to the woman. "The

diamond is yours."

The woman pointed one pale finger to the brightest, largest carat. The bartender held out a frosted martini glass for the jeweler. He dropped in her chosen diamond, and it sank like a fallen star.

"À votre santé," said the jeweler as the bartender departed with the rattling cart.

The woman, still grinning, lifted her fingers as if she might pluck out the jewel. The old man beside her grabbed her wrist—

"I said the diamond was yours. I didn't say you could take it out of the fucking glass."

The woman appeared stung. She looked from the glass to the man, her eyes narrowing.

"I'm fucking serious," he said, even as he laughed. "If you want it so badly, you can find it in tomorrow's filth."

The woman was clearly disgusted. For a moment, I thought she might throw the drink in his face. Across the room, our eyes met. She drained the glass in one go, diamond and all. And then lifted her chin in defiance, her gaze full of ugly recognition: *You are starving prey. Just like me.*

I hid it well, but she was right: I was always hungry. A single moment of either madness or mystery had shaped my life. Ever since, I have sought proof of the impossible and bent my whole life around the feeding of it.

I fanned out the pages on the marble table, studying my notes for next week's speech on the myth of Melusine. The print before me showed Melusine with tangled, waist-length hair, bat wings, and a coiling, serpent tail. Her hands were clasped in demure horror, as if she were clinging to some last vestige of genteel shock before she could abandon her husband for his betrayal.

Melusine had been made famous in Jean d'Arras's

fourteenth-century writing. Depending on the source material, she was something of a mermaid or a siren. One day, a nobleman came across her in a forest glade and begged her to be his wife. She agreed on the condition that he never spy on her while she bathed. The nobleman agreed, and for a time they were happy. But eventually, curiosity overwhelmed him and, one day, he spied on her as she bathed, saw her true nature, and lost her forever.

I have always been intrigued by these not-quite women, whether they were sirens or mermaids, kinnari or selkie. The world can't seem to decide whether to condemn, covet, or celebrate them. They're damned as reminders of lust, and yet the House of Luxembourg enthusiastically claimed descent from Melusine's unnatural bloodline, and inside an eleventh-century church in Durham Castle there lived a mermaid carved in stone. Hundreds of years ago, perhaps some pagan entering a church to escape the cold would have seen that carving as a message. A password, of sorts, that even in this strange place and strange religion lay something familiar . . .

Even if she is a devil.

"Sir?"

I looked up, ready to admit defeat to the waitress and leave when I saw that she was holding a platter with two drinks. She held out an envelope: "A gift from another guest."

The two drinks looked identical: a rich amber whiskey with a perfectly clear sphere of ice. I opened the letter.

The drink on the left will fill your belly for the rest of your days, but you will only be able to speak truths.

The drink on your right will leave you hungrier than before, but it will polish every lie that leaves your tongue.

I looked around the room; a strange tingling worked its way up from the base of my skull. Even before I reached for the glass on the right, I imagined that magic liquid gilding my tongue. I drank. The whiskey tasted like a hot knife, burnt and metallic.

Seconds later, I heard the softest laugh. I turned in my seat, and that was when I first laid eyes on Indigo Maxwell-Casteñada. Not a man at all, but a woman.

She leaned against the wall, hardly ten feet from me, wearing a column dress of shirred navy silk that looked as if it had been poured onto her body. Sapphires winked at her throat and ears. Silver flashed on her wrists.

She moved lightly. I want to say that it was gentle and serene, like a fawn through snow. But Indigo's grace was restrained, calculated, as if she knew that people like her could stomp the world into submission and she had no wish to bruise it further.

At first glance, Indigo was attractive. She did not become striking until one looked closer, noticed the way she held herself, or rather, how the light held her. As if she were something precious. Her skin was richly bronzed, her eyes large and dark, nose lightly snubbed, and her lips had a curious fullness—the bottom lip not quite as ripe as the top. This asymmetry transfixed me.

She made her way to my table, sank into the chair opposite me, and announced: "I am Indigo and *you* chose to go hungry." Her voice was low and rich. I had the deliciously absurd thought that each syllable was steeped in onyx and chords of music. "Why?"

"Between the two choices, I may not be able to live long without food, but I don't have a life worth living without the other."

She smiled.

Some individuals are like portals, the knowing of them makes the world a far vaster place. In Indigo's presence my world widened. Brightened. There was something about her that made the eye linger. It wasn't her beauty; it was the way she seemed superimposed on the room. A mirage that might vanish if I looked away.

"What do you recommend I drink?" she asked.

This ease, this exchange of nonsense with Indigo Maxwell-Casteñada, could not possibly be real. Thus it was from a place of disbelief that I spoke in whimsy.

"I was hoping they might serve us something less human," I said. "Ambrosia, if they have it."

"Is it hard to come by?"

"A little. The ancient Hindus believe it resides in an ocean of cosmic milk."

"The sea is too far," said Indigo with a melodic sigh I could feel on my skin. "Maybe liquid gold? Or is that unappetizing?"

"Diane de Poitiers, a famous mistress of Henry II no less, drank gold to preserve her youth."

"Did it work?"

"Supposedly she died of it, which is to say, she didn't get any older."

Indigo laughed. I caught her perfume. I thought she'd smell of amber and night-blooming jasmine, but she was adolescently sweet with the sort of synthetic, sugary green apple fragrance I associated with high school girls. On Indigo, it was like cover-up, a wolf rubbing sheep's fat into its fur as camouflage.

She snapped her fingers and a waiter appeared, bearing two glasses of Champagne.

"To hope," said Indigo, clinking her glass to mine. "And to all the beautiful ways in which we can forget its fatality."

After a sip, she eyed me over the rim of her flute. "Are you not starved for something?"

That famished chamber of myself shivered. "I'm always starved."

"Good," said Indigo.

Platters of food began to arrive: tins of caviar in silver bowls filled with ice; quail braised in pomegranate molasses and wine; a rack of lamb so succulent the meat slid off the bone without protest.

Indigo made no mention of my request to see the grimoire from her private collection. Instead, she began by asking what I thought the eternal would taste like, which season I would want to live in for a decade and why. If I tried to speak about my life, her smile dropped. If I spoke about current events, she'd turn her head. About an hour or so into our meal, I grew too curious.

"It seems that I'm offending you every time I bring up reality," I said.

"Reality?" she repeated, with a touch of scorn. "Reality is what you make of your surroundings. And the world outside my own cannot touch me." There was a note of sadness when she said this, as if she were a ghost and her hands now passed through things once reached for with ease.

"I know you feel the same way," she said in that smoked voice. "I've looked you up, Professor. I've even read your books."

The thought of Indigo trailing her elegant finger across one of my sentences made me feel exposed. She had not laid a hand on me, but I already knew the texture of her skin.

"You're fascinated with the world we cannot see, the creatures that might have lived within them but now only exist as fairy tales. I suppose that's why I wished to meet you." A shy softness flitted across her face. She hesitated, her full lips jutting into a pout before she continued. "You see, I wish to live a certain way, and I'm interviewing companions for that life."

Whenever I think of our first meeting, I am reminded that the word "seduction" comes from *seducer*, to draw aside. But Indigo did not draw me aside so much as she drew aside the world I had always lived in and showed me a way of living a world apart.

She saw straight to my naked hunger and smiled. Her chair scraped back as she leaned across the table. The flames danced; candlelight gilded her skin. She became a question, and the answer she saw on my face made her close the space between us and kiss me.

In her kiss lay wonders—the humming of firefly wings and the secret of alchemy. On her tongue was the ghost of roasted plums, forgotten poems. I was so entranced that I almost didn't notice when she bit down. When I pulled back, her teeth looked rusty.

And only then did I realize she'd drawn blood.

Chapter Two

THE BRIDEGROOM

I was convinced Indigo would leave the moment I ceased to entertain her. I could already picture my midnight walk back to the cheap student housing in the Latin Quarter. I'd probably wait a whole day beside the landline and never see or hear from her again. I would never be able to talk—much less gloat—about the encounter. No one would believe me.

That might drive another man insane, but I'd had more than twenty years to make peace with the lightless space between what you cannot believe is a truth and what you know must be a lie.

Here was one: I had a brother once.

Even now, I could conjure the smell of blown-out birthday candles, the rough cotton of my mother's dress pulling tight over her belly. That was the day she told me she was growing a friend for me.

As a child, I liked this idea so much I tried to grow other friends so my brother and I would never be lonely. I planted sneakers, a book, and a whistle. In time, I figured they would become a warrior, a storyteller, and a musician.

When my brother was born, my mother taught me how to

support his head when I held him. I marveled at the warm weight of it, the swirl of hair so fine it looked etched. He smelled like milk and dust.

"He's yours now," my mother said in her soft, rose-petal voice.

I grew taller that day. Or maybe it was that my soul shot up in size, trying to make enough room to hold him within it.

Growing up together provided endless adventure. There were quests through the woods, playtime as pirates, hide-and-seek with our father pretending not to see us under the bed. One birthday, my mother gave me a book of fairy tales. That was when I first learned about thresholds, places where the mortal world thinned into the realm of Faerie. They could look like anything: A door in a graffiti-covered alley, a dark shadow beneath an apple tree. An ordinary closet.

I used to take that book with me everywhere. Sometimes, I even hid in the great cedar armoire at the end of our hallway to read it. I liked crouching on the warm wood with a flashlight in my lap, the sleeves of winter coats resting on my shoulders like tame birds. Best of all, I liked seeing what was lost—and could be discovered—in the belly of the armoire. Misplaced hats, pennies, the left hands of gloves, the occasional key.

I lost something there, too, though I could never be sure what it was.

One day, when I was seven years old, I saw that the armoire doors had been left open. I called for my brother, thinking he must be inside waiting for me. He often crawled into the armoire and sat by my feet while I read him a story by flashlight. We loved to pretend that the smooth wall of the closet was secretly a door to Faerie.

I called for him over and over. Finally, I went to the kitchen to ask my mother where he had gone.

She blinked at me. "Sweetheart, what do you mean? You don't have a brother."

I didn't believe her at first. I looked for his clothes, his toys. I hunted for his smudgy handprints on the wall from when he had gotten into the jam jar, the notch on the doorframe when he begged to see how tall he was growing. Everything was gone.

I had no choice but to believe my mother. Now, though, as the years have softened my memories, there are days when I cannot decide whether this is a truth I cannot accept, or a lie I cannot let go of.

My brother's absence, real or imagined, lived inside me. Because of him, I became obsessed with finding proof of the impossible. I shrouded this search in the semi-respectability of comparative mythology and folklore, but that need drove me all the same.

Until Indigo, I was lost in that search, hidden in my own thoughts. But she saw something in me. Something that turned her kiss into a knife that cut me free from the dark.

IN FAIRY TALES, A KISS MARKS A THRESHOLD—BETWEEN THE state of being cursed or cured lies a kiss. But not all kisses cure; some kill. Thresholds go both ways, after all. I wasn't thinking about this when Indigo drew me to her beneath the chandeliers of her Paris hotel. At the time, I wished only to trap her laughter under glass. I could not hear, back then, how uncannily triumphant the sound was.

Indigo pulled back from our kiss and reclined in her chair. The glittering world of the Casteñada bar intruded once again. Everything about this place now offended the senses, from the electronic lounge music to the fused smell of cigarettes and cologne.

Indigo stood to leave, and I braced myself to be abandoned. She reached into her slim black purse and withdrew a single key.

"Follow me," she said.

As if I could do anything else.

I followed her past the gleaming bar, the velvet chairs, the chandeliers glinting overhead and into the main hallway of the hotel. It was cool and empty. Everything was vaulted ceilings and milky marble, which stood in contrast to the rich scarlet and brocade rug spread on the floor like a trail of blood. Indigo led me up a staircase of gold and iron, and into a private hallway, where a doorman in a red jacket stood with his hands clasped.

"I can manage alone this time," said Indigo.

The light-skinned doorman tilted his head. He pressed a single button, which opened a private elevator cleverly disguised as a tall, cracked painting of the dryad Daphne caught mid-transformation into a laurel tree. The moment we were alone, Indigo moved closer. She was tall, but still she had to tilt up her head to meet my eyes. She put her hand on my belt.

"Do you know the tale of Eros and Psyche?" she asked.

The elevator began to climb and so did her fingers.

"Yes," I said. Her fingers stilled. She wanted me to tell the tale, and so I did. "The god of love fell in love with Psyche, a mortal princess whose beauty rivaled even Aphrodite's. He stole her away on a sweet wind, cloaked her in darkness, and brought her to his palace."

I touched Indigo's hand. Her skin was hot, pressed silk. I moved my thumb over her wrist and felt her pulse. Calm, even.

"He made her swear not to look on him. He folded away his wings and visited her in the darkness and in midnights they grew to know one another," I said. I lifted Indigo's hand and kissed the inside of her wrist. "But then Psyche broke her promise. She looked at him while he slept and for that betrayal, he left her."

"And then what?" asked Indigo.

"Then she had to prove she could find him," I said. "She endured misery after misery to be with him."

Indigo's silk dress scratched against the cheap fabric of my blazer. Her synthetic apple scent washed over me. I forgot about the elevator until it chimed, opening into a wide vestibule. The floor-to-ceiling windows of Indigo's penthouse boasted the jeweled skyline of Paris. Off to the side, a white staircase spiraled into lavish upper suites. On the main level, antique winged chairs, gilt mirrors, and a single white couch adorned an elegantly austere room.

"So you know the tale in theory," said Indigo, one hand on my chest as she pushed me into the foyer. "But not in practice."

I reached for her. She drew back and undid the silk tie at her waist, held it out to me. She raised an eyebrow and looked at the floor. Slowly, I knelt at her feet.

"We can play at gods," she said. "What do you say . . . will you play with me?"

Play, worship, follow. It was all the same to me. I nodded. She lowered the silk over my eyes. It was still warm from her skin.

Her lips skimmed mine. "Don't look."

She raised me up, and I stumbled after her. The floor changed beneath me, from smooth oak to the expensive pile of her wool carpet. Moments later, Indigo pulled my wrist, and I was falling, my back on the firm cushion of her couch. Silk rustled. Her warm legs fell to either side of my hips.

"Don't look," she repeated.

I stilled beneath her. The first time she said it felt like a reminder. The second time was different. A test.

In the tales, the moment Psyche glimpsed Eros in his true form, he left her. But that was what made it a tale worth telling . . . that there was light to be found in the dark.

"Don't—" Indigo said.

I yanked off the blindfold and she startled. The city lights revealed her in sacred squares of gold—the delicate wing of her collarbone, a beauty mark on her sternum, her small, high breasts—as if this was all my mortal eyes were allowed.

"You looked," she said, her voice more curious than wounded. "Why would you do that when you know it will only make a god leave?"

I tried to look into her eyes. She was backlit by the city, her face obscured in darkness like a hidden cosmos, a whole universe I longed to know.

"To prove that I am not afraid of being tested," I said.

"Is that so?" asked Indigo. She settled more fully into my lap. My hands, which had braced her hips, climbed reverently up her waist to her breasts.

"Yes," I said.

Her lips moved to my neck. "And what if that test kills you?"

"Then it kills me."

I felt her smile against my skin, her teeth cool and slick.

"And what waits for us in the end? When you survive all my tests?" she asked. She rose then, guiding me to her. "Tell me. Now."

"Bliss," I said. "Bliss eternal."

After that the city and all its glitter were lost to me. In that second, I knew I would love Indigo forever.

I didn't know what it would cost me.

THE NEXT MORNING, INDIGO TOOK ME TO VIEW HER PRIVATE collection. After a twenty-minute drive, her black car pulled up to a wrought-iron archway. On either side, ivy and wisteria choked the high stone walls. A large, grinning crescent moon dangled from the gate, as if Indigo had speared it from the sky and kept it like a trophy.

Half-hidden in the ivy, a rectangular iron plaque announced: LE MUSÉE DE LA BEAUTÉ PERDUE. The museum of lost beauty. We got out of the car, and I followed Indigo down a white-gravel driveway and into a small labyrinth where ivory seraphim rested their wings atop shoulder-high hedges.

At the end of the labyrinth appeared a large cottage. From outside it looked rusted and forgotten, its only purpose to prop up trellises of tea roses. Inside, it was sleek and modern, the gallery walls spotless so as not to detract from the encased fragments of manuscripts and the iron pedestals holding diorite miniatures of ancient scribes and priestesses. A pair of sliding-glass doors at the far end of the room blew a climate-controlled lullaby over a trove of rare books.

"This is what you wished to see," said Indigo, leading me to a glass-topped table.

When I looked down, there was a single torn page from a grimoire. It was highly decorated, illustrated in gold leaf and lapis lazuli. There was nothing left of the spells but a crude depiction of the sun beside a handful of Aramaic characters. It was likely nothing more than a fifteenth-century copy of the *Clavicula Salomonis*, and a poor one at that.

"I'm told it once held a spell that let people cross time and space," said Indigo, looking at me out of the corner of her eye.

She wore a heavy sable coat, unseasonably warm for early November. Her red lips were a slash of blood.

"Why did you want to see this?" she asked.

"Sometimes I think I had a brother who left me for a different place," I said, the words clumsy and raw, unused to being uttered aloud. "I've been trying to find a way to live in this world. Barring that, I was looking for a way to leave it."

Indigo's gaze held a certainty I wished to rest my life against. "And now?"

"And now I wish only to stay."

Indigo smiled, though there was a split second where her face was blank. Haunted, even. I knew that look. She might smile at me, but she, too, had hunted this spell for a reason.

Who were you looking for? I wondered. *What were you running from?*

Indigo kissed me. I removed her coat and spread it on the floor beneath us. Soon, the sound of her sharp, panting breaths drove all other questions from my mind. I may have entered her world that day, but soon she became all of mine.

In Indigo's realm, the days might begin with picnics in the Jardin des Rosiers and end on the prow of a gleaming boat in the middle of the Adriatic Sea. The evenings summoned private concerts and our nights were filled with games. In these games, we took turns at being monstrous or mortal, grotesque or godly.

But at least now, no matter what we were, we were never alone.

"I WANT TO START SOMETHING NEW WITH YOU," INDIGO SAID A few months later. We were lying in her bed watching the dusk erase the city skyline. "A new chapter. A new story. There will be no glancing at the pages that came before this one. Can you live with that?"

At that point, I had a vague understanding of Indigo's life before we met. Her parents died when she was young, she was raised by an aunt she no longer spoke to—sad and strange, but stranger still was that she possessed a past at all.

Indigo was so much like the fairy tales she loved that I suspected she was one. It didn't matter how many times I touched her, fucked her, held her. She was a phantasm to me, proof of the impossible and thus a talisman against the absence that had haunted my adult life.

I knew how these tales went. I knew that her condition bordered on the sacred, and if I crossed it, I would lose all the magic of her. So I agreed.

"Yes," I said. "I can live with that."

This was a lie I kept secret, even from myself.

Chapter Three

THE BRIDEGROOM

There are two kinds of love—one born from smiles, and the other from screams. Ours sprang from the latter. I had been enchanted with Indigo from the moment I met her, but I must confess that I did not truly love her until our wedding night dissolved into nightmare.

On a Sunday morning beneath a copse of oak trees and a canopy of pale orchids, Indigo and I were wed. She wore a gown the color of bone, a small crown of ivy and white anemone. She said there would be no one else in our marriage, and thus no need for witnesses. Our scant attendees—the officiant, and the trio of musicians—all wore blindfolds. When the ceremony concluded and the papers were signed, we took Indigo's plane to a villa nestled in the rolling hills of Tuscany. And it was there, after a feast of wild boar stuffed with apples, glasses of red wine so dark they were nearly black, after I had peeled the lace from Indigo's body, traced the echoes of its patterns on her skin . . . that the nightmare found me.

For months, I thought I was cured. I believed the nightmare could not reach me from where I slept in Indigo's bed. I was wrong.

My nightmare is always the same.

I am naked and surrounded by shadows. The dark turns solid. It drapes across my knees, encircles my chest. It feels like velvet and smells of wood polish.

At first, it is a caress. And then it is not. Pressure builds in my chest, weighing me down until the shadows are over my eyes and my nose, prying apart my teeth and pouring down my mouth, my lungs are burning, and the air is full of cloth—

I woke screaming.

When I opened my eyes, I found Indigo propped on her elbow, watching me. Our large room was cast in darkness, and from the cracked window a peacock's midnight cry broke the silence. The tapered candles Indigo had lit for our wedding night encircled us in frail golden light. In their glow, her unflinching stare reminded me of a cathedral icon's knowing gaze.

I lay there, panting and mortified. I tried to move, but Indigo splayed her free hand across my chest and pushed me down. She took my shaking hand, brought it to the side of her throat, and held it there, breathing slowly, pulling me from the nightmare until all I could feel was her pulse hitting my fingertips in a delicate percussive dance. Then she sat up, her hair over her breasts and the sheets around her waist, and with her other hand touched where my own pulse strained against my skin.

Indigo did not speak. But our heartbeats shared the same rhythm. It said: *Here is the dialect of the living and I am living alongside you.* It said: *I know this, too, and I can share it with you.*

I've had many lovers comfort me in the aftermath of my nightmare over the years. They've soothed me, coddled me. A few even sang. What Indigo did was closer to prayer—her body bent, her head bowed. She was a different creature by night. Vulnerable, if not forthcoming. That night, I fell asleep to the sound of her heart beating.

For the first moment in years, I knew the lost peace of childhood, when autumns were endless and secrets unheard of, and even time revealed its coveted workings. I remembered how I once knew how to tame and lure whole hours to my side where they might doze like sleeping beasts until I wished for them to pass.

Safety was its own spell, and whatever Indigo had cast on me, I loved her for it.

I have since learned that marriage is nothing more than a spell strengthened by daily ritual. The spell requires libations: mundane musings hoarded and pored over, the repetition of small dismays, the knowledge of how your spouse takes their coffee. Marriage asks for that crust of time you were selfishly saving for yourself. Marriage demands blood, for it says: *Here is what is inside me, and I tithe it to you.*

A marriage cannot live on honest midnights alone.

AFTER OUR WEDDING, INDIGO AND I MOVED INTO HER HOUSE OF glass, on a stretch of uninterrupted coast along the Pacific Northwest. Her home sat on several acres surrounded by red cedar and hemlock trees, sprawling pines and Sitka spruces that looked as if they were creeping toward the ocean more each day. But for all its grand space, there was nowhere to be alone. There were only two rooms that locked. One was our bedroom. The second was a study, which Indigo gifted for my exclusive use. Connecting them was a hallway Indigo called the Gallery of Beasts. It was lined with the cast bronze heads or figures of rabbits, oryxes, sphinxes, wyverns, crocodiles, and stags. I always walked quickly down that hall. It had an odd tang of blood from all the metal.

From the living room, I used to watch Indigo move through the transparent bones of our home. I knew her melting gait, the way she sank into armchairs and immediately—childishly—folded her feet beneath her. I knew how she held her pen, how she stacked dishes, how she lit candles by striking the match against her teeth. Our translucent house was a compromise: I could see all of her, but never know all of her.

Such a compromise initially proved easy. Soon after we married, I left the History Department and became something of a nomadic scholar. I published and held the occasional lecture, but by day my primary work—if one could call such an indulgence work—was as a concept development consultant for new and existing Casteñada properties.

At night, there were an endless number of games for us to play. Sometimes she was Theseus fleeing the labyrinth, and I was the savaging Minotaur trying to sink my teeth into her. Occasionally, I was Endymion and she was Selene, the moon goddess draped in silver who crawled onto my lap and fit me inside her.

One night, Indigo lay beside me in bed. I lifted her hand, watching the light catch on the white crescent scar on her palm. My fingers skimmed up her arm and the hollow between her collarbones to the curve of her cheek.

"What are you doing?" she asked.

"Memorizing you."

She smiled. "For what purpose?"

In case you disappear, I wanted to say. But I didn't dare. When I looked at Indigo then, her eyes were soft and wet, and for a single moment I knew the very texture of her soul.

"I wish I could win your hand like in the stories," I said. "I'd fetch you the feather from the tail of a firebird. I'd fit the ocean in a walnut shell. Or find you Cinderella's glass slippers."

Indigo laughed. "What would I do with glass slippers?"

"Dance in them, of course."

SOMETIMES, FAIRY TALES ARE LITTLE MORE THAN A LITANY DE-tailing acts of devotion. Sisters knit shirts of stinging thistles for brothers turned to swans. Wives wear out iron shoes. Princes scale mountains of glass. I supposed it was a matter of will. What would you do to be happy? To be loved?

Our first wedding anniversary happened to coincide with the opening of a new property near Wistman's Wood in Devon, England. Beneath a chandelier of antlers and before a small, be-jeweled crowd, I presented my wife with a pair of handblown glass slippers from an artisan I had found in Nakano City. To the laughter and delight of the crowd, she insisted on wearing them.

I will never forget how she sparkled—her dress the color of bruises, a collar of amethysts at her throat. When the musicians in their fox masks struck up the first slow waltz, we danced on a platform disguised as a large, gilded nest.

Indigo's smile never wavered. Her composure never slipped. She nodded at the crowd, and they poured in from the fringes of the ballroom to join us. After that first dance, I led her to one of the golden tables that circled the room.

It was only when she sat and the hem of her dress lifted that I noticed the blood pooling in her glass slippers, the fine crack along one side.

Indigo removed the shoes carefully. Two of her toes were blue. Later, we would discover they were broken. Later, I would cradle her ankles and tell her I loved her and insist on carrying her up the stairs and all throughout the house.

I had always found the rejected stepsisters of Cinderella far more captivating than the story's namesake, and now I knew why. When the shoe did not fit, they cut off their toes, sliced off their heels, squeezed their feet into glass, and lowered their skirts to cover the pain. Perhaps, in the end, the prince made the wrong choice. Such devotion is hard to come by, after all.

Look how I will carve myself to fit into your life. Who will not do less?

In Indigo's blue toes and ruined skin, I saw a love letter. Gruesome, yes, but for all that it became in the end, it must be said that it was always true.

I TRIED NOT TO BE CURIOUS ABOUT MY WIFE'S PAST, THOUGH I sometimes felt I could detect its shape in her silences.

I'd watch her pause before the photographs tucked into the far edge of the study she rarely entered. The pictures showed her childhood home, Domus Somnia. The House of Dreams. It was a sprawling estate on an island off the coast of Washington. Now it was occupied by her aunt, a woman with whom Indigo communicated through a network of caretakers, assistants, and solicitors, and nothing more.

I didn't ask her the reason for their estrangement or about the House of Dreams. I sensed this was a line that was not to be crossed. Besides, I knew how these stories went. There was always a hapless youth or milk-skinned maiden who makes a promise they cannot keep and invites pain into the only happiness they have ever known.

How ungrateful, how foolish, one might say. But they do not know us. They know neither the contours of our hearts nor the cold hands that shaped them.

We are the ones accustomed to making our beds in fireplaces, to bending our will to sharp-toothed stepsiblings, to standing alone in the woods with nothing but a trail of rapidly vanishing crumbs to guide our way home. Pain is inexplicably vital to us. It pins us to the very fabric of our lives, that which joy and comfort and *warmth* have made alien and foreign. Pain speaks to us in a voice that carries the hallowed certainty of hymns:

I know exactly what you deserve, and I shall give it to you.

Chapter Four

THE BRIDEGROOM

By the end of our third year of marriage, I understood that the secret to everlasting love was fear. Fear tethered love in place. Without the terror that came from imagining a life without your beloved, there was no urgency in loving them.

I tried to love Indigo as she wished.

I learned not to question the glazed, haunted expression that snuck into her eyes when she thought I wasn't looking. Once, she walked out of a movie theater without an explanation. The film had seemed innocent enough—a tale of two sisters—though the specifics escape me now. Another time, I found her sobbing in the garden over a dead bird. I told her we could go into town and buy her a pair of birds if she was so unsettled. She only stared at me in confusion.

One day, I came across a piece of Indigo's secret. It was a piece of hair crooked like a beckoning finger in the Gallery of Beasts. The hair was trapped beneath the paw of a granite sphinx positioned near the entrance of the bedroom.

At first, I only stared at the braided strand. I had touched the sphinx's talons too many times to count on my way to our bedroom. This time I traced the groove where its wrist and arm joined, and it slid to the side, revealing a small hollow where the braid of hair ended in a loop. The hair was cool to the touch and nearly as dark as Indigo's, shiny like brushed silk. At the end of the braid, a pair of teeth dangled. One of them had been engraved with the letter *A*.

"What are you doing?"

I shoved the braid back into the hollow, but it was too late. Indigo stood at the other end of the hall. Rain plastered her hair. A smell like metal and ozone seeped into the hallway and I briefly wondered if the thunder outside had followed her into the house.

"It was sticking out," I said. "I thought—"

"You were prying," said Indigo, her voice flat with fury. "You know you're not supposed to do that."

"It was an accident, Indigo," I said, taking a step toward her. She trembled, and I hoped it was from the cold. "Let's forget this happened. It was a mistake."

"I don't believe you," she said. "I told you not to pry."

"I'm only human, Indigo," I said, trying to keep my voice light. "Don't tell me you'll leave me for the crime of occasional instances of mortality."

At this, she went utterly still. I did not recognize her in that moment, the way the whites of her eyes nearly glowed, the tension of her jaw.

"I am scared of you," she said in a quiet voice. "You terrify me, and that is how I know I love you . . . but you're not scared of me at all, are you?"

Without another word, she left me there in the Gallery of Beasts. I didn't follow her. I told myself she was overreacting, and my own guilt made me even more adamant in this belief.

I went about my day, pushed the bracelet of hair and the engraved tooth from my mind, though I couldn't stop thinking about the exquisite temperature of the hair, only a few degrees cooler than Indigo's. I avoided the Gallery of Beasts even as my tooth—the same cuspid that had been marked with the letter *A*—started to ache.

By evening, my pride had crumbled. I went to the dining room prepared to apologize. Indigo wasn't there and the table had been set for one. She never came to our bedroom that night either. That was a first for her, but I told myself her anger would pass.

The next day was the same.

And the next.

And the next.

I began to count the clothes in her closet each morning and evening, hunting for some sign of my wife's presence, hoping she had entered our room and I had not known. I walked the house for hours. I wandered the gardens at night. I interrogated the staff, though they refused to answer my questions. I left our bed and started sleeping in the living room. The day after that, I dragged pillows and blankets into the hall before the front door, determined to catch her. On the eighth day of her absence, I began to dream.

I dreamt of the sharp smell of cedar, splinters beneath my nails, my fists bloodied from knocking repeatedly on a door that wouldn't open. I knew my brother was on the other side. I wondered if Indigo might be there, too, whether I had once more been judged and found wanting.

You forgot me, I screamed at them. *You left me behind.*

This fear had stalked my entire life. My parents, already old when I was born, had died while I was still in university. At the time, I felt grateful at their passing. Not because I wasn't saddened at their loss but because now I could be certain there was no one left to leave me.

On the tenth day of her absence, I woke from my nightmare to find her standing at the foot of my crumpled blankets. I had piled them into a heap at the end of the hall, where I waited. At the sight of her, a terrible relief snapped through my ribs.

"Well?" she asked.

"I am scared of you," I croaked.

She smiled.

AFTER THAT, SOMETHING CHANGED BETWEEN US.

I could feel her secrets exerting a gravitational force in the months that followed, pulling her into some other realm. She spent hours walking alone by the shore, sitting in our garden of hemlock, nightshade, and other venomous flowers, staring at various books whose pages never turned. Sometimes she'd raise her chin, eyes alert, as if someone had spoken her name. I thought of the tales of selkie wives. In the end, they were always called back to the sea.

I watched her every day, looking for some sign that her time with me had come to an end, and I began to notice little things: how quickly she passed through the Gallery of Beasts, how she traced the small, crescent-shaped scar on her palm as she dressed for bed, the way she ate with the feral quickness of an animal that doesn't know where it will find its next meal.

We played our games out of desperation. Only through the guise of myth could we speak to each other. Only beneath the borrowed light of a fairy tale could I look at Indigo for as long as I wanted.

Lately, though, I had begun to hate our games.

My wife still loved me. I could see it in her eyes, how her

fingers lingered on my jaw, how she moved my hand to her pulse and held me in the dark when I woke screaming. But after three years, her love wasn't enough to keep her by my side.

One spring afternoon, the phone rang. I did not know it at the time, but this was the moment when everything changed. I was reviewing plans for a new project while Indigo read through some correspondence from her charitable organizations. We rarely received direct calls on the landline, and Indigo startled.

"Yes?" She held the receiver away from her. Her lips flattened. The pen dropped from her hand. I watched her draw some shutter over herself even before she raised her eyes to look at me.

"Of course," she said to the person on the other end.

She hung up. I waited.

"Tati, my aunt, is dying," she said. "She needs to see us. I don't know how much time she has left."

"When do we leave?"

Indigo looked out the window toward the sea. When she spoke, I had the impression she was addressing someone who was not in the room.

"We leave for the House of Dreams tomorrow."

Chapter Five

THE BRIDEGROOM

As a scholar, I have always found dreams to be frustrating—if not lazy—motifs. They might be portents or prophecies, messages or mysteries. Dreams might pass through gates of horn and speak true, or sneak through gates of ivory and speak false. At its heart, a dream is a door.

Sometimes there is nothing behind the door, only the stacked faces of strangers. Sometimes the door holds row upon row of indignities plucked and preserved like fruit out of season. And sometimes the door is a piece of yourself that has been exiled and severed for reasons you have been made to forget, and it is only in dream that it dares to show itself.

The night before we left for the House of Dreams, my brother came to me.

He has never come to me in dreams. Or in nightmare. He has only ever existed in the twilight of waking when I considered the impossible and folded it away before the sun could see.

In the dream, my brother's back is turned to me as he crawls to the great cedar armoire in my parents' hallway. My brother, forever on the cusp of six years old, clambers inside. I yell for him. I watch his pink toes as he melts into the dark. I am reminded of the jackets in the armoire, of my father's wool coat that I once wore around the house, trumpeting the sleeve as if I were an elephant. For a moment, I hear my brother laugh.

A small, pudgy hand reaches out from the dark of the closet. I walk toward him, intent upon touching him when I catch a whiff of apples. Indigo is here too. She crawls past me, her heels kicked off, her bronze hand clasping my brother's as he pulls her into the armoire.

"Wait!" I scream to them.

But they have crossed into a world where I cannot follow.

"Indigo," I call out, but there is no point.

She is already beyond me. I am simply the thing that marks the journey, that which is left behind to bear witness. Perhaps I am the door.

Perhaps I am the dream.

I HAVE STUDIED THE PHOTOGRAPH OF THE HOUSE OF DREAMS so often I thought I would recognize it instantly. But I underestimated how the House acquired its name. I'd thought it was some affectation of the rich as they planned their Washington island estate back in 1901. But Domus Somnia fit the structure perfectly.

The House was an architectural gem boasting four stories of crimson brick. Its steep, gabled roofs were supported by figurines of frowning satyrs and narrow-waisted caryatids. Huge, stained-glass bay windows graced its exterior. Rosebushes decorated the entrance, but they looked all wrong and far too bright, like lipstick on a corpse's mouth. In a slender turret, my gaze caught on an oddly shaped window.

It was an eye.

Blue and unblinking, the pupil a perfect circle of gold.

From Indigo's photograph, the House of Dreams had seemed nostalgic in its beauty, a grand and faded souvenir of a dead era. In person, the House felt alive. Even the passing clouds cast an illusion of the brick bulging and narrowing. Breathing.

I stared at the wrought-iron door. It creaked open and an answering ache unfastened inside me. I saw a pair of small, pale feet crawling across its shadowed threshold. For the first time in years, my mind taunted me with familiar images—jam-stained fingers, a hiccupping laugh, a handful of wishing dandelions.

You never had a brother, my parents had said.

But he was here, I realized. My brother was here, and if I walked into the House, I would find him—

Inside the car, Indigo's hand closed over mine. The touch of her skin dragged me back to myself. I blinked. The shadows around the House skittered like a laugh.

This was the first time the House whispered to me.

It would not be the last.

"The last time I was here, Tati told me she was glad that she was blind because she'd never have to set eyes on me again," said Indigo, staring out the window.

This was the most she had said since receiving the call. When Indigo was in one of her moods, she might as well have been made of smoke for all that I could hold her. A week ago, I might have savored this morsel of her past. Today, the sentence seemed laid out like a trap.

"I'm sorry," I said.

Indigo was wrapped in her favorite black sable coat. She wore dark pants, heavy boots, a cream blouse that crawled up her neck, red gloves, and a mink hat pulled over her ears. On someone else it would be an ordinary, albeit elegant, ensemble for winter. But on Indigo, each piece of cloth was an intentional boundary separating her from the world.

"Don't be," she said, her face expressionless. "She loved me. She still does." Indigo turned back to the wrought-iron door, now half-open and bearing witness to conversations out of earshot as the chauffeur announced our arrival. "I'm merely unrecognizable to her."

Her. Hippolyta Maxwell-Casteñada.

If you looked hard enough—and I did—you could find photos of Hippolyta and Indigo from various functions, back when Hippolyta had agreed to be the face of the Maxwell-Casteñada hospitality empire. In every one she is turning Indigo away from the camera. There's a fierce, almost wounded, look in Hippolyta's gaze. She has—or at least had—the wide-set, expressive eyes of a martyr, and Indigo was always a scrap of magenta taffeta or blue frills, a child half-steeped in shadow.

I looked up at the sound of footsteps crunching gravel. The chauffeur opened our door. My breath plumed in the cold. About a hundred feet away, an older woman whose skin was nearly as white as her hair walked down the front steps, then stopped short the moment she saw Indigo.

"It's you," said the older woman.

At first, I thought this was Hippolyta, but that was impossible. Hippolyta was supposedly blind—though I hadn't known that until Indigo spoke of it—and there was something too neat about the woman's black dress and pulled-back hair that suggested a daily uniform. Her voice was rich with memory. I reached for Indigo's gloved hand, and she trembled and stiffened. She was afraid, though I could not guess why.

"I can't believe it's you!" said the woman, opening her arms. "Indigo, how long has it been? Ten years?"

"Eleven," said Indigo, her voice a touch short of warm. She bent in time to be embraced. When she pulled back, the older woman had tears in her eyes.

"Look at me," she said, laughing as she wiped them away. "Old and sentimental as anything." She clasped her hands, nodding at me. "I'm Mrs. Revand, the housekeeper. I knew this one before she became this hopelessly elegant woman." Mrs. Revand stepped back, admiring Indigo. "You look just like her, you know. Your mother."

Indigo demurred. "Impossible, but thank you."

"And you're married!" said Mrs. Revand. She winked. "He's almost as beautiful as you."

"Almost," I said, with an indulgent, bored smile even as my mind was creeping up the stairs of the House.

Indigo had always treated her past as if it were dead. So I planned to approach this visit like an autopsy. I wanted to see mundane things—pieces of homework left in drawers, a book holding her adolescent handwriting. She had given me so little that even the thought of knowing how she curled her g's and dotted her i's tempted sacrilege.

"The House has been through some changes since the last time you were here," said Mrs. Revand. The warmth of her expression cooled. "We have, of course, honored you and your aunt's wishes regarding the presence of maintenance workers on the estate, though I do have to wonder why we can't make some necessary repairs? The roof, for instance, has severe water damage. The pipes need replacing too—"

While Mrs. Revand droned on about maintenance, I scanned the facade. Far above me loomed the turret, the eye-shaped window, and, standing against it, a figure in white. I blinked. When I looked back, the figure was gone.

"Forgive me," said Mrs. Revand, shaking her head. "I'm be-ing unforgivably rude. No doubt you wish to see your aunt, but she . . . she had another episode this morning, I'm afraid. We had to sedate her. There's no use waiting, my dear. I'd come back tomorrow."

Indigo frowned. She touched my arm. "Would you give us a moment alone? Maybe you should head back to the car."

I made my farewells to Mrs. Revand. The only thing I heard as I moved out of earshot was Indigo's smoky voice:

"What has she been saying about me?"

The car was still parked right in front. Some distance away, our driver—a young, dark-skinned man from the mainland— smoked a cigarette beside a maple tree. I'd nearly reached the door when a soft chirping song rose from the ground.

I stepped onto the lawn, following the sound a few feet away to something small and dark, quivering in the grass. A bird with a midnight-blue belly, green wings edged in gold, speckled white with a glossy, iridescent head. The starling twitched, one wing still, the other twisted at an odd angle. I bent to pick it up when I noticed little marks moving across its plumage—

Ants. Dozens of ants. Ants squirming in its eyes, lifting its broken talons, crawling in the gaps of its wing.

It was being eaten alive, and yet it sang.

"What a waste of time," Indigo said as she ducked into the car, the door slamming shut.

The chauffeur held open my side. "Sir?"

The starling's threnody followed me. I found myself thinking of omens and cedar wood, the slow turn of strange faces and the sound of a door closing. Indigo curled against me in the back seat. I tried to feel the warmth of her, but I thought only of those ants, of their thousand wet mouths opening and closing.

All full of teeth.

BY THE TIME WE ARRIVED AT THE CASTEÑADA HOTEL, IT WAS completely dark. The drive from the car and subsequent ferry trip to the mainland left us tired. As the valet stacked our bags and the night manager enthusiastically greeted Indigo—and, by a far lesser extent, me—I recognized my handprint on the property.

Over the past few years, I had conceptualized and brought to life more than half a dozen homages to my wife. Here I rediscovered a love letter in the lapis lazuli and bronze tiles of the lobby, its nacreous tables and chandeliers of pearls and windowpane oyster shells.

"Melusine," I said.

I had told Indigo the tale of Melusine early in our courtship. We were in the bathtub of her Paris penthouse, slightly intoxicated and muzzy from a day spent in bed.

"Tell me a tale," she had begun, climbing into my lap.

I caught the slow glint of hunger building in her eyes. I gripped her waist, held her in place. She squirmed as if she were trapped.

This was part of our game.

"Once upon a time," I said, "there was a man who married a water spirit named Melusine. Except he didn't know what she was. Before they married, she made him promise that for one day out of the week, he would let her bathe in private and never disturb her."

"Did he keep his promise?"

"He was a weak man," I said, running my thumb along her full bottom lip. "Of course he did not."

She liked the way I said that and rewarded me with a kiss.

"One day, curiosity overcame the husband and he spied on her through a hole in the door, and that's when he realized his wife was not fully mortal. Below the waist"—here, I paused to demonstrate, and Indigo sighed as I stroked her—"she was a serpent."

Indigo gripped my shoulders. "Then what?"

"Then Melusine abandoned him for the sea."

"Poor Melusine," said Indigo as she shifted to let me in. "You can tell she really loved him."

"Is that so?"

By then, I was distracted by her fingers in my hair, the heat of her thighs. And yet I never forgot what she said as she lowered her mouth to my ear.

"She kept him alive when she should've done so much worse."

Indigo's voice now reached me through the memory. A soft, tired smile curved her mouth. The chandelier lights picked out hues of ruby in her hair.

"Do you remember when you told me this story?"

How could I forget?

"Maybe you can tell me again tonight?" Indigo said, right as a voice called across the lobby.

"Azure!"

All softness left Indigo's eyes. That name, *Azure*, iced over her. Across the lobby, a young Black woman waved and walked toward us. She had large, dark eyes and her hair was a bouncing golden halo, like the corona of a saint.

"Azure!" she said again.

That name. Azure. *A.* Like the letter carved on the tooth at the end of a bracelet of hair. I watched as the name snared and tightened around my wife.

"You're mistaken," said Indigo. "Have we even met?"

"We went to high school together! You guys had that crazy graduation party?" The woman paused. Frowned. "Oh my God, I'm so sorry. You're not Azure . . . Indigo?"

The way she said the name. There was a distaste to it. The other woman's mouth crimped, and I wondered what memory she held behind her teeth.

Indigo's smile turned brittle. "The one and only."

Indigo gestured at the hotel. It was a sign: *You are in my realm.*

The other woman managed a laugh. "Oh my God, it's been ages! I'm visiting family, haven't been back in years. How are you? Do you and Azure still talk?"

"No," said Indigo. "I haven't seen her in years. She left the island."

Within seconds, Indigo summoned a frosty, regal sheen, as if she were made of gems and even her shadow were too precious to step on. The other woman picked it up like a scent.

"Right," the woman said, matching Indigo's coolness. "Sorry to hear that. You two always seemed close."

"Life rarely goes as planned," said Indigo. "I hope you have a pleasant stay on the property."

"Thanks," said the woman, nodding at me once before turning on her heel.

My head started to ache. By the time we were alone in our rooms, I could not remember how we had got there. My mouth tasted of salt.

I couldn't stop thinking of the pain on Indigo's face. All these years, she had carried a secret wound. I'd known it existed, though she had forbidden me from asking any questions. In that time, a chasm had widened between us. And now I knew it had a name.

"Who is Azure?"

Indigo stiffened. I had never once broken her rules, but I could not ignore that. Not when it was so boldly thrown in my face. Indigo sat at the foot of the bed, digging her thumbs into the arches of her reddened feet.

"She was my best friend," she said, not looking at me, not repeating her name. "We had a fight. She ran away after gradua- tion." Indigo breathed carefully, as if the air had been disturbed by her admission. "She was the closest I had to a sister growing up. It's hard to speak of her."

For months now, I had dreamt of the engraved *A* and the cool braid of dark hair. I told myself it was a hundred different things . . . an odd souvenir from a lost love, a magic spell to ward off evil, a keepsake of her mother's. But the *A* was for Azure.

Indigo disappeared into the bathroom. When she emerged, she wore a long, white nightgown I had never seen before. It re- minded me of the figure in the window.

"Are you coming to bed?"

"Soon."

I drew a bath and stared at the water. I wondered about Melusine's husband breaking his promise. Folklore categorized Melusine a mermaid, but never clarified whether that's what her husband saw. I wondered about the moment when he caught the muscular flex of her tail, the red in her scales like so much gore, the knowledge of how she must have cramped her otherworldli- ness to fit into something as silly as a tub of water. When he broke his promise, did he see a mermaid, a maiden, or a monster?

If I broke my promise to Indigo, what would I see?

Chapter Six

THE BRIDEGROOM

The next morning, the blue bitterness of Azure's name remained coiled in my jaw.

"You're awake."

Indigo sat up in bed, staring at me.

"I don't want to be," I said.

I turned from where I had been leaning against the large windows that looked out over the wind-wrinkled sea. I have never liked swimming in open water. I hated the cold void of the ocean, the disturbing weightlessness of my own limbs. Indigo's eyes were cold and depthless, and I felt that same sensation, a pebbled seafloor pulling my feet out from under me.

"Bad dreams?" she said, throwing back the duvet.

"I'm still thinking about Azure."

She rose from the bed, naked, and reached for the robe hanging on the lapis-and-Capiz-tiled wall.

"That's to be expected," she said lightly. "It's the last name you heard before sleep."

"Indigo—"

"I need to get ready," she said, tying the robe. "Tati will be waiting for us. Hopefully, this time she'll be lucid."

Tati. I'd forgotten she would finally see us today.

If Indigo and Azure had been friends since childhood, then that meant Tati knew her too. *Indigo and Azure*. Both of their names conjured blue—sea skies and livid bruises, gas flames and rich cloth. Their hues were close enough that one might be considered the sister of the other.

When Indigo stepped out of the shower, she appeared unbothered. She paused before my armchair by the window. Droplets splattered onto my pants as she leaned over, taking my face in her hands, kissing me. She drew back, then pressed her forehead to mine so that I saw only her lips move as she spoke—

"This place is poisonous to my very soul, and I am sorry for how it's changed me. But soon we'll go home," she whispered. "Just know that no matter how I am, I haven't forgotten that you are all I have in this world."

As she drew back, the sun broke through the clouds behind me, mottling her bare skin in rainbows. Scrubbed and bare, Indigo had something of the inhuman about her, and I was reminded of the promise she had extracted from me.

Do not look.

Do not ask.

Do not pry.

I have long imagined that my wife was cursed and that my silence might one day break it. But today, as the light rendered her lovely and alien, an idea slipped into my skull and my vision sheered sapphire, cerulean. A question edged in blue found my tongue:

What if the breaking of the promise is the breaking of a spell?

The thought was blasphemy, and yet it tasted like snowfall and rare sugar. My mouth watered.

"I love you," said Indigo, and shame curled in my stomach.

Was this not some kind of test? If I could stand the taunt of curiosity, then perhaps she would no longer feel so hunted and whatever disjointedness had come between us would disappear.

I reached for her hand, kissed the inside of her wrist, her map of veins and dewed skin. "I love you too."

Indigo's shoulders relaxed, though she didn't smile. When she touched my cheek, her hands were frigid, her nails sharp. "Don't let me doubt it."

I WOULD NOT CALL THE HOUSE OF DREAMS A HOME.

There was something flimsy about it, a quality to its shadows that suggested it was not always in one place. That if I arrived unannounced, it would not be there. It was aptly named in that sense, though I was unsure whether its provenance belonged to dreams or nightmare . . . or something else entirely. Like the substance of fairy tales.

I have lost count of the number of stories I knew that dealt in fae glamour. In some tales, the Fair Folk can make a handful of leaves appear like coins. Their homes might be richly appointed in one light and turn out to be nothing more than a pile of rough twigs and damp straw. To glamour was to lie, and that made it dangerous.

The moment Indigo and I stepped out of her car and onto the gravel driveway, I felt the House comb through me.

I see what you cannot, it whispered.

I tried to focus on Indigo. But it was as if her proximity to the House had drawn an uncanny, animal-like quality out of her. When she smiled, her teeth appeared sharper.

"I should warn you about Tati," said Indigo. "She's not fully present these days. Not after her injury years ago."

I caught sight of the turret. I remembered the pale figure before the glass.

"Is there anyone else here aside from Mrs. Revand?"

Indigo looked at me sharply. "No. Why?"

The car came to a stop, and I pointed up at the turret and its curious window. "I thought I saw someone there yesterday."

Indigo followed the line of my finger, and her mouth pinched.

"Nobody uses that room," she said. "Not anymore."

I SHOULD HAVE KNOWN WHAT WOULD HAPPEN WHEN WE crossed the threshold of the House of Dreams. I knew all the tales. I understood the texture of enchantment.

But I had forgotten how certain places can be so old they are alive. So alive that they do not simply hunger; they learn to hunt.

If you follow a white stag into an enchanted glen, or open a golden door in an abandoned alley, or find that a mirror's surface is liquid to your touch—it is never by chance. It is because something has need of you. It has laid its autumn leaves just so, coaxed woodsmoke from thin air, cut the light through the branches so that it spells an invitation.

Gone was my wariness when we entered. Instead, I was grateful that Mrs. Revand and Indigo spoke in hushed tones so that I could wonder at this place that had molded my bride. It felt like cupping my hands around a secret.

The inside was beautiful. The floors were polished chestnut, cut to resemble interlocking stars. A rich, faded blue rug stretched across the entrance, which opened into a sitting room of ornate Venetian furniture and bronze statues of goddesses in repose. From the center of a soaring, pressed-silver ceiling hung a chandelier. Slender windows with cream drapes bound by golden ropes hinted at the water beyond.

I tried to imagine Indigo growing up here—young, too skinny. I tried to imagine her padding barefoot across the carpet, running inside after a swim, leaving puddles of water on the expensive silk couches. I tried to imagine her slouched, boneless, against the ebony stairs, a book propped on her bronze knees.

I could not picture it. There was no sign of the girl Indigo had been. She might as well have been cobbled together from dust motes and shadow, her charred brown eyes a gift of color from the chestnut floors.

I did not realize that as I stared hungrily at the House, the House was staring hungrily at me.

"It hasn't changed at all," said Indigo.

Mrs. Revand disappeared down a hallway at the top of the stairs.

"She's gone to let her know we're here," said Indigo. When she looked at me, a flicker of misgiving filled her eyes. "You should know that she will—"

Her phone went off and Indigo groaned.

We did not bother with cell phones until recently. They were ugly and bulky. The attorneys had advised Indigo to purchase one, given the state of Hippolyta's health. They'd even gone so far as to send her the latest contraption toted by all the teens on the mainland: an insect-red Nokia with a stubby antenna. Indigo glared at the device.

"I imagine I'll need to take this," she said. "I'll only be a moment."

Indigo usually moved with grace, but her gait as she walked away was almost militant. As if preparing for a fight.

From the top of the stairs, Mrs. Revand gestured to me.

Come, she mouthed.

I looked back to where Indigo had vanished and told myself she would simply meet me there. As I made my way up the stairwell, the sea stretched out beyond the tall windows. The water flexed, muscular as a great tail beneath the sunlight. I thought of Melusine bathing in the dark, anchored to her wild body in the hopes that her husband might let her have this one privacy, might even break the spell.

If only he remembered not to look.

UPSTAIRS, THE WALLS WERE A DULL, MEATY RED AND THE AIR carried the sour, musty tang of an unrinsed mouth. The wall sconces held dead lightbulbs. I found this odd, but what difference would it make to a blind woman?

"Miss Hippolyta?" called the housekeeper, knocking on a pale golden door right off the landing.

From within, an answering creak of bedsprings.

"He's here, alone," said Mrs. Revand with a guilty look at me. I understood, too late, that Indigo would not like this, but I could not make myself turn and leave. "Just as you asked."

I stepped inside. Thin drapes covered the windows, the high-ceilinged room only barely illuminated. Strange art in gilded frames lined the walls—trees and curlicues, hearts, crosses, black-and-white roses. A dozen vases filled with flowers made from a material I couldn't identify were shoved into a corner. At the center of the room lay a huge, circular bed. Its sheets were as red as the brick outside.

"Are you beautiful?" came a rasping voice followed by a sharp laugh. "She always collected exquisite things."

My eyes were still adjusting to the light, and so Hippolyta appeared as little more than a small, wriggling shape on the bed.

She turned her head, speaking to some invisible thing beside her.

"No, hush hush, I know. There's only so much time," she said before sniffing in my direction. "Come, come. Come closer to me."

I moved to her bedside and Hippolyta came fully into view. She was small, bald, and dark as a chestnut. Her frilled night-gown was doll pink and hung raggedly off her body. Her thin neck and thinner wrists were adorned in braided jewelry. Her face was not beautiful, but it was arresting. Those wide-set, mar-tyr eyes I had seen in the press photos now milky and mottled blue. Her mouth was a lopsided slash, framed by wrinkles. Thick, raised scars made her skin appear oddly folded, and when she opened her mouth to speak, I smelled the rot on her breath.

She cocked her head to one side. "Well? Are you?"

"Pardon?"

"Are you beautiful?"

I considered this, faintly amused. I was aware of how men and women looked at me, of how Indigo had looked at me that first night we met and every night after.

"Yes."

Hippolyta's gray tongue snaked out from her lips.

"They say you're good at finding things," she said. "Baubles, stories . . . secrets."

"I try," I said, thinking she was referring to my work as a historian.

"You see, I lost a secret . . . it was very poorly done of me," said Hippolyta, shaking her head. "It was not a secret I was supposed to lose. Maybe it is not a secret at all, but an idea grown up in the dark and fed on dusks and twilights. Don't you think?"

The question was not directed to me, but to the invisible thing beside her. I felt like the House was playing tricks on me, the walls leaning at an angle. Again, I thought Indigo wouldn't like this, and the thought made me straighten my back, look over my shoulder to the door. It was closed.

I did not remember closing it.

"I don't think I can help you, ma'am," I said, moving backward. Hippolyta's hand darted out with surprising speed and grabbed me. Her bracelet slid down her thin arm, hitting my skin. The material felt wrong. Warm, somehow. Too soft. Not like twine or silk. Something tickled the back of my throat.

"You're wrong, beautiful," she said. "Tell me, how well do you know your bride?"

I slid my tongue around my mouth, working out whatever was stuck at the back of my throat, moving it to the front of my teeth. Perhaps it was a piece of wool from my scarf.

"Does she love you?" asked Hippolyta. Her milky eyes found mine. "Does Indigo love you?"

"Yes," I managed.

Hippolyta laughed. I could not take it anymore. I reached between my lips and my fingers closed on something caught on my tongue. When I pulled, I saw that I was holding a strand of long, black hair. I had seen it before, I realized. Twisted into a bracelet, a tooth hanging off the end with a single engraved letter:

A.

Azure.

Chapter Seven

AZURE

The first thing you have to understand is that I loved her.

I loved Indigo from the moment I saw her outside the House of Dreams. She was carrying a crystal punch bowl of milk and blood in her arms, the splay of her shadow and the rhythm of her steps summoning magic in her wake.

My mother and I had moved into the town of Hawk Harbor two weeks earlier. Our house back in Oregon was small and red, surrounded by fields of sunflowers. Maybe we would have lived there forever if Jupiter hadn't shown up at the diner where my mother waitressed on weekends.

Jupiter seemed to possess some magic of his own because he took one look at my mother's red mouth and empty eyes and fit himself into those hollows until all she could see was him.

The first time I met Jupiter, he tried to give me a bag of candy. I really wanted the candy. Still, I wouldn't go near him. I hated how his eyes tracked me, how he smiled with his mouth closed. Like he was trying to hide his teeth. A month later, my mother came home flushed and bright-eyed as she showed off a dull stone on her hand.

Within weeks, we were making plans to move to Jupiter's

thin, squat house. I'd only ever seen pictures of it. It was hidden behind a sunken driveway, the windows peering out over the grass like the half-lidded eyes of a predatory animal.

I didn't expect the town to be anything special that day when Jupiter met us at the ferry. The place of my earliest childhood years wasn't much either. A general store, a church, a white-slatted sign announcing a school game, a boat dock, the wharfs.

So when we rounded a corner and the House of Dreams appeared, I thought it couldn't be real. I sucked in my breath, nearly slapping the car window.

"*That*," said Jupiter, as he slowed the car, "is the Casteñada family home. They named it something fancy and Latin. You know how rich people are."

My mother cranked down the window and glared at it.

The moment I saw the House, I knew it held magic. That dragons slumbered beneath its floorboards, that the trees on its property grew wish-granting fruit, and that in the highest turret lived a queen and when she combed her hair, jewels clattered to the ground. For the first time, I became aware of what my life looked like in comparison. Greasy and cheap, a construction of cardboard to the wonder baked into those red bricks. If I'd known better, I would have shut my eyes and never looked at the House again. But I couldn't stop staring.

"All that for one family?" said my mother, wrinkling her nose.

"Not even *one*," said Jupiter. "Parents got drunk on a plane and crashed it." He laughed, shaking his head. "Now the *whole* thing belongs to some ten-year-old girl with a crazy fucking aunt—oops—" Jupiter paused, as if remembering I was in the back seat. "Sorry, princess."

"I think it's tacky," said my mother, rolling up her window.

Jupiter met my gaze in the rearview mirror. "And what do

you think of the house, princess? The little girl who lives there is about your age. Imagine if we were the ones who lived in that place? We could play hide-and-seek for hours." He smiled, flashing his too-white teeth.

My mother paused. The lipstick tube in her hand halfway to her mouth.

"She hates that game, J," she said. I didn't understand why she sounded annoyed, like she'd been left out of something. "She'd probably hide under the bed to read another book. You'd be searching for days."

"I don't mind waiting," said Jupiter, tapping the side of his nose.

The car started moving again.

EVERY CHANCE I COULD, I TOOK MY BIKE PAST THE HOUSE OF Dreams. It wasn't more than a fifteen-minute walk from Jupiter's, though it had the air of another world entirely. Everything seemed brighter, *better* when I was near the House. I could only imagine what it must be like to live there, reading by a massive fire, finding gold coins in one's teacup, coaxing your pet leopard on an afternoon walk.

I decided to do a little experiment to test the House's magic. I took two identical strawberries—both scarlet, shiny, fat as a ruby. I ate one in Jupiter's house, and it tasted sour. I kept the second in my hand as I pedaled to the House of Dreams. I held the fruit up to the sunlight bouncing off the wrought-iron finials. I took a bite. Sweet, fragrant juice spilled over my lips.

It was the first time I understood that beauty has its own power. Beauty transformed. Its presence could coax ambrosia from sour fruit or take an ordinary, rained-upon sidewalk and dew it with diamonds. I wanted beauty to touch me, change me, declare me worthy of its notice.

At that moment, the front door clanged open. I jumped, dropping my half-eaten berry, and grabbed my bike. I thought an adult was going to yell at me to leave. Instead appeared a girl my age.

I had only to look at her once to understand that one day she'd be beautiful. She was coltish and long-femured, the joints of her shoulders so tanned and glossy her bones shone. She wore a dress that was far too big for her, and her feet were bare and dusty.

A crystal bowl caught the light in her hands. She had a carton of milk tucked under her arm. I silenced the bell of my bicycle and tried to make myself small behind the brick pillar of the gate.

I watched as she set the glass bowl onto the front steps and poured milk into it. She reached into the dress's front pocket and drew out a knife. Without pausing, she pricked her palm and squeezed the blood onto the milk's surface. When she was done, she shoved the bowl of milk and blood beneath a hydrangea bush, stepped back, and closed her eyes.

I knew what would happen next. I'd read all about it. She'd made a sacrifice. The air would wrinkle, a star-flecked hand would grab her wrist and yank her into some new place where I couldn't follow. A place full of magic. Where she'd become a queen.

"Wait!" I yelled, forgetting all about my bike. "Take me with you!"

The girl looked up from where she stood by the hydrangeas. She tilted her head in acknowledgment, though she didn't move. In her silence, my face started to burn with embarrassment. I pointed to the bowl of milk and blood.

"I thought you were . . . going somewhere."

Her eyes widened.

"Where?" she asked. "Where do you think I'd go?"

Her voice was slightly raspy, each word elegantly articulated. I'd never heard anyone speak like her. I wished I could speak like that.

I wondered what I looked like to her. The October sunlight lacquered her skin and hair. Around her, the trees on the property wore traces of gold, as if they'd donned it just for her, for the moment she'd step outside.

I wanted to tell her about all the books I'd read, the ones my mom had told me we couldn't bring with us when we moved here. Books about Aztec sacrifices, gods with two heads. Tales where one step into the shadow of an apple tree could yank you out of this world altogether. But I couldn't fit all of this into my answer.

"Somewhere else," I said. The girl seemed disappointed. She looked behind her. She was going to leave and I couldn't let her do that.

"I read somewhere that faeries like bowls of sweet milk . . . that they'll come if you leave them something like that."

"I know," she said, bored. "They're supposed to come get me one day. I'm their family." She pushed her thick black hair over her shoulder. "I thought the blood and milk would speed up the process."

When she didn't say anything else, I traced the edge of my bike handles, convinced that in a few seconds she would tell me to leave.

The girl eyed me. "Do you *really* want to come with me?"

I didn't trust myself to speak, so I nodded.

The girl lifted one burnished shoulder. "I'm sure they have

room for us. I bet they've got a palace."

She walked forward and unlocked the gate that separated us. It opened with a screech. She took my hand and led me to the hydrangea bush, where she offered me the knife.

"Are you brave enough to go to Faerie with me?"

I thought so. I even had a sticker to prove it. I was absurdly proud of that sticker—a quarter-size, neon smiley face with sunglasses—and did my best to preserve it when the glue wore off and the smile began to lift from my sweater. It had since held pride of place in the pocket of a clear plastic folder I took with me to school. The nurse had given it to me when I got my before-school shots in a cold white office that stank of ethanol.

"You're the bravest one out of the bunch!" she'd said. I hadn't made a sound when she injected me. She stretched a Band-Aid covered in watermelons over the wound. "Normally, these kids are howling left and right, but not you." She beamed at my mom. "You should be proud of your girl."

My mother, who had been sitting in the examining-room chair, listlessly flipping through a magazine, glanced at the nurse and at me. She rolled her eyes, arched one eyebrow. The exchange was conspiratorial. It said: *Of course I am.*

My mother's arch look crystallized that moment for me. If I could've turned it into a pendant and worn it around my neck, I would have. In those days, I would've rendered all the glances my mother spared me into jewels and treasured them as such. I thought of the sticker in my clear plastic folder as I stuck out my hand to the girl.

"I'm brave enough," I said, and took the knife.

I brought it to the heel of my palm and dug in the tip. The girl held out the bowl. My blood ribboned across the surface. Afterward, she put the bowl back under the hydrangea bush, and when she returned, she smiled.

"I'm Indigo."

INSIDE THAT BOWL OF MILK AND SUGAR, OUR BLOOD ENTWINED. Maybe a blue petal from the hydrangea bush touched the milky surface while our spell cured in the moonlight, and that was all it took for the connection between us to be sealed. Even if I didn't know what it was, I knew that *something* had happened, because the next day, I could feel Indigo waiting for me. I sensed her like my own pulse.

It was a Sunday, and my mother and Jupiter were at the movies, so I rode my bike to the House of Dreams, and there she was—sitting on her front steps with a book in her hand, two glasses of apple juice beside her. I was not only expected; I was wanted. The knowledge glowed inside me.

The day after that, Indigo and I walked to school hand in hand. At lunch we sat together, and later that afternoon, we looked for faeries by the stream next to the House. This became the shape of our days. When the bowls of milk and blood didn't lure the faeries to us, we tried adding honey, and then maple syrup. I even stole one of my mother's earrings to drop into the bowl, hoping the jewels would sweeten the bargain.

I spent every weekend at Indigo's house, wearing gowns that didn't fit, bracelets that slid off my wrists. At night, we poured salt along the windows and woke at midnight to eat sugar from a crystal bowl. I drank from her cup, and she fell asleep in my lap, and when we braided our hair together, we hung pendants in the woven strands.

Time melted our first autumn into glassy winter, and by spring, magic grudgingly revealed itself to us. Now we could see that the knotty root of a tree beside her house was the abandoned dining table of a garden gnome. The thin creek behind the school was the home of a rusalka with dappled hair like a sparrow's breast.

Back then, I was always looking for the right currency to enter magical realms: a special coin, a rock with a perfect hole at its center, a butterfly wing glittering with dust. Things that could be traced with a fingertip.

Later, I would understand that the entrance to another world craves that which cannot be traced. It wants the mouthy weight of a nickname no longer uttered, the soft-furred throat of the dreams that pad quietly after you from one year to the next. To belong to the Otherworld, you must not belong to yourself.

I know this because it granted me entry. It was not a realm full of sunlight or a place where the moon could be dented with a spoon long enough to reach it. It was the space wrought between me and Indigo, a spectrum of blue where the world reknitted around us as if we were a walking wound burning a hole through its glamour.

A YEAR HAD PASSED SINCE I'D HELD OUT MY HAND FOR INDIGO'S knife. We now had matching scars on our palms, pale little divots like the slap of twin fish tails. Today, sunlight lay thick on the trees. The air shimmered, panting from the heat.

Indigo and I sat at the dining-room table, halfheartedly piecing together a puzzle that she told me would become a door to the kingdom of mermaids if we finished it before midnight. I glanced at the clock. It was hardly noon. Midnight was far away.

Around us, the House hummed drowsily. Even after a year, I had not gotten used to this place. It dazzled me, putting on a show of radiance rippling through stained-glass windows. Every room seemed too precious to sit in, let alone steal its air. I loved the heavy velvet curtains, the cabinets full of crystals, the priceless vases and spoons laid out on the formal dining table, where one of the dozen staff members polished them until they shone like pieces of moonlight.

"The House likes you," Indigo had said the first time I stepped inside.

"How do you know?" I asked, secretly pleased.

She pointed at the elaborately carved front door. "See? It shut all the way on the first try. It doesn't do that unless it likes you enough to keep you."

We were stuck inside that day, though not by choice. I yawned, glancing out the window to the backyard, the creek that fed into the river. We had tried swimming in the waters earlier. It was so cold, my toes cramped immediately. The staff must've known because halfway up the garden walk someone had left a pair of thick towels. I was still wrapped in mine.

"What are you girls doing inside on a day like this?"

I looked up to see Tati standing in the doorway of the kitchens. Sometimes Indigo would make a kitten-cry and wrap her arms around Tati and call her Tottlepop. Tati loved it when Indigo called her that. She would kiss Indigo on the head, and for a moment they'd look like mother and daughter.

I tried not to watch them when they were like this. My mother never held me. Maybe she wanted to, but whenever she came home from operating the ferry's ticketing office, Jupiter was always there to gather her up and so there was nothing left for me.

Tati approached us, and Indigo straightened in her seat. When she got all stiff like that and called Tati "the guardian," Tati's face closed. But Tati couldn't see Indigo's expression at that moment.

"You're wasting all that sunlight," she said, perching her chin on Indigo's head and winking at me.

Beyond the shape of their eyes and color of their hair, Tati and Indigo didn't look much alike, even though she was the older sister of Indigo's mother. Tati's features were wide, squashy, and friendly. Indigo was drawn with a more restrained, elegant hand.

"She's not nearly as beautiful as my mother," Indigo had told me. "But I still love her."

I didn't need Tati to be beautiful to love her. I loved her the moment I had entered the House, and Tati feigned a gasp: "Indigo! Is this your long-lost sister, or did you finally bring one of your shadows to life?"

I had beamed when she said that. Here, I belonged. I didn't mind if that meant being someone else's shadow.

Most days, Tati wore colorful scarves on her head, and when she hugged me, it was like she was using up all her strength for that one embrace. Tati was a witch, which is to say she was a kind of artist. She worked, she told us, in "the medium of memory" and smelled like hot glue and dried roses.

"It's gross outside," said Indigo, studying the puzzle, ignoring Tati's arms wrapped around her.

"We tried swimming in the creek," I offered.

"Too cold," said Indigo.

"Oooh, there's an idea!" said Tati. "Why don't I have a pool built for you girls? I can put it in the backyard—"

"I don't want a pool in *my* backyard," said Indigo, enunciating each word.

"Oh, sweetheart, are you sure? I think you girls would love it—"

Indigo pushed her hair back and chose that moment to toss

her head, hitting Tati's face. Tati winced, her hand flying to her mouth. Tears of pain welled in her eyes. Indigo turned to glance at her. I thought she would apologize, but she didn't.

"I don't want a pool on *my* property," said Indigo, annoyed. "The end."

I slid from my chair. "Are you hurt, Tati?"

"I'm fine," she said through clenched teeth.

When she lowered her hand, I saw blood on her fingertips. She quickly wiped her hand along her dark skirt.

"Then why don't you girls go to the local pool?" she asked. She tried to smile, but the warmth had vanished from her voice, replaced with something soft and yielding. It reminded me of the way my mother spoke to Jupiter. "I'll write a note so they let you in."

A FEW HOURS LATER, WE SAT IN THE SHADE CAST BY THE LIFE-guard's chair, our feet dangling in the water. The public pool was crowded, and it smelled like sunblock and sweat. I kept glancing at Indigo, wondering if she'd say anything about Tati. I felt guilty for accepting Tati's hug before we left. Indigo had shrugged her off, and so I had let Tati hold me as close as she'd ever held Indigo.

Indigo stared across the water. "Did you know that if you possess someone's true name, they'll belong to you forever?"

"What's a true name?"

"Like a secret name," said Indigo solemnly. "Everyone has a true name. Trees, monsters . . . even people. What's yours?"

"Azure," I said.

Indigo shuddered. "I can't believe you said it out loud!"

"So?"

I tried to appear nonchalant, though I worried I had given up something priceless.

"Sometimes your real name is the name people call you. But it's only important if someone *knows* that it's true," said Indigo, eyeing me. "And once they know it's true, then they own you and you can never gain your freedom unless they give it back to you."

I thought about this. "You're the only one who heard me, so give it back." I tried to say it like I was joking, but I wanted to cry.

Indigo looked at me, one corner of her mouth tilted up. Her eyebrow arched. "It's mine now!"

I tried to grab her. She shrieked and dove into the pool. After that, we played for hours. We stood with our legs wide apart in the water and took turns wriggling through like slick mermaids. Sometimes, we pretended to trap each other. We did handstands and opened our eyes and looked up at the sun through the cold blue. It wasn't until I went home that night that I realized Indigo had never given me back my name. It was just a formality though.

From the moment I met her, I had always belonged to Indigo.

Chapter Eight

THE BRIDEGROOM

How well do you know your bride?

I had not moved from my place at Hippolyta's bedside, and yet her voice was now transposed over a rhyme so old there was moss in its joints—

Turn back, turn back, thou bonnie bride, nor in this house of death abide.

I had seen the words, but I had never heard them so clearly until now. It was a familiar-enough motif; its skeleton found in everything from Grimm and Perrault to a neat dissection in the Aarne-Thompson-Uther folkloric index. A young maiden visits the house of her betrothed, and there finds an old woman who bids her to hide behind the oven. The girl waits. Soon the door opens and her beloved stomps in, dragging a dead girl by her hair and heaving her onto the table. He tells the old woman that he means to eat well tonight and cuts the dead girl into her choicest bits. Behind the stove, the girl sees the firelight fall upon her beloved's treasures. In the corner, he keeps a pile of snowy breasts. His rich rugs are shining strands of raven, ginger, and golden hair. His precious porcelain is made of glazed pelvic bowls, and his many gems are teeth set in gold. In the betrothed's haste to carve the meat, the dead girl's little finger flies into the lap of the hiding maiden who, by now, has realized her beloved is not what he seemed. And all the while, the old woman sings.

Turn back, turn back, thou bonnie bride, nor in this house of death abide.

Hippolyta was clearly not sane. Her words were not to be trusted.

So why could I not stop listening?

"Let me tell you a tale, beauty," said Hippolyta. "One day there was a beautiful revel and a sky of azure and a sky of indigo walked hand in hand into the Otherworld, but only one of them came out. Do you understand me? Only *one* came out."

I heard a creaking on the staircase.

"Miss Hippolyta?" called the housekeeper from the other side of the door.

"You must find my Azure," said Hippolyta. "Oh, the House misses her so much you can feel its ache in the floors! Only Indigo knows where she went, but my Indigo is a slippery girl, always has been. She kept Azure as close as a secret. You have no idea how much they loved each other."

"Let me go—" I said, but Hippolyta held tight.

"The Otherworld knows the girls' secrets; perhaps you can ask it where Azure went? Why she never visits?" said Hippolyta, frowning and pouting like a child. "But who can get into the Otherworld without a pair of wings?"

"I can't help you."

Hippolyta's bony fingers caught my face, drawing me to her. Her fingers left damp and sour marks on my skin. I held still.

"I can hear your longing like a heartbeat," said Hippolyta. "If you find Azure, the House will reward you. The House knows your deepest desires. The House always provides."

Mrs. Revand knocked on the door. "Miss Hippolyta?"

Hippolyta released me. I stumbled back as the door opened.

"Good visit, I hope?" asked Mrs. Revand with false brightness. "This way, sir."

Mrs. Revand gave us a moment of privacy. I glanced over my shoulder to see Hippolyta slowly sinking into her covers.

"You say she loves you, but what is she anyway?" said Hippolyta, and then she closed her eyes and sang: "*My sly blue-sky girl, too good to be true, and all of one hue, you're my girl so blue blue blue.*"

Hippolyta laughed and I closed the door behind me. I hardly registered Mrs. Revand asking me to wait so she could see what Indigo wished to do next. I sank onto the stair landing.

Indigo would be furious that I had met Hippolyta without her. It wouldn't matter that I had kept my promise and not pried. Perhaps she knew that Hippolyta wished to taunt me. I wished I could tell the old crone that it made no difference. What I knew of Indigo I loved, and that was enough.

And is it still enough?

I didn't recognize the voice in my head. It was like a child's, high-pitched and breathy. The sound of it a finger of frost dragging down my neck.

"Yes," I said, though I did not know to whom I was speaking. "Yes, it is enough."

I knew the exact moment when I had decided that what my bride offered was enough. Indigo and I were in Paris, basking in those first, fresh months of knowing each other. It was too early in spring to be beautiful, and the city looked dull and groggy, an aging woman robbed of the winter season's diamonds.

One evening, we took aperitifs on her terrace. On the small wrought-iron table lay a plate of cheese, marbled slices of meat, and an odd glass terrarium nearly a foot high and full of smoke.

"I have a surprise for you," said Indigo, removing the glass.

Smoke unraveled in the air, revealing a tiered golden platter. Scattered across its three levels were tiny gold-skinned plums.

"Faerie fruit?" offered Indigo.

A feeble bit of sunlight broke through the gray clouds, illuminating her face. The wind tugged petulantly at her hair as she lifted her hand. For a moment, I thought she would push her palm against the air and the stitches of the world would rip and take us somewhere far away. I thought I heard my brother's voice on the wind:

Come with me. Come find me.

How? I thought.

But the answer was staring at me. Indigo sat in one of the little iron chairs and reached for a plum. Gold foil glittered her lips, and I smelled the marzipan paste that had molded the fruits.

"Well?" she asked. "Don't you want a bite?"

"They're not real."

I sounded like a wounded child. Indigo only laughed. "How do you know?"

"What do you mean?"

"True faerie fruit is the taste of the threshold," said Indigo, parroting the words of my own research papers back to me. "The alchemical properties of which might transmute all that we are. It can allow us to move through spaces humans were not meant to occupy. It can give us powers. It can let us see through glamour. Who is to say what it truly looks like?"

Indigo held out the fruit. I understood then that she was not offering a doorway of escape but a means by which to live.

"Faerie fruit is exceptionally dangerous," I said. "It is beautiful to behold, but they say death laces its ambrosial flavor."

The ripe fullness of Indigo's mouth was now the gold of a pagan god. I loved how she sat with her long legs folded beneath her, an artful carelessness to her limbs as if she only briefly inhabited this form.

"Sounds far too treacherous for me," I said, bending to run my thumb along her bottom lip.

"Don't worry," said Indigo, smiling. "If you're good, I'll keep you safe."

"Promise?" I asked.

"Of course," she said. "Now, close your eyes."

I did as I was told, and she placed the plum between my teeth. It tasted like gold and honey with an echo of iron and salt. It was the taste of a threshold crossed; a bargain struck. In all that time, I have kept my eyes closed and Indigo has kept me safe.

I knew that Hippolyta's words were merely words, and yet they conjured an image all the same. As I slouched against her door and caught my breath, I thought of the maiden in the robber bridegroom tale, of the way she must have gasped when the dead girl's little finger landed in her lap, how she must have counted all the times she had kissed her betrothed's mouth and thought of the sweetness of his breath, while on the other side of the oven, he sucked marrow from a girl's femur.

Later, I would recognize this as the moment when the House of Dreams struck. This was the nature of clever places. I thought there was no knowledge the House could tempt me with to convince me to do its bidding. I was wrong.

One moment, I was staring at my feet. The next, I heard that same childish voice sigh.

You lie. It is not enough.

Abruptly, I was thrust into an image that held the shape and weight of memory.

I saw my mother as she looked when I was seven years old. She was too strong-jawed for beauty, and yet she had the most delicate, doe-wide green eyes. We're standing in the kitchen and someone tugs my hand. It is my brother, chubby and jam-stained, squirming and laughing as I twirl him on the spot. In my mother's hand is a cigarette. We freeze at the sound of my father's heavy footsteps in the garage. My mother grins and taps her ashes into the sink.

"Are you ready to play, boys?"

I blinked. I was still outside Hippolyta's door. The sound of my father's footsteps melted into Mrs. Revand's clipped gait as she walked up the stairs. The image vanished entirely. I traced the edges of it in my mind, disturbed at how neatly that lie fit within.

How could such a thing be possible?

In answer, sunlight moved through the stained-glass windows. When I looked down, my hands were soaked in blue.

If you find Azure, the House will reward you.

The House always provides.

Chapter Nine

AZURE

My hair was the one thing I possessed that was finer than Indigo's, and I treasured it as if it were my soul exposed. To me, each strand held a version of my life as it had once been, and I believed if I tended to it, then that version would return.

As a child, my mother used to rub sweet almond oil into my hair, combing it until it poured down my back like a starless night sky. In those days, she would tell me the tale of Rudaba, a Persian princess whose hair was a river of night and who let it spill over the ramparts of her castle so that her lover, King Zal, might use it to climb his way to her chambers.

"You're my precious fairy-tale girl," she once said.

That was before she worked extra jobs and the skin beneath her eyes wore shadows. When we moved to Hawk Harbor, I still held on to the dream that things might be as they once were. That first week in the new house, I wore my hope in every knot and tangle of my unwashed and unkempt hair.

I wanted my mother to scold, to sigh, to plant me before her with her knees against my back. I wanted her to comb my hair and hum through the bobby pins clenched between her teeth. It was not her attention I caught though. It was his. At the end of that first week I sat at the breakfast table and Jupiter whistled.

"Well, where'd this little wild thing come from?" He laughed and smiled teasingly at my mother. But when he looked at me, his smile didn't match his eyes. The air of the breakfast nook turned humid and small, and even though I was hot in my sweatshirt and pajama pants, I wished my hair were long enough to cover me up and swallow me whole.

Jupiter wet his lips with his bright-pink tongue. "Your hair is so long I could use it as a blindfold and still not be able to catch you."

My mother sat folded up in her chair, legs to her chest, a coffee mug balanced on her bony knees. When Jupiter spoke, she slammed her hand on the table and stood so fast I flinched.

"Why are you *always* trying to embarrass me, Azure?" she'd said, grabbing my arm and hauling me to the hallway bathroom. "You're making me look bad," she snarled. "Look at you. Your hair is . . . *disgusting.* I've been working myself to death to take care of you and you can't bother to take care of yourself?"

She let go of my arm, breathing heavily as she shoved me into the bathroom.

"Either braid it or cut it off," she said, slamming the door.

After that, I never wore it down at home. But in the House of Dreams, Indigo insisted I always wear it loose. Only then did I let its heavy, fragrant weight rest on my shoulders.

"It's like magic," she would say, combing her warm fingers across my scalp. Her voice stretched tight with yearning. "I bet it *is* magic . . ."

I had always wanted magic in my life, but one Saturday morning, in the winter of my thirteenth birthday, I didn't want it anymore. That day, I dressed to go to the House like usual. I didn't ask for my mother's permission. I avoided mentioning

Indigo around her because her face would twist, and her voice become silken and venomous: "Running back to Miss Casteña-da's house? She's going to think you're clingy, honey. And nobody likes a clingy girl."

As much as she sneered when she uttered Indigo's name, I knew my mother was secretly grateful for her too. Without Indigo, I'd be home.

With her.

With Jupiter.

In those days I could always feel Jupiter's shadow—a gluttonous, sticky thing—clinging to my skin no matter where I went. When I opened the bathroom, he'd be there, smiling and surprised with a towel slung low around his waist. I would be forced to look at him then, forced to squeeze around the space he took up all around me.

I hated looking at him.

Jupiter was tall, thin, and narrow in the shoulders with a taut, hardened pouch of flesh around his navel that reminded me of an egg sac. He was the color of a tooth. That's how I thought of him. One long fang of a man, and my mother caught up in him like a piece of wedged-in meat.

But his face was different.

"The face of a movie star," my mother would say, leaning over to caress his cheek.

Jupiter had straight white teeth, a square jaw, yellow hair he kept at shoulder length, and heavy-lidded gray eyes that always seemed on the verge of sleep. There were paintings of angels in Indigo's house that I couldn't look at because their faces reminded me of him.

I didn't hear him enter my bedroom that morning as I was packing my bag.

I never spent much time in the room that was supposedly mine. I never decorated or hung posters on the wall, though Jupiter had bought plenty for me. I didn't want to claim any part of that place.

"I got a present for your mama, princess."

By the time I turned, he was already a foot away. A golden chain dangled from his fingers.

"You want to try it on?" he asked before closing the bedroom door. I was reminded of the room's smallness. He lowered his voice. "It can be our secret."

"No thanks, I'm okay," I said, fighting to keep my voice even.

I'd learned to stay still around him. If I was jumpy or my voice squeaked, he would hug me to calm me, and I didn't like it when he hugged me.

"Shh, shh," he soothed. "Look at you, so sweet you don't want to try on your own mom's gift no matter how much you want it? You're my good girl, and good girls get rewarded."

I held still as he moved closer.

"Turn around," he said.

I told myself that if I did what he wanted, then he would leave. So I turned. His breath was cloying and rancid. He lowered the golden chain around my neck. The cold locket thudded against my collarbones. He spun me around. We both faced my bedroom mirror. I watched as he moved my braid aside and bent so we were eye level, his face rising like a horrible moon behind my shoulder.

"Beautiful," he said. "I wish you'd wear your hair down more, Azure. It makes you look like a younger version of your mother."

Maybe he could sense that I wanted to move away then because his fingers tightened on my shoulders.

"You know, princess—" he started when the door swung open.

My mother stood there. Jupiter released me instantly, breaking the necklace as he snapped it off my neck. I was so happy to see my mother, tears came to my eyes. I didn't realize I was shaking until I grabbed my jacket off the bed and my fingers couldn't catch the zipper.

"Azure, why don't you go to Indigo's?" said my mother.

Her voice was fire. I inched out of the room, staring at her, something vast expanding in my ribs. I clutched the end of my braid. My mother looked primal and huge in the doorway, and Jupiter's face turned so pale I could see the spidering veins in his forehead.

"Honey," he said, raising his hands.

The locket winked in the light.

"Why were you alone with her?"

"I wasn't!"

"The door was closed," she said.

Jupiter's square chin jutted out. His face turned mulish. "The door must've shut by accident! Honey, I was showing her a surprise I got for *you*—"

"You're always trying to spend time with her, and honestly, I don't like it."

I hovered out of sight. Indigo was expecting me, but maybe . . . maybe my mother *needed* me. I imagined us sitting on the couch. I pictured my head in her lap, her fingers in my hair. I held my braid so tight, my hand ached. My mother's shoulders sagged, her voice hitched in a sob—

"Why do you always look for *her*?" she asked. "What about *me*?"

I let go of my hair.

I left.

OUTSIDE JUPITER'S SQUATTING STUCCO HOUSE, THE AIR WAS cold and metallic. Just breathing it stung my nose. Tears froze on my lashes.

The moment I opened the gate to the House of Dreams, reality inverted. The air shifted. Wind stirred my bones like they were wooden chimes and I might be translated into song. And when Indigo opened the door, I became a held breath finally exhaled.

Indigo took one look at me. "What is it?"

I touched the end of my braid as I entered. Normally, I felt a fine sift of electricity travel along each strand, its magic waking in the presence of the House. But my mother's words lingered and now that magic felt less like power, and more like poison.

What about me? Why do you always look for her and not me?

I tugged the end of my damp, cold braid.

"I want to cut it," I said. "I want to sacrifice it. Make Tati do it. Please."

Indigo's eyes widened. "What do you want to gain?"

I was glad she didn't try to stop me. I thought of the heat rising off Jupiter's body, the cold locket on my skin.

"I want to be invisible," I said.

Indigo was silent and then she nodded. She glanced toward the staircase, held a finger to her lips. "We'll have to ask Tati, but step quietly. I think the House is napping."

As I slipped off my shoes, I noticed that the House *did* seem more quiet than usual. All the staff had already left for the night. Tati preferred everyone, even the housekeeper, to live away from the grounds. I wondered if the House preferred it that way too.

The House was more than a building, you see. It was a body. The dark oak floors smooth as skin. The smell of mulled spices wafted in a rhythm like breathing. In the twin fireplaces on either side of the vast sitting room, sparks lazily spiraled through the air like a sequence of dreams.

Quietly, we took to the stairs.

I skimmed my hand along the mahogany banister. The carpeted steps purred beneath my bare feet. I loved Tati, but I had never liked her wing of the House. Here, the walls were painted scarlet, the crimson rugs woven with gold. Intricately cut lanterns flickered through the narrow hallway as if it were a pulsing artery. It even smelled like blood, salted and rich in iron.

The door to Tati's workshop was red and slender, affixed with a small centered doorknob shaped like a child's hand cast in gold. Indigo pushed open the door and announced: "Azure wants you to cut off her hair."

As I entered Tati's workspace, my heart began to race. Seven small windows shaped like stars let in the afternoon light. On the left wall, a series of seven white columns held up black jet vases with dozens of bouquets. The wall to the right was covered in gold oval frames showing everything from abstract curlicues on a white background and illustrations of a three-legged horse to elaborate black lacework and ships sailing across a thready sea.

All of it made from human hair.

Tati called it mourning jewelry.

"You know why she does it, right?" Indigo had once whispered to me in the night. I couldn't see her face, though I knew she was smiling. "Tati was married once, but her husband ran away when their baby died, and she had to bury it alone and so she shaved its head and turned its hair into a rose. She wears it sometimes."

On the rare occasions when I went to Tati's studio, I avoided looking too closely at the pieces, especially the ones where only the smallest wisps of hair had been used to make a flower. It was unsettling to me, the knowledge that a wreath had been made from the crimped, gray strands of a dead woman.

"Sometimes I think it should be called memory jewelry instead," Tati once told us. "A strand of hair is a thing of remembrance—it bears witness to our joys and our pain. It is nothing to be afraid of."

Tati looked up from her work. In front of her was a tall black stool with a hole in the middle. Strands of hair weighted down by steel bobbins hung over it. Today she wore a black silk scarf around her head. I wasn't sure whether she had any hair of her own.

"Azure needs you to cut off her hair," repeated Indigo.

Tati frowned, setting down her tweezers and the boar-bristle brush she always used. "That's rather drastic for a Saturday, don't you think?"

"She needs it as a sacrifice so she can turn invisible," said Indigo matter-of-factly.

"And why would a beautiful girl like you want to be invisible?"

I opened my mouth then quickly closed it. If I said it, I would make the reason I needed this power real. I knew there was danger in naming things. I treated the truth like a monster that could be summoned by speech alone.

"You know what I do every day?" asked Tati, smiling.

"Witchcraft," said Indigo, a note of longing touching her voice.

"Of a kind, perhaps," said Tati. "I preserve."

"With hair," I added, relieved that I didn't have to explain why I wanted this magic so badly.

"With *hair*," Tati repeated, nodding. "Hair has power. It helps us communicate to the outside world how we wish to be seen, or not be seen. It is a language of identity."

Tati got up from her table and walked over to us.

"Look, sweetheart," she said, placing her hands on my

shoulders and turning me toward the wall.

A small mirror hung there, its borders decorated in elaborate curlicues of finely worked hair.

"If you cut off all your beautiful hair, you would be making a great sacrifice, but it's a sacrifice of yourself," said Tati. "You would be *severing* a part of you."

A spot of cold opened behind my ribs. I ignored it. Maybe that was true, but I didn't want this part of me. I stared straight into Tati's face and felt the pressure of Jupiter's fingertips on my bare shoulder.

"Please," I said.

Tati sighed. "I'm not doing anything unless I've got your mother's permission. Why don't you ask her and then we'll talk?"

But talking to my mother meant I had to go home. I'd left so quickly I didn't have any of my things for school, but after spending the day hiding, I had no choice. I let the House relinquish me back into the cold. I could tell it didn't want me to go. My foot caught on a trail of ivy poking out of the ground. The iron finial of the gate bit down on my scarf as I left.

"I'll be back soon," I said.

As if to express its displeasure, a harsh wind blew through me, and it no longer felt like music. The sky on the walk home was gray and stripped of its diamonds, and with every step, the end of my braid slapped dully against my back.

I hated walking through Jupiter's front door. Even when all the windows were open, the air in the house was cloying. A damp smell, like mushrooms and dirt, seeped up through the carpet and mixed with the intensely sweet candles my mother lit in the evenings.

I kept my jacket zipped to my neck as I walked through the foyer. I planned to disappear into my bedroom, but then I heard my mother humming. I could smell onions sizzling in butter and knew she was making my favorite pasta. An ache went through me. For a moment, I felt that same hum against my scalp as she rubbed oil in my hair. Beside the front door, the key holder was empty. Jupiter was not home.

"Mom?"

She poked her head into the entryway. Sometimes I forgot how beautiful she was, tall and dark-skinned. She wore her hair in ringlets that hit the top of her collarbones. She had on a red dress and her lily-of-the-valley perfume.

"Oh," she said, her shoulders falling. "I thought you were Jay. He stepped out to grab some wine. We're having a date night at home."

I walked into the kitchen. The dining table was set for two with a long white candle flickering in the middle.

"I'll bring the food to your room," my mother said, her voice too bright as if selling me something. "With *two* pieces of cake."

She was trying, but it wasn't for me. I reached to touch my hair and found that my braid had come undone by the wind and fallen around me like a protective cloak. Her words stung right through it.

"What do you think?" she asked, smoothing her dress. "How do I look?"

"Beautiful."

She almost smiled then, and I should've left it at that. But I had an odd glimmer of understanding. It was like reaching for a knife just to know its weight.

"Jupiter says I look like you," I said. "But when you were younger."

Her smile turned so brittle I thought it would snap her face. Her gaze went to my unkempt hair.

"You look like a slut with your hair down like that," she said. "Get out of my sight."

I STUFFED MY SCHOOL THINGS IN A BAG, GRABBED AN EXTRA SET of clothes, locked my bedroom door, and climbed through the window. An hour later, I sat on the edge of Indigo's copper bathtub. A pair of kitchen shears lay in my lap. I held out my hair to her, my palms upturned like a supplicant. In the candlelight, Indigo looked like a priestess.

"Take it from me," I said.

I felt nothing but the loss of weight as each lock hit the bottom of her tub. With every snip, my spine straightened. Indigo worked with quiet focus, her fingers hot on my neck as she shielded me from the blades. When it was finished, she took my face in her hands.

"There," she said. "It is done."

I closed my eyes.

"How do you feel?" she asked.

Each sacrificed strand translated to a piece of armor. It was invisible, yes, but I felt it shimmer all around me. I flexed my fingers, stretched my neck from side to side, marveling at the lightness.

"Safe," I said, opening my eyes. I touched the sawed-off edges of my hair. "I feel safe."

"We should offer it to the faeries," Indigo said.

I wasn't sure what the faeries would get from it—maybe they could spin memories from its strands. Maybe their mattresses were filled with girl hair.

That night, we pulled on Tati's old fur coats and leather boots. I stroked the House's sides as we walked down the stairs, and moonlight twisted on the floor like a laugh etched in silver. Outside, we threw the fistfuls of hair onto the lawn and I knew that no matter what, I would always be safe with Indigo.

Chapter Ten

THE BRIDEGROOM

Perhaps I could have sat in the parlor and waited for Indigo, but I didn't want to spend another minute in that House. I rubbed my thumb along the brass handle of the front door. The metal had been worn shiny by a dozen hands. Normally, such a repetitive exercise drew me back into the present. But I couldn't shake the image that had invaded my mind.

The false memory had triggered a second one, and when I blinked, I saw an old canvas backpack filled with saltine crackers, two tins of sardines, and a pair of socks. It was midnight, and I was helping my brother into the cedar armoire, telling him: *"Go. I'll follow you to Faerie."*

But none of it was real. I never had a brother. This was nothing more than the House tempting me to break my promise, convincing me to pry where I should not.

I looked back up the stairs. The door to Hippolyta's room was closed, though there was another wing I had not explored. I'd glimpsed it only briefly on my way to the entrance, and even that brief glimpse had unnerved me.

At the far end of that hallway, a slender set of wrought-iron stairs spiraled upward into some unknown space. An odd fragrance had drifted toward me when I noticed it. Apples and honey. A slanted twin of the perfume Indigo daubed on her neck and wrists each morning. I pictured the House's exterior. There was only one place those stairs could lead.

The turret.

Nobody uses that room. Not anymore.

So whose room was it?

Without thinking, I found myself climbing the stairs once more and turning down the other side of the hall. Here, time stood still. Even the golden dust motes remained suspended in the air. A small recessed niche caught my attention. Its three chestnut shelves were empty except for a tube of lipstick on the top shelf. I opened it. The shade was deep plum and bore the crescent imprint of a mouth.

Indigo's mouth? I wondered.

Or Azure's.

I returned it to the shelf and noticed a ribbon dangling. I tugged lightly, and something broke loose. It must have fallen between the shelf and the wall—

A mask.

Made of blue satin, studded with pockmarks that might have once held rhinestones. It was casual and blithe, and I hated it. In all the years Indigo and I had played, she never once reached for a mask. It would've been redundant. But here was proof that once upon a time she had so thoroughly been herself as to need a disguise.

"Careful with that."

Mrs. Revand appeared on the main stairs, one of her gray hands clutching the banister. Indigo was not with her. I was both relieved and disappointed.

"My apologies," I said, placing it back on the shelf.

Mrs. Revand flashed a tight smile. "She's very particular about maintaining the grounds and this side of the House. Not even the cleaning crews or maintenance staff are allowed there," she said, glancing at the staircase.

I nodded. "Well, Hippolyta seemed—"

"Oh dear, not Miss Hippolyta," said Mrs. Revand. "Indigo is the one who sets the rules." A breeze moved through the House, and it moaned as if from neglect. Mrs. Revand laughed. "The House is clearly as nostalgic as Indigo. Pardon me, *Miss* Indigo. Old habit from knowing her when she was so young."

I thought of that divot in the lipstick, the satin mask that might have touched her face. At the back of my head spun the image of my brother disappearing into the armoire, and I asked, ever so lightly, for I knew I was testing the boundaries of a promise—

"What were they like? Indigo and . . . Azure?"

Mrs. Revand sighed and folded her pale hands across her belly.

"Beautiful," she said. "They were walking heartbreak. But mischievous, sweet, always running around outside in their other world. Always playing with their hair, trying out new things . . . I remember one day Azure just clean chopped it off with no warning! Miss Hippolyta was so sad. She *loved* long hair, you know."

"Why did Azure leave town?" I asked.

Mrs. Revand shook her head. "I have no idea. One day they were two halves of the same soul. The next . . . separate. I think the last time I saw Azure was at the girls' graduation party." Mrs. Revand licked her lips. "Friendships are like that sometimes. Especially with young girls."

I looked more closely at the housekeeper. Her hair was gray, frizzed. Her face softened with jowls. Her lips wore the creases of years. Her eyes, though, were a surprisingly bright shade of blue. I couldn't picture a time when she was beautiful, but maybe she had been. Perhaps she had also been half of someone's soul once.

"You and Miss Hippolyta never tried to get in touch with her?"

"God no. It was her choice to leave, and it's her choice to reach out," said Mrs. Revand. She looked beyond me to the dusty carpet, the iron staircase. "Besides, some girls aren't meant to be found. Memories make their own houses, even more magical than this one, and that's where girls from the past live." She touched the wooden handrail. "In those houses, dust can't touch them. Time never colors their hair silver. Wrinkles never crease their face. They can stay untouched and perfect forever. And that's how I like it." She smiled, and I wondered how many times she had thought what she'd just spoken aloud. "In my memories, Indigo and Azure are always happy. Always dancing."

Chapter Eleven

AZURE

You can picture it, can't you? The moment when time caught up to us, the slant of light in which the familiar turned strange. I studied our faces side by side and felt a *lack* of myself as the first touch of frost crept into our eternal summer.

I never used to notice time passing, but my indifference was one-sided. Time watched us spit our baby teeth into our palms, pull sequined dresses from Tati's closets, and pretend we were monsters. Time followed us to school every morning and afternoon. It sat on our shoulders while we dreamt of faeries, heard us sigh when we were lulled into sleep, traced where our knees touched across Indigo's green bed, smelled our bones lengthening in the afternoons, and watched how as the years blurred and softened, so did we.

At fourteen, Indigo was already beautiful in a way that made people uncomfortable. It wasn't her body. At least, not yet. It was in the sureness of her gaze, the certainty with which she held her chin.

Sometimes when we went swimming in the creek behind her house, Indigo would snap off her bathing suit, lift her arms, and raise her hips off the ground. "Look. I'm starting to change, and

I've got hair now. See?"

I could only nod. She'd begun to smell different, too, a tang of salt to her skin. Even her sweat smelled fruited, like she was ripening beneath the moonlight. Meanwhile, I was thoroughly invisible. I had asked for this power the moment I tithed my hair, but I hadn't imagined how methodically it would cloak me. My mother had curled her lip in disgust when she saw my shorn head. Jupiter's gaze had gone unfocused with disinterest, and if I held my power tightly, I could escape his notice for days at a time. That invisibility coated my skin, my body, my bones.

I tried not to stare at Indigo during those swims. I couldn't help it though. I wanted the water to lap at new, secret parts of me too. I wanted to emerge from it smelling like something other than pond scrim. But I was as scentless and hairless as a rock.

Every time we dried ourselves and lay down in the grass, I watched for new gaps between us. I waited for her fingers to flinch away from mine, for her eyes to drift sideways while I spoke, for a yawn to be stifled, but all was the same.

Until the day before fall break.

I woke beside Indigo that Friday. Her eyes were bright and her hair—recently cut to match my own collarbone-grazing length—still damp and spreading puddles on my pillow.

"Time to go to school," she said.

"But you're not dressed?"

"I'm not going," said Indigo. "But *you* are."

She tugged me upright, and I tasted panic on my tongue. "Go to school without you?"

Indigo beamed, nodding. I stared at her. We'd never willingly been apart. I didn't understand. My clothes bruised as I shrugged them on.

I studied Indigo out the corner of my eye, trying to figure

out what I might have done wrong. Had I said something in my sleep? How had I offended? Why was she banishing me?

Indigo finger-combed her damp hair, feet tucked beneath her on the bed. She had changed from her set of night-sky pajamas to a thin shift that turned translucent in the autumn light. The trees outside her bedroom window burned scarlet. I felt that color sear through me as if it were an inferno consuming all that I had known and come to love.

"Go on, Azure," she said, smiling and pointing her chin to the door.

I walked to the door.

"Wait!" said Indigo, her voice warm and playful. She sprang from the bed, ran to me, and kissed my cheek. "Okay now go. Go, go, go."

I could barely put my feet on those stairs. Was that her goodbye? A fond kiss? I touched the walls of the House. It was cool and silent, too early for it to be awake and thus as mute as any ordinary structure. The staff bustled around me, and I tried not to cry. What if I never returned?

A wreath of berries and gold-foiled branches had been netted over the chandelier in the main foyer. The smell of caramel and cardamom wafted through the House, and I couldn't move. What if the House could turn me into a statue? Then I'd never have to leave. A loud rumbling echoed from somewhere on the grounds. I froze, leaning over the handrail as Mrs. Revand made a tut-tutting sound.

"Don't mind that, sweetheart," she said with a wide smile. "It's not for you to see."

The words landed like a slap. I was a guest who had outstayed their welcome. I stared at Mrs. Revand—warm, plum-shaped with henna-dyed hair, crepe-paper skin. She used to praise me for my nice manners, now all that praise looked like pity.

I fled.

THE DAY WAS A BLUR WITHOUT INDIGO. I MOVED LIKE A SHORN thing through the halls at school. With every hour that slid by, my fears gained weight and sharpness, hunting me all the way home. Without Indigo, colors bled from the trees. I breathed and tasted only petrol and woodsmoke where the day before I smelled windfall apples and frost.

When I reached Jupiter's house, I decided on a plan. I would change my clothes and return to the House of Dreams. I would ask Indigo's forgiveness for whatever I had done wrong—

"Indigo called," my mother announced the moment I stepped through the door.

Indigo never called. She'd never even been to Jupiter's place. I used to ask her before our tithe of magic had given me the power to get through those evenings alone. I didn't even know she had the landline number. My mother's face was blank, bored, and betrayed nothing. That, at least, was familiar.

"Well, technically Hippolyta Maxwell-Casteñada"—my mother theatrically deepened her voice at this—"called on Indigo's behalf." She paused, eyebrows raised. "They asked that you *not* trouble yourself to come over for the weekend and said they'll see you on Monday."

"What?" I repeated.

"Their words," said my mother, lifting her shoulder. But her grin was savage. "What'd I tell you? That family will *burn* straight through you. Now that you're older, she's probably getting bored—"

My mother paused. I didn't know what she saw in my face,

but her grin vanished. She shook her head as if remembering where she was, and then stepped toward me. Her hand raised for an instant, only to fall back to her hip.

"Maybe you don't see it now, but this is a good thing, Azure."

Her eyes met mine. I couldn't remember the last time my mother had looked at me so directly. I felt it like a touch, and I shuddered.

"If she kept you around, she would break you into little pieces," she said. "You'd never be able to put yourself back together. I've seen her type before. Trust me."

But trust was all I had, and it was not my mother who held it. The details of that weekend escaped me—bland mounds of rice, thimblefuls of water, hours lost in the shower waiting for my fingers to prune. I registered those days without Indigo as a single held breath, the release of which came only as I made my way to the House of Dreams on Monday morning.

I rehearsed my apologies and clenched my fists. The fifteen-minute walk from Jupiter's gravel driveway to the oak-and-alder-shaded sidewalks of Indigo's estate stretched out for a century. But then, soon enough, there she was: Indigo. A silhouette transposed, the world around her soft with shadows. She wore knee-high green crocodile boots, a high-necked black lace dress beneath a silk robe carelessly belted at the waist.

"Tati has a surprise for us!" she said, and I felt her smile in my bones. "I didn't want us to look over the weekend because you *know* we would, but now we get to see it! Azure . . . Azure, why are you crying?"

Indigo came to me. I lifted my arms to hug her, but she held me apart. Her grip was stern:

"Stop crying," she said, annoyed. "You know we don't do that. You know They might be watching."

They. The fae. The ones we sometimes tried to lure to us. The ones who let us see their magic, even if they never showed their faces.

"Tears are bits of your soul," said Indigo, her face inches from mine. "We can't risk letting them hit the ground."

I lifted my hand to wipe them away as Indigo leaned forward: "What a waste." Her tongue was hot and smooth as it darted out, tracing the curve of my cheekbone. She smacked her lips as she pulled back.

"C'mon," she said, turning on her heel.

I followed her, so ecstatic at what I felt had been a near brush with exile that I never paused to wonder why she had taken my tears for herself. In the stories we read, tears were no less precious than a god's golden blood. I should have told Indigo they were not hers to take. But I would've offered anything to follow her anywhere.

THE OTHERWORLD.

That was what we named our gift from Tati, though we never considered it as something so ordinary as a "present." It had been meant for us.

It had *always* been meant for us.

Destiny shifted into place the moment we walked down the stairs of the back balcony and onto the vast acreage of Indigo's estate. The gardens had been modeled after a French palace somewhere I had never heard of, and from lawn level the sea was nothing but a flash of silver hundreds of feet away, nearly obscured by the thick row of linden trees that marked the land's slow melt into the surrounding water.

Today, the grounds were empty. No gardeners pruned the

trellis of roses arced over the stone-step pathway we often took to play in the creek. No staff member raced back to the house carrying platters of cut peonies and violets for the sitting rooms. The October wind stirred our hair, nipped gently at our ears.

"This way," said Indigo, her voice effervescent with excitement.

A tapping sound made me turn my head. Tati stared down at us through the windows of the sitting room. Her smile was wide, and she made a happy shooing motion with her hand. I waved at her, and she blew me a kiss. I caught her kiss and held it to my cheek.

"Tati isn't coming?" I asked.

"Of course not," said Indigo, skipping ahead down the path. Light dappled her hair, and when she reached for my hand, my heartbeat had never seemed so loud. "It's *our* gift. She said so. She said it was intended for us, so I made Tati swear that whatever it was she'd never trespass." Indigo stilled, turning to me as her voice took on an air of prophecy. "It's not for her to see. Other people wouldn't understand, Azure. Their eyes wouldn't be able to take it."

We usually never walked farther than the creek. As far as I knew, there was nothing out there except the remains of a mill that had burned down in the 1700s, and whose giant stones had served as temple ruins and sacrificial altars when we were younger. The mill was surrounded by a high stone wall. From the House it was nearly invisible, hidden behind the tall cypress and spruces lining the lawns. After a worker broke their ankle clearing the place of rocks a few years ago, Tati forbade us from playing there. It was a rule we had agreed to follow in return for access to all her old costumes.

Indigo tugged me farther down the path until we stood before the gate of the mill. It had changed. It was no longer a skeleton of stones but something tall and ornate, wrought of iron with panels of stained glass in every shade of blue. Salt from the nearby sea stung my nose. From here, I could no longer see the House of Dreams. We'd been released somewhere feral and far outside the world we knew.

Indigo reached for my hand, placed something warm and fluttering in my palm.

"Look," said Indigo, her eyes aglow. "Tati had a blacksmith make them for us."

I looked down to see a pair of starlings. Each iridescent feather iron-cast with a beveled ruby jewel for one eye and a winking sapphire for the other. I could have sworn they breathed, the feathers rustling in the wind, and even before I realized they were keys, I knew they had unlocked magic, drawing into focus the wonders we'd long glimpsed out the corners of our eyes.

Indigo took the key with the blue eye, and a fine silver chain unraveled from the starling's mouth. "This way!"

She slid the key into the padlock of the new gate. It sighed as it swung open, and for the first time we beheld our Otherworld. We stepped across the threshold hand in hand, and I felt the slightest resistance in the air, the breaking of the thinnest of membranes. When I looked down, my arms were damp, christened by an unearthly dew.

The light had an opaque quality as if—only here, in this place—we might card it from the air like wool, drape it over our bodies. An inhuman music reached me: the wet unraveling of apple blossoms and the delicate, percussive dance of a line of ants as they threaded through the oak leaves. Gone was that savory autumn smell of bruised leaves and rained-upon cement. It had been replaced with something rare and distilled, a perfect chord of music dissolved in honey and poured liberally over the ground.

"Do you feel that?" asked Indigo, looking at me.

I nodded.

The millstones were gone, re-formed into a high turret the color of thunderclouds. Beside the turret stretched an old oak, flanked by silver firs and red alders, scraggly apple trees, and a lonely willow, its branches languidly drifting in the creek that hugged part of our small kingdom. The land was roughly a half acre sectioned off from Indigo's property by the rock wall, bursting with deer and sword ferns, fairy bells and pink columbine, dog's tooth violets and hyacinths.

From that moment on, we stopped playing games in which we looked for the Otherworld, and instead, we went to it directly. It was our responsibility, and Indigo and I took our role as guardians seriously. Now that we knew where it was, it felt wrong to exploit it. We left out dishes of milk for the solitary fae, threw raw meat for the selkie in the streams. But we no longer tried to summon them. We didn't want to force magic's hand.

Instead, we tried to be worthy of it.

We were educated the way monarchs might be, fed on a steady diet of history and poetry, dance, and music, all the graces that might serve us in the realm we were meant to rule. But what we were most fascinated with, the one thing that held us in constant thrall and swayed from hubris and humility depending on the time of day, was, of course, ourselves.

Why had the Otherworld revealed itself to us?

Why had magic curled about our feet?

Who were we?

Soon, we were fifteen years old. The air smelled of heartbroken daffodils crushed by April's rain, but it was still cold enough that we dragged blankets from the House to our Otherworld and lay bundled on the turret roof. We did this most evenings after school, which seemed less like a place and more like a penance. In those halls, we moved like ghosts and existed only to each other. I thought we were invisible, but as I would find out, Time was not the only thing that watched us.

"Maybe we're exiles," Indigo mused.

"Oh."

I didn't like the idea that I had been thrown out of something, but I was comforted by the thought that at least we'd been thrown out together.

"Supernatural beings cursed to a mortal life," said Indigo. "Like this life is one grand test and if we grow up wrong, then we'll end up as Cast-Out Susans."

Her mouth pinched at the idea. That week, Indigo and I had finished rereading the Chronicles of Narnia and were once again obsessed with Susan Pevensie. A queen locked out of the realm she'd once ruled, exiled for the crime of growing up.

Susan Pevensie was our nightmare.

"We're not going to end up like that," said Indigo, curling her fist beneath her chin and closing her eyes. "I'm not worried."

But I was.

I pictured my mother as she had once been—burning and bright—before she began to collapse. My mother had given me little of herself. Not her mouth or her height or her laugh, and I was terrified that of all the things she hadn't passed down it would be this slow unrecognizableness that I inherited, like a vicious disease that would eat me from the inside out.

"Let's look into the future," I said.

Indigo blinked open one eye. "Why?"

"Just to be sure."

She looked at me, waiting for me to elaborate. I said nothing. The branches scratched, catlike and curious, against the walls of the turret.

"All right, fine," said Indigo.

It turned out there were thousands of ways to divine the future. There was aruspicina, alomancy, daphnomancy, gelescopy, ceraunoscopy; the examination of entrails, the study of a trail of salt, the divine hidden in the smoke of burning laurel leaves, hints of the future layered in the cadence of someone's laughter, the revelation of time through a pattern of lightning.

I didn't want to kill something. The salt merely blew in the wind. We couldn't find any laurel leaves. I didn't understand what I was supposed to be looking for in someone's laugh, and the lightning disappeared too quickly.

For two weeks, which seemed interminably long to us, I tried everything I could think of.

"Boiling the shoulder blades of donkeys and reading the fissures of their bones?" read Indigo aloud from my research notebook.

She laughed. I wanted to laugh too. But soon the spring would ripen and end, and we were growing too fast, and there were days when my mom summoned me home to her and Jupiter, and I didn't have a choice except to lie there and listen to them scream and pant through the wall we shared. I looked out over the jagged edge of the turret and beheld the Otherworld. This was our realm of honeyed light and apple blossoms, a place so steeped in wonder that if we were to plant a sonnet in the shade of the oak, we might return the next day to find it had become a tree that grew poem-plums and all who ate of it would speak sweetly.

I imagined being shut out of it, unable to cross the bridge, and

I began to cry.

"Azure?" said Indigo, reaching for me.

I didn't know how to share my fears with her, and I didn't have to: Indigo knew. Of course she knew.

"There's no need to worry about the future," she said. "I've already seen it."

"You have? What happens next?"

She wrapped her arms around me. "This is our home forever, Azure. One day, our bones will go in the ground and our soul will wriggle into the House of Dreams and we can grow ballrooms on Sundays, eat shadows for dinner . . . we can do whatever we want."

I laughed. My whole heart was warm because she hadn't said "souls" but "soul." Just the one. Indigo twined her fingers through my hair, and her voice cut through the wind: "Nothing matters except us. Nothing is even real on the other side. You know that."

I smiled.

"We'll be here forever," said Indigo. "I swear it."

Chapter Twelve

THE BRIDEGROOM

If you combed through enough fairy tales, untangled their roots, and shook out their branches, you would find that they are infested with oaths. Oaths are brittle things, not unlike an egg. Though they go by different names depending on the myth—troths and geis, vows and tynged—there is one thing they all share: they must be broken for there to be a story. Only a shattered promise yields a rich, glittering yolk of a tale.

I could feel the promise I had kept for so long, tipping back and forth on the ledge of my own conviction. *Promise me you will not pry. Can you live with that?*

I am trying, I wanted to say. *Truly, I am.*

But when I blinked, I saw Hippolyta's glowing teeth as she laughed: *You say she loves you, but what is she anyway?*

What was Indigo? She was my bride, and she was my love, but there was something of the inhuman that clung to her. A grace and indifference that struck me as alluring one moment and alien the next.

TWO YEARS AGO, WHILE I WAS IN THE MIDDLE OF TRANSLATING

a thirteenth-century Breton lai, a lyric poem popularized in me-dieval France, I became fascinated with oaths and broken prom-ises. I carefully selected each poem so that I might examine the gaps in a story, the details dropped in favor of others. For what is said is not nearly as interesting as what is held back.

My research led me to Wales, and the timing happened to co-incide with our second wedding anniversary. Indigo had planned a surprise for us, and thus I found myself in a castle she had bought out for the occasion in the town of Merthyr Tydfil, a place nestled amidst auburn hills and twisting trees, babbling streams and boulders that once knew the heavy tread of a Roman sol-dier's boot.

"Sometimes, I can't believe you're real," I said.

Indigo smiled. "Who said that I am?"

We were in the topmost room of the castle, lying in a carved four-poster bed made of wood so dark and glossy it looked wet. A heavy red canopy draped over us. Tapestries of bulging-eyed horses and bears danced on the walls, and outside the narrow windows, rain slicked the countryside.

"True," I allowed. "Like Blodeuedd. Have I told you the tale of the flower bride?"

"No," said Indigo with mock hurt. "You have not."

I wrapped my arms around her, resting my chin on top of her cool, silky head. "Once upon a time, there was a hero who was placed under a curse by his own mother that he might never take a human wife. For many years, he was lonely. In the early evenings, he went on long walks just to see his shadow stretched out so long before him that it seemed to belong to someone else entirely.

"Fortunately, the man was not alone, and a pair of great ma-gicians found a way around the curse. They gathered flowers of broom and meadowsweet and oak, and from this, they fashioned a woman of extraordinary beauty and named her Blodeuedd, or 'Flower-Faced,' and gave her as a bride to the lonely hero so that, finally, he had a wife of his own."

"She was made for him," said Indigo, walking her fingers up and down my chest. "Crafted for him *just so* despite his curse."

I smiled. "Curses are made to be broken. They aren't so static as one might think."

"He never broke his mother's curse."

"No?"

"No," said Indigo, her smile sly and lupine. "He couldn't have a human wife, so he was given a bride of flowers. His flower bride was never real at all, but he didn't care because she had been made to please him."

There was more to the tale of Blodeuedd—it ended unhappily, as so many of these tales do—but I had to leave for my lecture, and so I was gone from her side that whole day. By the time I returned, I had almost forgotten the story. Indigo had not though. That night, I found the castle cold and silent, the table set with food, silverware, and thick, flickering candles.

"Hello?" I called out.

No one answered.

I made my way up the narrow stone steps and into the bedroom with its vaulted ceiling. There, Indigo greeted me from a bed thick with flowers—rose petals, hibiscus whorls, meadowsweet, and broom. She greeted me shyly, eyes warm, a marigold perched in the curve of her neck.

Indigo had never looked more beautiful to me than she did in that moment. It wasn't her features—though they had always been lovely—it was the way she molded the atmosphere of the room. She looked like the nostalgia that settles in your ribs at the end of a story you have never read, yet nevertheless know.

In the dark sheaf of her hair, I saw the forest floors where wolves stalked milk-skinned maidens. In the hollow of her neck, I saw the light of precious jewels kept safe in the stinking jaws of a slumbering sea monster. In her parted lips, I glimpsed something that—in my own unpracticed, sloppy awe—struck me as holy. For a moment, I saw a window and not my wife. When I walked to her, it was like peering straight into something primordial and desperate, where the inscrutable space between stars had once birthed myths and gods, built palaces of story and scripture in which human doubts found a place to rest their weary brows.

"If you are a figment of my imagination, some wild dream, I hope I never wake," I said.

Indigo reached for me, drew me down to her, and I forgot everything else in the hot press of petals and skin.

When I woke the next morning, I was bloodied. We hadn't noticed the small thorns forgotten in the bouquets the night before. Indigo was horrified.

"There weren't supposed to be any thorns," she said, touching my broken skin.

I was scratched, but she was unscathed.

I remembered that night, those petals, the marigold falling from her neck when she rose up on her knees to touch me.

His flower bride was never real at all, but he didn't care because she had been made to please him.

I have closed my eyes to be with Indigo. I have chosen not to care about the waking world.

Now, waiting in the hall for Indigo to take us away from this place, I looked at my palm and noted the small scar, puckered and colorless on the heel of my hand, a reminder of that night. In this, too, I saw a warning:

Even an illusion can wound.

Perhaps more so than anything.

Later, I would remember this as the moment where some part of me knew that I would break my vow. Later, the knowledge would be sharp, bright as a match struck in the darkness.

But even so, I could never have foreseen how it would end.

"WOULD YOU LIKE SOME TEA WHILE YOU WAIT FOR MISS INDIGO?" asked Mrs. Revand. I had been standing near the front entrance for the better part of an hour, some animal part of my brain itching to get away from the House's reach. But I could not leave without Indigo. "The lawyers have her tied up, I'm afraid."

Mrs. Revand led me into a parlor on the main level. It was full of stately upholstered chairs and had that sweetly musty scent of disuse that I've long associated with aristocratic decay. A massive bay window looked out over the spectacular grounds and water. My eye caught on something else entirely though.

Against one of the seafoam-colored walls stood a large armoire. It was dull and blocky, the color of blood-soaked wood. Beside it, an ugly industrial-size fan with sharp blades whirred. The longer I looked at the armoire, the more my mouth turned dry. I began to cough.

"Sir?" prompted the housekeeper. "Are you all right?"

I cleared my throat, my cough over as suddenly as it had begun.

"Tea, yes?" asked Mrs. Revand, edging toward an ebony door that stood half-ajar. I could not see what lay on the other side.

I nodded.

"I apologize for the presence of this unsightly fan, sir," she said, glaring at the whirring blades. "The room must be kept at a particular temperature, and the cooling system is under repair."

"That's fine."

The housekeeper left me alone in the parlor. I was glad Indigo was preoccupied. She would want to know what Tati had said, and I didn't yet know what to tell her.

A sky of azure and a sky of indigo walked hand in hand into the Otherworld, but only one of them came out.

I walked to the window facing the sprawling grounds of the House of Dreams. A labyrinth of stone walkways disappeared beneath sculpted vine arches and passages of knitted honeysuckle and ivy. A row of silver lindens marked a pathway to the water.

I imagined there was a private harbor for the Maxwell-Casteñada family. A boat, perhaps, named after some river goddess. But when I looked closer, a structure knifed out from the top of the trees—thin and slender, a shadow of that black turret I had first glimpsed from the driveway.

I breathed deep. Gone was the sense of heavy omens. There was nothing except the plodding whir of the fan. Whatever I had felt in the upstairs hallway couldn't toy with my senses here, and I saw the House for what it was—an old, creaking pile of wood. Nothing more.

I raised an eyebrow, feeling smug in this knowledge.

I thought if there was anything at all to be deciphered in this House, I would be the one to do it. After all, I had much practice. Even as a child, I had been fascinated with the ways the ancients interpreted the world. I'd turn branches of bleached driftwood in a fire and imagine I was heating the shoulder blades of slaughtered goats. I'd eat spaghetti with my hands and think of a Roman haruspex kneeling over an altar, the entrails of beasts running between his fingers in thick, uneven ribbons.

Even now, I preferred the idea that the universe preferred to speak through lightning and shadows. I stared out at the water, lost in daydream—for it certainly could not be a memory—of a brother who rarely used his voice. If we were in different rooms or levels of the house, we would speak in our own language. He'd knock on the floor or a shared wall, and I'd come to him.

What followed was a series of images I knew to be true—my father's playfulness, how my mother sang, the smell of cigarette smoke and violet candies, the scratchy houndstooth coat with the missing button, my fairy-tale book with the split spine and my father's ketchup thumbprint on the first page that looked so much like blood I thought it had been used for ink. Our family once played endless games of hide-and-seek. My favorite spot was under the checkered tablecloth of the dining table. I could picture the illusion of a brother fitting neatly into those memories—how we would have crouched under the table, knees huddled, the milky smell of his breath as we waited to be found.

I was lost in that image when I heard a thud. For a moment, I was convinced I had imagined it. But the sound came again—a clatter, and then, softly, a loud and resolute knock.

It was coming from inside the armoire.

Chapter Thirteen

AZURE

For Indigo's sixteenth birthday, Tati planned a masquerade, and the entire school was invited. The graduating class of Hawk Harbor was barely a hundred people. The House could easily fit them all inside. But Indigo didn't want them there, and for this I was selfishly happy.

"It's time to show face," Tati said, the day the invitations were sent out. "It's not only for the island, Indigo. The investors are coming in from overseas, shareholders want to know the girl who will take her parents' place. People want to know who *you* are."

I thought—hoped—that Indigo would fight Tati as she usually did, but even if she didn't like how bossy Tati was acting, she liked being a part of the Casteñada tradition. Her father had been formally introduced to his father's business associates the day he turned sixteen, and his father before him.

"Think of all the people, the dresses, the cakes . . ." Tati said. We were standing in the kitchen while she examined the final stack of invitations—heavy blue cardstock with silver foil and a navy silk ribbon. "You'll love it, Azure."

I knew I wouldn't. When Tati had insisted on inviting every-one, I'd been terrified that my mother and Jupiter would come and only slightly relieved when my mother turned up her nose and said they'd be too busy on vacation to "celebrate a poor little rich girl." But even without Jupiter and my mother there, the party would be a disaster.

I could already picture it—Indigo on one side of the room, me on the other, a sea of people between us, the House rendered strange underfoot. I sensed the way people would stare at the grand windows and brilliant chandeliers, the sweeping grounds, and the hall of portraits. None of it was mine, and I knew that. But it wasn't ownership I cared about. I had been a part of the House for so long that it now held pieces of me, and by the end of the party, I would feel rummaged through, like the House, stained by all who'd entered.

Before Indigo's party invitations, I had thought our classmates never noticed us. We were a pair of silent, dark-haired cuckoo chicks sitting in a nest of cream-colored finches. We never lined up for the ferries to go shopping on the mainland or attended the beach bonfires, drinking beer out of canteens. We rarely spoke to anyone other than each other. But the Monday after the invitations were mailed, I realized that what I had thought was apathy was actually awe.

I felt the change the moment I stepped into homeroom, an electric hum tracing the lines of my skull. Indigo and I had entered the building together that morning, as we always did, but the principal had pulled her away for a quick word and scowled when I tried to follow, so I arrived alone.

The classroom seemed defined for once, all its edges articulated—the chalkboard decorated in crimped, painted cardboard, the square arrangement of sixteen blue plastic chairs, the sun-warmed smell of chalk mixed with my classmates' sweat and hair products. And underneath it all: the sour, unripened scent of youth.

Our teacher hadn't arrived yet, leaving me with twelve pairs of eyes that had never beheld me so closely until now. I stepped back, as if to melt into the wall behind me, when one of them, a boy named Barrett with a gentle voice and a constantly red face, spoke:

"What's it like inside there?"

The eleven other students shifted in their seats, blinking away only for a moment before resuming their staring.

"What?"

"The House," he said, licking his lips. "You're always inside the Casteñada house."

"Is it actually haunted?" asked a girl. It took me a moment to find her name: Anna. She had lank blond hair and small, hooded eyes that flicked over my outfit: a pair of red velvet pants and a lacy black sweater cinched at the wrists with a high neck. A slow, vicious heat climbed my skin. The clothes belonged to Indigo, and Anna knew it. She smirked.

"Are we all really supposed to wear masks?" asked Emmanuel. His skin was the color of black marble, and he had the hands of a grown man at fifteen. "Like Halloween masks?"

My heart stammered. I didn't like their focus. I didn't like feeling pinned by their eyes. I thought of Jupiter across a room, some poison in his gaze paralyzing my muscles, and I could not find air.

"Are you guys related?" asked another.

I opened my mouth, then balked. How could I explain that we were two halves of the same soul? But I didn't have to. Indigo stood in the doorway. She looked at the girl who had asked, and a corner of her mouth tilted up.

"Something like that," said Indigo in her low, honeyed voice.

I exhaled, she caught my hand, and we transformed. I could not tell you where that magic came from, whether it was some unseen element insinuating itself into our atoms or if I served as mirror and moon to Indigo's incandescence. All I knew was that together we were lustrous.

The classroom fell silent. I felt the tiniest thrill to see their lips part, their eyes unfocus. But then the teacher stepped inside, and the spell we'd cast upon them broke.

IN THE DAYS LEADING UP TO INDIGO'S PARTY, I THOUGHT THE House would be happy. Usually, it loved decorations. It always appeared grander, more elegant with the presence of flowers and wreaths, garlands and lights. Plus, it was constantly fussed over in preparation. Mrs. Revand arrived early and left late, directing the maids to scrub and polish every inch of the interior. I watched from the staircase as she ordered slabs of ice sent to the basement, snapped at boys wheeling ropes of fairy lights to string them across the grounds, signed for deliveries of carts of orchids and violets.

But the House was sullen. A sourness crept into the wood, and no matter how many candles were lit, the staff wrinkled their noses whenever they stepped past the threshold. Carpets newly flattened bunched, rolling ankles at every hour of the day. Curtains unraveled from their hooks, painting shadows over the walls and turning the rooms hunched and small.

"It'll be over soon," I said to the House, patting its topmost stair. "It's only one party."

It did not seem convinced.

The week of the event, Indigo and I hid in the Otherworld for as long as we could, emerging only to eat and sleep and attend school. Tati was to blame, but still I felt sorry for her. Tati needed our thoughts on decorations, wanted our measurements taken for dresses. She made us taste cake samples and Indigo write thank-you cards in advance. She wanted us—as I overheard her saying one evening when I was supposed to be in the bath—"to take this seriously."

"I hate her," Indigo said, her words dropping like stones. The party was two days away, and the House was still shrugging off any attempt at festivity. Today it had loosened a whole string of lights from two of its pillars.

"You don't mean that," I said, thinking of Tati's hopeful smile and her bruised mood from each of Indigo's refusals.

A couple of days earlier Tati had shown me a sketch of a mask she was commissioning just for me. It was made of blue satin and sprinkled with small blue rhinestones. Light and playful. I touched the drawing, imagining the satin's watery smoothness against my skin, and smiled up at her.

"I'm so glad you like it, sweetheart," she said.

She opened her arms to me, and I hugged her tight. I could tell from the way she held me that she was imagining Indigo, soft and sweet. I tried not to mind. I kept all that warmth for myself and daydreamed about the jeweled mask.

I loved that mask in a way that made my teeth ache from the guilt. I wished I could be more like Indigo. I wished I didn't notice every gleaming stone set into the bathroom mosaics, all the polished silver laid out on the mahogany table, each marble surface anointed with golden bowls of rare fruits and exquisite truffles. It's true we shared one soul, but I was the one who had to return to Jupiter's house, who had to venture between light and dark, and whose eyes needed time to adjust.

The evening before the event, what had once been frosty

between Indigo and Tati iced over and snapped. Since the tables were covered in decorations, we had to eat dinner in the formal dining room, the Camera Secretum. It was Indigo's favorite place, and my least favorite, in the House. The translation of its name was the Room of Secrets, though it only ever gave me nightmares.

Lined with the skulls of animals on one side and the heads of taxidermied beasts on the other, it was where Indigo's grandfather displayed his hunting trophies. Indigo said it was the best place for dreaming. While I read in the library, Indigo hid in the Room of Secrets, sketching pictures of what we would look like when our true, fae spirit made itself known. She never let me see her work.

"Until I'm finished, it's a secret even from me," she would say.

Which was probably why she loved the Camera Secretum so much in the first place. Tati once told us that Indigo's grandfather had insisted on conducting every business meeting within the walls of that room.

"Only the dead know how to keep secrets," Tati told us with a dramatic wink.

I thought of that again when Tati stood in the archway of the dining room. Her face was stony, and her hands clenched at her sides.

"Indigo," she said, flashing a tight smile at me. "I need to speak with you. *Now.*"

Indigo looked mutinous. After a moment, she pushed her chair back from the table and stood. I set my napkin down to follow, but Tati shook her head at me.

"I'll be right back," said Indigo. "Wait here."

Without Indigo beside me, the jaws of the animal skulls lengthened and grinned. My back prickled from the gaze of a lynx frozen in a snarl. I pushed my food around my plate for what felt like hours but what was probably minutes and then ran from the room.

Firelight flickered in the parlor down the hall from the kitchen. I meant to go straight to the stairs and up to Indigo's bedroom, but a sharp, animal sob drew me back. I had never heard Indigo weeping before, and the sound—fragile as a glass bell—tore into me. I crept to the parlor, holding close to the wall, peeking inside only to see Tati crumpled on the ground. She was backlit by the fireplace, her face bloated with tears.

Indigo stood over her, the light shining through her thin nightdress. She looked like an icon from ancient times, draped in fire and linen, her hands impassively clasped in front.

"How could you say that?" sobbed Tati.

Tati's hand flew to a brooch pinned to her long black nightgown. It was the rose, the one made of fine baby hair. Tati's fingers dropped. She stared up at Indigo. "I didn't become your guardian because of *money*. I stayed because I love you, Indigo. I am human and I make mistakes, but I am trying my best to raise you, to help get you ready for the world, and that means showing them who you are . . . the niece I *love*."

Tati reached out to touch Indigo's dress. Indigo didn't move away from her, though her expression didn't soften.

"I don't care about the settlement," said Tati. "I care about you. You are all I have left in this world."

Tati crouched like an animal, and when Indigo still didn't move, Tati crawled forward, resting her shaking forehead against Indigo's knee until, finally, Indigo's glowing hand molded to her skull.

I stopped watching, and after that went to bed. This was not the first time I had seen Tati plead with Indigo, though it was the first time I'd seen her crumpled on the ground. I imagined being in Indigo's position, watching someone you love kneel at your feet, knowing you can make them stand or fall with a single word. Before I fell asleep, I saw my mother kneeling before the firelight, and it was not Indigo's hand she begged to absolve her, but my own.

AN HOUR BEFORE THE PARTY BEGAN, INDIGO AND I WERE WAIT-ing in her room, watching the cars pull up the driveway. I had never seen so many elegant people in my life—women in shining dresses, men in gleaming suits, masks wrought of pearls and silk ribbons. Our classmates walked past the driveway in a daze, staring at the cars, up at the House, at their reflections as if they were bewildered by what they saw, and I felt my chest swell with borrowed pride.

Indigo and I were already dressed. Tati had bought me a short, cap-sleeved, black velvet dress with an empire waist decorated with small blue jewels to match my mask. Indigo wore a long, off-shoulder blue gown that gathered in the back to form an elaborate train. Her mask was a simple length of black tulle, and her hair—now grown past her breasts—fell heavily against the middle of her back. My hair had grown out to the same length. I'd thought that with every inch I gained, I'd lose the magic of invisibility, but my power seemed to have grown with me, fitting me as close as a second skin.

"Tati says I have to show the world who I am," said Indigo, carding her fingers through my hair. "So, let's show them."

"What do you mean?"

"Let's show them who we are," said Indigo. "*What* we are." I closed my eyes and let her words reach into me. "That we're two halves of a soul, Azure. That when we're together, we weave magic. I bet the Otherworld will notice and gift us with more power. It'll be proud of us."

I opened my eyes. My pulse climbed into the hollow of my neck.

"We don't look the same," I said.

People had always told us we could be related, but that was only because we were both dark-haired with the same golden tint to our skin. My mother sometimes called herself Persian; other times she said her family hailed from an island off the coast of India. Indigo once told me her mother was adopted from a tribe of Bedouins. We never knew, really, but we were always aware that there was something *other* about us, something Indigo said even the faeries had noticed, and that's why they obsessed over us as we did them.

Beyond those broad strokes of likeness, we looked nothing alike. Where my nose was big, Indigo's was daintily snubbed. My mouth was frog-large, and hers was sweetly ripe. My eyes were brown and my eyelashes sparse. Her eyes were a rich mahogany with a fan of soot-colored lashes. Our hair was nearly the same shade. But where hers was the color of charred wood, mine was flatter . . . blacker. In the summertime, her hair was warm and smelled like hay and syrup. Mine always seemed a few degrees cooler. Indigo said it smelled like snow.

"It has nothing to do with 'likeness,'" said Indigo, eyes feverish and alight with her idea. "Come on, we barely have an hour."

"But, Indigo—"

"Don't you want magic?" she asked, grabbing my wrist.

Indigo unzipped my dress. Her fingers brushed heat down my spine as she tugged off her gown and handed it to me. Next, she undid the neat coils of my hair, brushing them out and rubbing something that smelled like violets into their ends. When she was done, I looked down. I wore Indigo's clothes like an animal pelt. I wore her scent like a talisman.

"Go," said Indigo, tying my mask around her face and grinning. "Go and enjoy our party."

"Where will you be?"

"Right beside you," said Indigo, squeezing my hand.

I walked out of Indigo's bedroom and into the hallways overflowing with music. Strands of light braided across the ceiling, flowers of freesia and peonies hung in thick, perfumed veils. I walked down the stairs, my fingers trailing against the wall of the House. I felt it purr in delight.

The crowd swelled through the entryway and servers instantly threaded through them, balancing platters of fizzing drinks and dainty bite-size pastry cups with spoons of tartare. I wondered if this was how Indigo felt when she walked down these same stairs, as though the world was not something she stepped into, but *on.*

People I didn't know smiled warmly at me. I was embraced. I was exclaimed over.

"You look lovelier every year," whispered a woman whose swanlike neck was roped in pearls. She touched my cheek, smiling, before melting into the crowd. Indigo moved behind me—a cool, sly shadow.

"Happy birthday, my dear," said a tall, dark-skinned man. He was handsome, with wide eyes and crooked teeth. He bowed neatly over my wrist.

He had an accent. I'd never heard an accent before. I couldn't place it.

"You must visit the Paris flagship, *non?* You will love it."

Behind me, I felt Indigo recoil. I wanted to shake my head or say no, but his words had already conjured an enticing image—boulevards and bougainvillea, the trill of a language stamping the air and the brief, abrupt collapse of the walls of my life where other cities winked in the distance.

"Indigo?"

I looked up to see Tati now standing beside the man. Her face white beneath her domino mask and matching headscarf.

"Hippolyta," said the elegant man. "I was just telling Mademoiselle Casteñada that she must visit before she's all grown up and inherits the world." He laughed, and it was warm and booming. He turned to Indigo and nodded politely. "She can bring her friend too."

In the span of seconds, I turned from a giant to a gnat. I hadn't even known to dream about a life outside of Hawk Harbor, but Indigo could slip into new cities with a snap of her fingers. All I could do was hope she might want to take me along.

"How generous," said Tati, still staring at me.

Cake was cut. Music was played. Indigo and I ran upstairs and down, our gowns rumpled from switching, our half souls blurring to one. Our feet ached from hours spent dancing and running, and when midnight came and the House yawned in irritation at the remaining trail of guests, Tati found me in the hallway, where Indigo and I had stolen the cake and eaten it by the handful in the dark.

"You enjoyed yourselves," she said.

I nodded. Indigo was curled onto my lap, fast asleep. I pushed her hair off her face, adjusted my mask, which was set at a jaunty angle on her cheek.

"That could have been very bad, Azure," said Tati, her voice quiet, but sharp as a piece of glass.

I was flush with power, and so I lifted my chin and said

nothing. Indigo and I shared a soul. Her boldness could be mine too.

"Don't get confused, child. You and I are not like the Indigos of the world," said Tati. "People like her can remake reality as they so wish, but we are forced to live in the lands they leave behind."

Tati was wrong. This power answered to me as much as it answered to Indigo. I had just never thought to test it before.

The next day, I returned to Jupiter's house. I found him waiting for me in the hallway, and this time I did not stiffen. I had relied too long on the invisible armor of my hair, but that was only to slip past him. Not show him that I could not be caught. Not now, not ever.

"Look who's here!" he said. "Our long-lost princess."

He moved to ruffle the top of my head. He was wearing his golden watch with the broken link. Sometimes, Jupiter's watch got tangled in my curls. He would say: *Don't worry. I've got it, princess. I'll get you free.*

I used to feel every contour of those minutes. I would count the seconds it took before he moved his arm and even then, I would feel the ghostly echo of his touch hours later. Jupiter's flesh was almost hot and uncannily soft and pulpy, the peeled paleness of a squashed fruit.

This time, when he reached for me, his fingers glided off my hair. His watch didn't snag and when he opened his mouth to say *Gotcha, princess*, I smiled with all my teeth because he was wrong. He had not gotten any part of me.

My power had a slippery quality. I was oiled in it. I could glide into places, armored and unseen. My hair reflected gazes. When I showered, I could sculpt it sleekly over my breasts and stand in the water and know that nothing could touch me.

"I LIKE US LIKE THIS," SAID INDIGO.

A few weeks had passed, and we were tucked into our Otherworld.

"Like what?" I asked.

I knew what she would say, though I still wanted to hear her say it. Lately, the muscles of my legs felt sleek, like they ached to shift into fins or backward into talons. The terrain of my body curved to make room, the way a vessel hollows to allow space for wonder. It was not a transforming but an unearthing, and I knew that what I was always meant to be was slowly pushing its way to the surface.

Indigo smiled, staring up at the sky. "Powerful."

Above, the oak branches groaned and leaned against the stone turret of the Otherworld, as if trying to gather us against its hard body. Indigo laughed and the silver ornaments hanging from the willow branches trilled and sang. If she had told me in that moment that all the world was a dream designed to delight us, I would not have doubted it.

"See?" she said, turning to me. "It knows."

Chapter Fourteen

THE BRIDEGROOM

One must never look with the eyes alone. Things transform with ease and without warning. In one tale, a dead mother becomes an ash tree and, in lieu of flowers and leaves, puts forth gowns of silver and gold for her only daughter. In another, the mutilated bodies of little boys bend into doves who coo and mourn their murder. The material form might be anything, but each tale relies on the ability to perceive the fantastical from the false.

I would be lying if I said I've never looked for my brother. On the days where logic thinned and I allowed myself to consider his existence, I imagined him in the silhouettes of the trees, in the sharp tilt of a raven's head. He would no longer look the same. I expected that his mortal body might have transformed into a slender deer, a bulging frog, a cold wind. But I would welcome him no matter what shape he took, for I knew the secret to such stories:

You must learn how to close your eyes and still look.

As I was looking now.

I could see nothing but the armoire, looming as huge as a planet in the middle of the parlor. With each insistent, deafening knock, I closed the distance between myself and an impossibility. In front of the armoire, the fan whirred. I thought of my secret, unspoken taunt to the House.

Well, what do you have to give me?

This, said the House. *Look.*

I reached for the knob; the thumping of the fan reminded me of a heartbeat. I drew a quick breath, my hands closing around the rough carved wood of the handle before pulling hard. The doors opened to a rush of air, a flat darkness, and then, unmistakably, a small childlike cry.

He came to me in a rush of wings and a flash of silver. He screamed once more, and in that shriek, I knew it was my brother. It made no sense. I knew I never had one. And yet I still lifted my hands to receive him.

At that moment, the door to the kitchen swung open and Mrs. Revand screamed. I turned my head for only a brief instant. In that second, the blades of the fan choked. The smell of iron hit the air and Mrs. Revand clutched the back of a settee, the tea tray trembling in her hand.

"Gods, not again," she said, lunging to unplug the fan. "I am so very sorry, sir. I have no idea how that bird got in here. Please allow me to get this cleaned up."

A black feather floated to my shoe. I caught sight of my pants. Blood spattered.

Before me, the blades of the fan clamped a starling's body, the wings bent, the neck clearly snapped. I was shaken, not by the sight of the corpse but by the unmistakable certainty that my brother had disappeared again. I had never felt this before, this belief that I truly had a brother. Yet now the conviction was solid and as irrevocably a part of me as my own bones.

I remembered the fairy tales. Forms are not to be trusted. Bodies might be inhabited and deserted, slipped on like so much cloth. Some forms are made to please and others to deceive. Here, a wolf pants in bed, the nightgown of an old woman thrown over its fur. There, a being places marigolds in its mouth and petals in its hair, and through a handful of flowers makes itself a wife. Now a brother is revealed and taken away, and the House of Dreams smiles because it knows I have been ensnared.

Mrs. Revand touched my arm. "Please, sir, this way. The driver will be here shortly, and I've asked them to retrieve you from the dining hall."

"What?"

Mrs. Revand blinked, and pity snuck into her eyes. "Miss Indigo left a few minutes ago. She has another meeting with the solicitors. She sent word for you to meet her at the hotel. The car should be here shortly."

"She left me here?" I repeated. "Didn't Indigo want to see Hippolyta?"

Mrs. Revand fell quiet. I recalled the guilt on her face when she'd summoned me, the look of apology when she'd closed the doors.

"Hippolyta didn't want to see her," I guessed.

Indigo must know that I had seen her aunt. I wondered if she also heard the House whispering to me, if she could somehow feel our wedding vows slipping between my fingers.

A thread now stretched between my brother, my bride, and Azure. I thought of promises made and broken, of the dark circles beneath Indigo's eyes and the engraved tooth.

What if my vow was another test?

Our first night together, Indigo and I played Eros and Psyche. It was only through the shattering of a promise that Psyche proved her love. Otherwise, Eros might have tired of her in the dark. Perhaps I had been given a chance to prove I would rescue my bride from whatever enchantment held her captive from me.

MRS. REVAND BROUGHT ME TO THE DINING ROOM TO WAIT while the staff cleaned the starling's blood, and there I beheld a curious echo. A small golden plaque hung on the wall outside the entrance: CAMERA SECRETUM. The Room of Secrets.

The ceiling of the dining room was domed and open, like the observatory of a planetarium. Golden fretwork curved beneath the glass. A long, uneven slab of white-veined onyx served as the dining table, which was bare except for a dusty candelabra at the center.

On one wall hung a series of taxidermied heads—an oryx with swordlike horns, three alpine goats, an ibex, pheasants, chamois, and musk oxen, and the radiant fall of a peacock's plumage through which a roe deer stared at me almost flirtatiously. The wall opposite held skulls and tusks. I recognized only a few of the creatures, but among them were mounted alligators and crocodiles, stately bison with polished horns, hog skulls, and the long, sinister ovals of a baboon's face stripped of flesh.

In our own home of glass, Indigo had a Gallery of Beasts. Her beasts were all made of stone, though they were no less menacing. I had found a clue to Indigo's secret hidden there. Even now, I could recall the cool temperature of Azure's hair, the smoothness of the engraved tooth. What secrets did this room keep for itself?

A button from my shirt plinked to the ground. I bent to pick it up and glanced at the underside of the onyx table. The House of Dreams was lying in wait, and the images of my brother that I had thought were false now crystallized into memory.

My brother and I had often played under our cherrywood dining table. Once, Father had come home while we were pretending to be wild wolves. My father threw some bread on the floor, and I picked it up off the rug.

If you're going to act like an animal, said my father, bending down to wink at us, *then you'll have to eat like one too.*

We ate under the table for a whole week, making animal sounds the entire time. Sometimes our parents joined us. Our father barked and howled.

I'd never laughed so hard.

But now the memory sheered, curled along its edges. The House sought to punish me for being so slow to take up its quest, and so it poisoned the details. Now my father showed his teeth, and beneath the dining table, my brother and I stared at our parents' feet and whimpered with hunger.

Open your eyes, said the House.

I straightened. Blood rushed to my head as the room came into focus. I would have yelled at the House for its impatience, but right then Mrs. Revand appeared in the entryway and smiled.

"The driver is here for you," she said. Her glance darted from the polished table to the flat hollows of the baboon skull. "You know, Indigo loved this room when she was little. It was her favorite place. Well, second favorite place."

I blinked and thought I saw a girl crouched beneath the table. But she was not my Indigo. This girl had long, black hair that puddled over thin, emaciated shoulders, and wide azure eyes. Her mouth hung open, her chin glossy with spit. A ghost girl in need of feeding.

"What was her first favorite place?"

"The Otherworld, of course. They used to spend *hours* there, my goodness," said Mrs. Revand with a laugh. "You would think they'd have put down real roots!"

And there it was. A hint laid bare, spoken this time in Hippolyta's rotting, rasping voice.

The Otherworld knows all their secrets.

Chapter Fifteen

AZURE

You notice power. Everyone does. It draws the eye, fills the mouth with saliva. Indigo's masquerade had drawn us into focus for our classmates, and the power we found afterward held us in place. They hadn't noticed us for the first time at the party because we were beautiful. They noticed us because we scared them. Their eyes tried to chisel us into pieces they could hold in their hand— brown eyes, dark hair, sullen mouths. When they smiled, they imagined us between their teeth, how we'd taste as they chewed on that glittering rind until all that was mysterious about us gave way to ordinary marrow.

Like most mornings, I'd show up at the House before school, shrug off the faded clothes my mother bought for me, and let Indigo carefully arrange our outfits. If she wore a headband of pearls, I wore a collar of them around my neck. If she wore a black dress with white boots, I wore a white dress with black boots. We blurred together when we walked the hallways, our long hair melting so we looked less like two distinct beings and more like a torn reflection.

If my power was to make sure the world never came too close, hers was to make sure the world couldn't get close enough.

It was a game for her, seeing what someone would do just to place themselves directly in our line of sight.

There was the boy who wrote us poems every day for a month, the girl who shyly offered all the cupcakes her mom had baked that morning, the upperclassmen who invited us to party before denouncing us as "fucking weirdos" when we refused, even as their eyes bored holes into our backs. Whenever someone dared approach us, I held myself still, wondering if they'd disappear if I remained silent. Indigo entertained their interest until they all, inevitably, disappointed her.

She didn't like the poems the boy wrote, the cupcakes tasted stale, the party was not a ball. For a moment, a pair of twins who started midterm caught her eye. They were short, pale-skinned, with fine, golden hair they both wore in a braid down their backs.

"Maybe they're like us," Indigo said.

It was the only time she offered to let anybody sit with us. I liked the twins. I liked their pink snubbed noses and cinnamon freckles, the watery blue of their eyes and their long, colorless lashes.

But soon, they bored her too.

One of them couldn't stop sniffling. The other couldn't stop speaking. Within minutes, the talkative one mourned their old home in Ohio and the neighborhood public pool, where only a few weeks ago, a boy with a boring name had stuck his hand up one of their shirts. Indigo never spoke to them again.

And then came Puck.

Puck was a year below us and once had a different name. It didn't really matter what it was, because this was the one she used around us. She was short, light-skinned, her body straight up and down. She had a large nose and larger eyes that were too close together.

I liked her mouth best. It was rosebud small, with even smaller, doll-size teeth. Indigo loved her hair. It was the kind of red that resembles a brushed-out flame, which she wore cropped to her chin. On the day she approached us, she was wearing a black sweater and red pants. She looked like a drop of blood.

"I know what you are," she declared.

Indigo raised one eyebrow. She had layered a white night-gown under a long, black fur coat. I was wearing a white leather trench and a long-sleeved black velvet dress that once belonged to Indigo's mom. We had split an apple between us, which I happily snacked on while reading Charles Perrault's book of fairy tales. Beside me, Indigo sketched. I knew better than to look at her drawings. Even the soul holds its secret caverns, and for us it was her art and my books.

"You know what we are?" Indigo said without looking up. "And what might that be?"

I eyed Puck curiously. She didn't seem like the type to stop by our table and mutter something unkind just for fun.

"Witches," she said, hushed. "Or . . . I dunno, fairy girls or something. I know you're not human."

My skin tingled. Indigo put down her pencil. The corner of her mouth quirked in a smile.

Nobody had ever said that to us before. There were rumors, of course, and they teased that we weren't human, but no one believed it. Puck was different.

Puck believed.

"I want to be like you," she said, her voice barely above a whisper.

Across the table, I felt a new heat rising off Indigo's skin. I almost grabbed Puck's hand. I almost told her to run. But one look at Puck's face, and I knew it wouldn't have made a difference.

Puck couldn't see us, not really. She saw only the blur of power, a shimmer that perhaps she imagined might feel like December sunshine on her skin.

"Sit with us," said Indigo imperiously.

Puck sat. She reached into her satchel for her bagged lunch. Indigo shook her head.

"We don't eat here."

"Sorry." Puck seemed ashamed. She folded her hands in her lap and looked down. "I won't do it again."

The deference in her voice made my stomach curl. But where I was embarrassed for her, Indigo was intrigued. She reached across the table, touched the ends of Puck's hair.

"Now your name is Puck, and you belong to us. Okay?"

"Okay," repeated Puck.

"Normally, you'd have to sign your name in blood to make the bond true," said Indigo.

I shot her a warning glance, but Indigo wasn't looking at me.

"Do you have something sharp with you?" asked Indigo.

Puck blushed again and shook her head.

"That's okay," said Indigo sweetly. "Come to the House after school and you can do it there. You know where it is, don't you?"

"Everyone knows where it is," said Puck, awed.

Indigo smiled again and I figured she had just wanted to hear it out loud.

"We'll see you there."

Dismissed, Puck gathered her things and stood. I felt a rush of relief that she was going. Maybe now I could talk Indigo out of whatever she was planning. Indigo wasn't finished though.

"Being like us means making sacrifices," said Indigo. "If you're serious about this then you cannot speak to a single human being for the rest of the day, Puck."

Puck froze. "I-I have a presentation to give in fifth period . . . but I promise I won't say anything else? Unless I'm called on or something?"

Indigo looked at her sharply. "Creatures of the Otherworld love loopholes. They love cleverness. If you can't make this sacrifice, then you're wasting our time."

Puck hesitated. Indigo sighed and slouched against me, laying her heavy, warm head in the crook of my neck. She smelled of apples. Usually when she did this, she was boneless and sleepy as a kitten. Now, I could feel the taut energy in her body, the careful way she arranged herself against me. I saw what Puck saw: a glossy-haired, elegant puzzle, a red fruit split between our hands. Indigo made us look like icon and enigma, less like sisters and more like two beatific halves. Puck gaped.

"I'll manage," said Puck.

When she left, Indigo lifted her head from my shoulder. I felt cold without her against me.

"What are we doing?" I asked.

Indigo shrugged. "Playing. I like her hair."

Puck met us after school before the wrought-iron gates of the House. I noticed that she had changed her clothes. She wore an oversize black pea coat, a white smock shirt, and black rain boots. A parody of Indigo's outfit.

Indigo had us wait on the other side of the fence, careful to maintain the separation. When Puck saw us, her pace sped up until she was almost running, clutching a pocketknife in her sweaty grip.

"I brought something sharp," said Puck, breathless and bright-eyed.

Indigo barely smiled. Puck never looked at me. I was a necessary, silent backdrop, both as expected and unremarkable as a cloud in the sky.

"Cut yourself," said Indigo.

"Um, where?" asked Puck, turning over her palm.

She had chubby wrists and stubby fingers and wore a power-bead bracelet of false jade around her wrist. It was too big for her and kept slipping down to her knuckles even as she shoved it farther up her arm.

"Blood is blood," said Indigo, impassive.

Puck screwed up her face, squeezing her eyes shut, and slashed the knife down her palm. She sucked in her breath, held out her bloodied hand.

"Press your hand into the earth," said Indigo. "And tell the earth your real name."

Puck cast about. On the outskirts of the House of Dreams, the ground was mostly sharp mulch, but she dutifully crouched down and pressed her hand to it.

"M-My name—"

"I forgot, you have to put your forehead on the ground," said Indigo. "It's called 'kowtowing.' You can look it up in history books. It's how you're supposed to greet powerful things, and the earth is extremely powerful."

"Oh, right," said Puck.

She knelt and placed her forehead in the dirt. Her jacket fell open, puddling around her. Her red hair flopped over her head. Indigo laughed silently. I glared at her, and she winked at me.

"My name is Puck," the girl said, her voice nasal in that position.

Finished, Puck stood, sniffling and blinking.

"Come inside, Puck," said Indigo, opening the gate. "Come into the House of Dreams."

I DIDN'T LIKE PUCK.

At first, I felt bad for her. I felt bad for the way she mimicked us, how she'd try to tuck her knees to her chest and fold delicately into chairs as Indigo did, or pull at her hair, as if by tugging it long and hard enough, she could make it grow like ours.

"Real faeries subsist off dew and forest fruits and the choicest of honeycombs," Indigo told her one day. She licked a bit of honey from her thumb. "You have to purify your body with our diet before you can become one of us."

After that, Puck pushed aside the cafeteria food and nibbled on apples, even drank from a birdbath when Indigo told her it was considered a delicacy amongst the Fair Folk. I should've stopped Indigo before it went this far, but by then, I had stopped feeling bad for Puck.

I hated how she breathed through her mouth, how she'd clutch at a scrap of Indigo's attention. A few times we kept her waiting outside the House, watching her from behind the trees just to see how long she could stand it. She looked weak—her shoulders curved in; her legs squeezed together as she rocked on her heels. Even her bored humming reminded me of a wounded thing mewling in the dark. Looking at her embarrassed me.

Two weeks after Puck joined us, Indigo invited her to the House for a second time.

"Are you serious?" I asked her.

"Of course not," she said, brushing out her hair. "It's not like I'd ever take her to the Otherworld. It's only a bit of fun, Azure."

That day, she greeted Puck wearing a floor-length emerald velvet duster—I had been given a matching gray one—and promptly looped their arms together. Puck turned slavish and adoring. Her eyes never left Indigo's face as she was led through the sunlit halls, and when we reached the Room of Secrets, she didn't even register the animal heads and skulls lining the walls.

"I have something for you," said Indigo, gesturing to the table.

A dozen ebony candles lined the long black table, along with twelve dainty crystal glasses filled with water. Indigo gestured me to her, leaving Puck stranded on the other side.

"This is the final test before you can truly be one of us," said Indigo. "One glass grants immortality, three are filled with poison, one will make you ugly, another will make you beautiful, four are filled with plain water, one will make you easily controllable, and one will make you lose your memory."

"I—" started Puck, looking confused as she took in the glasses on the table. "Can I have a minute to pick out—"

"No," said Indigo. "Your instinct will reveal if you're right or not."

Puck swallowed hard, then reached out, randomly grabbing one. She steeled herself, then threw back her head and downed its contents in one gulp. She looked at Indigo, her eyes wide.

For a moment, I wondered what Indigo had put in the glasses. It was sometimes hard to tell when she was playing and when she wasn't, and the only one who truly knew was her. Indigo winced, hissed in her breath, and exchanged a knowing glance with me.

"Oh, Puck," she said. "You chose the one that makes you easily controllable."

"I did?" said Puck. "But . . . but I don't feel any different?"

"No?" said Indigo. "Watch." She lifted her hand, her voice deepening in command. "Slap yourself."

I stared at Puck and realized that she was staring back at me, as if seeing me clearly for the first time. Her eyes held mine.

"I said . . . *slap yourself*," said Indigo.

I wished I could've seen my face in that moment, seen what

Puck saw. But she squeezed her eyes shut, raised her hand, and slapped her face.

"Again," said Indigo.

Puck slapped herself. Again and again. She sniffled loudly. Tears ran down her cheeks. One side of her face turned bright red, and yet her hand was still raised, ready.

"Told you, you picked the wrong glass," said Indigo. "But that's okay because you passed. The real test was to see whether or not magic even works on you."

Puck snuffled, nodding. An odd laugh broke free from her chest.

"Magic works on me," she repeated.

I looked at Indigo. She smiled, and it barely appeared human: a flash of glossy teeth, there and gone. Maybe she meant it to be a conspiratorial thing between us, but it only raised goose bumps along my arms. Indigo thought this whole situation was a joke, that of course there hadn't been any magic in this moment. She was wrong.

The magic was nothing so tangible as a crystal glass or an uttered incantation. It lay in how the House decanted the light, the aristocratic lines of the shadows cast on the floor. The magic was the spark in her brown eyes, rendering them an animal shade of amber. The magic was this: the supple sorcery of Indigo's words, such that your own hand became a blade you eagerly welcomed.

AFTER A FEW MONTHS OF PUCK TRAILING AFTER US, PARROTING Indigo's made-up nonsense, and, at one point, stealing her mother's engagement ring so that we might offer it as a gift to the faeries, Indigo began to grow bored.

She had run out of commandments and stories. She no longer

tried to dazzle. Maybe she thought Puck would grow bored with us, too, but it only humbled the other girl, made her sticky with gratitude.

One day, Indigo summoned Puck to the water behind the House of Dreams. The water was special to us, the place where all our worlds came together—the far-off glimmer of the city, the freezing shade offered by the yew and willow trees, the stone bridge that ran over the little stream we used to reach the Otherworld.

That was how I knew Indigo was never serious about Puck. For all that she granted her entry to the House and, on occasion, the lavender shadows of Indigo's bedroom, we never brought Puck to the Otherworld.

"The final test is to wash this mortal slime off you," said Indigo, touching Puck's face. She studied her for a moment, a true smile touching her lips. "You really are lovely, Puck."

Puck beamed even as she shivered and stood in one of Indigo's old nightgowns. Her red hair was a flattened flame against her neck. Her eyelashes looked fluorescent.

"Thank you," said Puck.

"Don't thank me," said Indigo. "The sky doesn't thank anyone for taking notice."

The tops of Puck's cheeks reddened. There was no cruelty in Indigo's voice, and I knew she meant what she said. Perhaps Indigo considered it a compliment to Puck that she would take a ruse this far. After all, faeries only tortured those who caught their attention in the first place.

"So, this is the last test?" asked Puck, shaking from the cold.

Indigo gave a curt nod. "You have to stay under the water. You can't come out, not even when your lungs feel like bursting—"

I frowned, reached for Indigo's hand. She smoothly folded

her arms out of my reach.

Puck—good, earnest, hopeful, stupid—was silent as she walked down the stone steps that led straight into the water. She stayed silent even as a frothy wave lapped at her narrow hips. She sucked in her breath and then, in one fluid motion, her head disappeared below the surface. The moment I couldn't see her red hair, I started getting nervous. The water turned still. A stream of bubbles rose to the top, swirling out like a breaking strand of pearls. Puck's little white fingers stabbed the surface once before vanishing into the dark.

"What if she drowns?" I asked.

"She won't," said Indigo, bored and already looking over her shoulder at the House in the distance.

We watched. The water turned still as ink poured onto a mirror. The bubbles vanished.

"It's been too long, Indigo," I said.

I stepped into the creek right as Puck surged out of the water. She gasped, spitting and clutching the railing of the stone steps. She stifled her sobs before blinking at us. Surely, she would yell and scream that we were crazy and that she could've died. Instead, she crumpled, and the nightgown ballooned around her as she offered up her pale, empty palms.

"I-I did everything you said," said Puck, speaking through her sobs. "I did everything right! Why didn't it work?"

I looked at Indigo. She wore a long, shaggy fur coat from a costume Tati had worn at some party years ago. I had forgotten who Tati said she'd dressed as, but I remembered the pair of papier-mâché claws she kept at the back of her closet, along with the sequined handbags she no longer used. On Tati, it looked like a costume. On Indigo, it was like another skin. Indigo sighed, and the wind lifted the fur off the coat as if she were bristling.

"I'm sorry, Puck," said Indigo. "You belong on the other side of the world."

Puck broke down and sobbed even harder. Indigo took off her coat and handed it to her.

"It'll be like a souvenir for you," she said, and then, with devastating gentleness: "Go home, Puck. You tried your best."

Tears streamed down Puck's cheeks as she whispered: "But I did everything right."

Indigo had nothing left to say. She lifted a shoulder and didn't even look as Puck left.

"We could've hurt her," I said.

Indigo rolled her eyes. "Nothing on this side of the Otherworld is real anyway. You know that. C'mon. Let's make some tea."

But I refused to move. I stood in the creek. The starling key fluttered against my ribs. I could feel the tug of the Otherworld behind me.

"Azure, come *on*," said Indigo, an edge to her voice.

I turned and followed her, still holding my ruby-eyed starling key. I watched Puck melt back into the world, now nothing more than a distant whip of fire slipping through the trees. I knew that side was mortal and mundane, choked with the noise of construction and exhaust fumes, stripped clean of magic. But it was also vast. I'd glimpsed this at Indigo's masquerade, the grown-ups with their foreign accents from foreign places, the fabric of their stories woven from places far away. When I stood in the creek, the water was a line of quicksilver dividing the world, and I wondered what it might feel like to be on the other side.

WE NEVER SAW PUCK AGAIN.

We saw a girl shaped like her walking the hallways at school, in line for cafeteria food, but she was no longer Puck. Every now and then I caught her staring at me. Once, I saw her outside in the parking lot, waiting to be picked up. Indigo had run back inside to grab a forgotten textbook and I was alone. Puck walked over to me, stopping a few feet away, a pitying smile on her lips.

"There's so much more out there than Indigo. If you don't wise up, you're going to end up miserable and alone," she said.

The words clung like a damp chill to the back of my neck.

I never told Indigo that Puck had spoken to me. I told myself she wouldn't be interested, but the truth was that Puck's comment was like a blade, and I didn't want Indigo to see the wound it left behind. I tried to push the words from my mind. I told them to leave me be, to let me live forever on the silver-bellied side of the Otherworld. But by now, the question contained within had grown too comfortable in my presence:

Are you sure? it asked.

Chapter Sixteen

THE BRIDEGROOM

Fairy tales often make demands of silence. Your lips must stay sealed. Even if you are standing on a pyre, knitting a shirt of thorns to break a spell for all your kin have turned to swans. Even if you are weak from childbirth and a maid replaces your babe—and there have been several since you became queen— with a rat. Even if you strike a bargain with the devil to offer the first thing you see and then return home to lock eyes with your only child.

We hear such tales, and we despise them. We point at loop-holes, the lack of logic, sneer at the characters and their passive-ness, yawn when some inevitable pain takes out the kindhearted girl, the last-born son, the fair-of-face fools we think we will never be. Our frustration is perhaps the point. These stories run on faith's inexhaustible fumes, and what is faith but an unknowable tangle? To know and to believe seems the difference between fact and fantasy, and it may have stayed that way for me forever had I not glimpsed my brother in a rush of silver and a flash of wings.

Until that moment, my life had been about the collecting of knowledge. Now, the House of Dreams was tempting me with a different ending if only I would do its bidding. This new ending promised I would not find myself alone, that it would fill my coffers with gold and silver, cloak me in the raiment of a king, and win me the hand of a peerless princess.

Thus, like all the fair-of-face fools before me, I rejected my knowledge and I believed.

WHEN INDIGO OPENED THE DOOR TO OUR HOTEL SUITE, I KISSED her with a closed mouth so the secret could not wriggle past my teeth. *I will free you*, I thought. *And I will find him.*

But the question of Azure gnawed at me too. I was certain Indigo knew where she had gone, but to press my wife on the subject would be to throw my vow in her face. And though I was sure I'd break it eventually, I was determined to do so quietly.

I thought the only price would be Indigo's fury. A fury I was convinced would be short-lived once she saw how I had freed her and how I loved her.

Indigo drew back from our kiss and sniffed the air. Perhaps she caught a whiff of the House's bargain on me.

"What happened to you?" she asked, her gaze traveling to the blood spatter on my pants.

"A bird flew into a fan."

"A starling?" she guessed.

I nodded.

"That's quite the omen," she said, stepping back to allow me to enter the room. She had not changed her clothes. Her coat was still buttoned, and she hadn't removed her gloves.

"The Romans believed that starlings spoke for the gods," I said.

"The future revealed in a murmuration of starlings," said

Indigo, raising her chin. "I already knew that."

About a year ago, we had seen such a murmuration at the Aberystwyth Pier in Ceredigion, Wales. Hundreds upon hundreds of starlings took to the skies like a scream given shape, flexing and pulling, dimpling into valleys and strange peaks that towered over the sea. I had been so transfixed that it was only after the birds dispersed that I realized Indigo was crying. I could not ask her then, and I could not ask her now, but the question lived in me all the same:

What did you see?

"I'm drawing you a bath," she said, heading toward the bathing suite. "I don't have much of a desire to go out and eat, so I've placed an order with the kitchens."

"Why did you leave me behind?"

The words hung in the air. We rarely spoke to each other so plainly. Indigo paused, her back to me.

"You clearly wanted to be alone," she said. "Otherwise, why would you go to her room without me? I was merely giving you what you wanted."

Ah, I thought. So this was how we would play.

"How do you know what I want?"

Indigo turned. Her lips slid over her teeth in the manner of a predator. It took me several seconds to understand that she was trying to smile. "Maybe I read it in an omen."

I pointed at my blood-spattered clothes. "And what omen do you read on me now?"

Indigo's smile briefly faltered. "Danger, certainly. Perhaps even death if you're foolish."

The light from the windows to my left slashed across her face, casting a shadow of prophecy over her words.

"Tati only has days left after all," said Indigo, her voice light again. "Although, if you really wanted to be certain of the future, you could've brought the bird. We could have picked apart its liver and heart like true soothsayers."

"Do you have a lot of experience looking into the future?"

Indigo stood beside the large clawfoot bathtub and turned on the faucet. It was difficult to hear her response over the rushing water.

"I used to. I even thought I knew the future. I was wrong." She looked up at me, and her smile turned haughty, almost pitying. "Three years of marriage and all it takes is one afternoon in that House for you to look at me as if I'm a stranger. As if you don't know me at all."

"Whatever you have let me know of you, I have loved," I said. "And still love."

Indigo turned off the faucet. With her hand still gloved, she touched the surface. "Your bath is ready."

I took off my clothes and stood before her. There were rusty smudges on my ankles. When I flexed my foot, the blood cracked. The heat of the water made me shiver. I sank into it anyway.

Indigo positioned a stool next to the tub and handed me a tin of lather. My razor dangled lazily from her fingers, inches away from my left hand. She liked helping me shave, said she liked the soft, scraping sound it made. We both knew that was a lie. What she really liked was the way my neck bobbed when the blade touched my skin. She loved my surrender.

"They're an odd custom, don't you think?" she asked.

She tapped my wedding ring with the end of her blade—a dented band of iron and tungsten.

"How so?"

"Everything about it . . ." she said, trailing the blade's tip over the ring past my knuckle and up my wrist. "Some believe that it connects to a vein of love, *vena amoris*, one that goes straight to your heart. But have you never wondered why it's a ring and not a necklace or a tattoo?"

Indigo twisted it now. "A circle is a fixed infinity. Even the way it looks when it's held up to the light is curious, as if it's a portal to some place of mystery and your choice to wear it means you've allowed your marriage to be a threshold to the unknown. And yet, even in the unknown, there is a demand of mutual trust."

I reached for her. "Indigo—"

"I know what she said to you," said Indigo, her eyes cutting to mine. "Let me guess, the House will answer some secret wish of yours if you find out where *she* went?"

She. Azure. I knew better than to lie. I nodded.

"No doubt she disparaged me or made it sound like *I* did something to make her leave . . . and no doubt, it got to you."

You say she loves you, but what is she anyway?

I caught Indigo's chin, holding on as she tried to move away.

"You let me walk into the dark, Indigo, and then you left me there. You can't be mad when I can't see properly."

And you cannot blame me for what I will do to set you free.

The set of her chin softened. She blew out her breath. I relaxed my grip, and she leaned her cheek into my palm, gentle as a dove. The steam from the bath pulled at her hair.

"Once Tati loved us like we were her own daughters," she said carefully, for this was surely a peace offering. Azure's name remained unspoken, a physical object she stepped around. "She was my sister in all but blood; then something changed. Tati couldn't see it. It was after the accident, and she wasn't the same anymore. Tati started seeing things that weren't there. Hearing things too. And when it came to . . ."

Again, the fragility around the name. The color of it was azure.

"I loved her in a way that almost made me wish never to love again until I met you." Her gaze turned pleading. "I would have kept her with me all her days. I would have killed for her. She was half my soul. Tati should know that I would have never done anything to hurt her.

"But I won't look for her either," said Indigo, her eyes lowering to the water, her thick lashes casting spikes across her cheeks. "There are some things we can never come back from. Not now. Not ever."

Indigo's face was soft, unlined, but when she lifted her gaze, her eyes seemed ancient. This was how I knew that grief had marked her. Only grief can make time change its tempo like that, expand seconds to centuries, with only our eyes marking the distance crossed.

"Do you believe me?"

I stepped around this trap. "I believe."

Indigo stroked my cheek. A bemused smile played on her mouth. "You need a shave."

I leaned my head against the tub and showed my wife my throat.

"You do it," I said, and she smiled.

ALL MARRIAGES POSSESS THEIR OWN TONGUE.

It is a lexicon discovered in that space between clipped sentences. Its poetry can be heard in the rustle of blankets as you shift to curl around the other in silent apology. In this way, I spoke to my wife. I let the slow drag of my thumb along her jaw say what I could not—

I have to do this for you, my love. My brother has left me, and maybe he won't come back. How shall I live if you leave me too?

We fell asleep midsentence.

That night, I dreamt once more of my brother. This time, we are in the House of Dreams. The armoire that my brother disappeared into now stands beneath a grinning baboon skull on the wall in the dining room. Hippolyta and Indigo sit on one side of the table. On the other, my mother and father.

Sit, my love, says Indigo. *Why are you standing?*

I'm waiting, I say, pointing at the closed armoire.

From within comes a soft knock. It grows louder as I reach for the handle. The knocking is the slow pulse of something coming alive, and when I open the door, I can feel another heartbeat lying atop mine.

My brother is inside. Our mother's violet scarf flops over his head. He sits with his legs crossed beneath him, pudgy hands in his lap. When he lifts his head, his mop of black curls gives way to a sharp, pointed face that is feathered and speckled. His face is a starling, and when he sees me, he cocks his head to one side and screeches.

I sat up in bed, turned on the light. I smelled iron and saw blood on my hands. I touched my nose, but it was dry. There was no blood on Indigo. She lay asleep, her face sweetly creased as she dreamt. I threw off the covers, checked my arms and legs.

But there was nothing.

I did not know whose blood was on my hands.

Chapter Seventeen

AZURE

By our sixteenth summer, I had grown accustomed to our usual itinerary. Indigo would hold elaborate picnics on the lawn, and we'd dress ourselves accordingly. We'd go down to the basement and rifle through chests lined with camphor, packed with lavender sachets, draw out her mother's old party clothes—plunging, velvet gowns embroidered with gold thread, tulle blouses thick as clouds, and sequined scarves that rippled over our palms like water. We laughed at how poorly they fit, giggled when they puddled around our feet.

But on this day, the clothes cinched tighter, and the hem that had once dragged on the floor now softly hit my ankles.

"What is it?" Indigo asked, lowering a broad-brimmed hat onto her head.

"It fits," I said, tugging at a gown the color of seafoam. "It's never fit before."

"So?" asked Indigo.

I didn't know why it mattered except that it seemed an inviolable rule that the costumes were not supposed to fit. Outside on the lawn, the tea was strong, and the cakes beautifully iced, and yet I struggled to concentrate on our game of chess.

Lately, I'd become convinced that Indigo had altered time somehow. Maybe she'd pulled each hour close to her body and the magic of it had warped my sight. The sky felt too close, and the House seemed smaller. The nights lasted for a blink, and the days limped along as if sprained.

Tati employed a skeleton staff for the season, and the House was quiet, listless, and sun-drunk, far too sleepy to do anything more than sigh underfoot. The Otherworld was the same. I could watch a leaf spiral through the air for hours. The creek murmured the same song on repeat. The pollen refused to fall to the ground.

One day in June, I saw Mrs. Revand standing outside the front door, peering through the glass. She worked part-time during the summer, and we weren't always sure when she'd arrive. I had been reading in the parlor—a book on Caravaggio's paintings that I had found in the library—while Tati was in her studio and Indigo sketched in the Camera Secretum. Sometimes she would spend hours in there, holed up with her papers and pastels, her eyes fever bright. Indigo didn't show her sketches to anyone, but they always took something from her. Whenever she finished one, she'd sleep for a whole day, leaving smudges of pink and blue on the bedsheets.

"Hello?" called Mrs. Revand.

I got up to answer, and the door yawned open. Mrs. Revand was not alone. A girl stood beside her, tall and reddened from the sun. She wore a white ribbed tank top and cut-off shorts. Her hair was shorn and dyed silver. A diamond winked in her nose.

"You must be Indigo," said the girl, smiling.

"This is Azure," said Mrs. Revand, stepping inside and cupping my cheek. "Indigo's sweeter shadow." She winked at me. "I only came to pick up some donation items Miss Hippolyta set outside her studio. Keep an eye on this one." She arched an eyebrow at the girl, who I understood must be her child, before smiling and adding, "My daughter has mischief in her bones."

I always imagined that Mrs. Revand ceased to exist when she stepped outside the House. Apparently, that wasn't true. The proof stood before me, and she had tan lines on her shoulders, inked words spiraling her wrists, and smile lines around her eyes that said she had let the world mark her. With Indigo, the world would never touch me.

"So . . . do you live here, Azure?" she asked.

"No," I said, crossing my arms.

I didn't want to look at this woman. Everything about her stood in stark contrast to my life at the House.

"I've *never* been in the old Casteñada home," she said, looking around and whistling. "It's gorgeous." She glanced down at the book in my arms. "Caravaggio?" she said admiringly. "You know, I was working in a hotel in Italy a few months ago and got to see his work in the Uffizi. The Medusa painting is wild. I think I stared at it for an hour."

I'd known it was a painting, but the idea that someone could stand before it, note the texture of the paint rising off the canvas, bump shoulders with strangers . . .

Time dimpled, and for a split second, the House turned to glass and the light of a life beyond it showed through its beams.

"Do you like ice cream?" she asked.

I nodded.

"Well, you've *never* had ice cream until you've had gelato heaped into a waffle cone while getting lost in the streets of Florence." She brought her fingers to her lips and kissed them. "Trust me, angels would fall out of heaven for this gelato."

"What are you telling this poor child?" asked Mrs. Revand

from the top of the stairs. She carried a huge box in her hands, which the girl rushed to take from her.

"Regaling her with tales of the forbidden substance . . . gelato," she said, winking at me.

Mrs. Revand smiled. I must have done something normal after that—nodded and waved, laughed, or said my goodbyes—but I only remember the moment when the door closed behind them. The sunlight moved over her shorn silver hair, and the wind tugged at the frays of her denim shorts, and I understood that Time was not obedient to her. Here, Indigo held Time captive, frozen, and because of this we revisited our favorite hours. But this woman did not hold Time. She spent it. She wasted minutes in the sun, threw away seconds on winding sidewalks, offered hours to paintings and ice cream and movement, and let herself be changed.

THAT EVENING WHEN WE SAT DOWN TO DINNER ON THE COV-
ered patio, dusk lay a thick coat of shadow on the grounds, and the periwinkle clouds held still enough to be admired.

"What a lovely evening, girls," said Tati, sighing into a chair.

Indigo wasn't hungry. She rarely was after a day spent sketching. Even so, she reached for a slice of peach, dipped it in honey, and held it out to me. I ate it from her fingers and handed her a glass of water. When she drank, I was no longer thirsty and when I ate, she was no longer hungry. This rhythm soothed me, and I might've forgotten about the woman altogether if Tati hadn't then taken a deep swig from her wineglass before swirling it in the air:

"And what shall we do with our summer, my dears? Take a gondola around the Venice canals? Hide away in the Florida

Keys?"

I didn't mean to respond. But the way Tati held her glass and the way she accented her phrasing brought back the elegant man from Indigo's masquerade. My hand tingled, remembering how he had bent over my wrist and spoke of a city where the skyline was jagged with life—

"We could travel," I said, and my voice rang alien in my ears. "We could go to Paris."

Indigo looked up from her empty plate. There were smudges of purple and red on her face, splotches of yellow and green on her arms. This latest project had consumed her. She referred to it only as "our gift," and whenever she sat down beside me looking as if she'd spent the afternoon wrestling a rainbow, my chest ached because I knew she loved me.

"Why would we leave?" asked Indigo, her gaze darting toward the Otherworld.

"I don't know," I said. I twisted the starling key around my neck. "I just thought—"

"I *love* this idea, girls," said Tati, clapping her hands together. "Indigo, you need to visit the Paris site anyway! Remember Guillaume? He was here for your birthday . . ."

Tati trailed off and I held my breath, wondering if she'd mention how Indigo and I had revealed ourselves that night. Ever since that one confrontation, Tati had mostly laughed it off, but there were moments when her face grew serious, and she would touch my hand and beg me never to do something like that again.

Tati smiled. "He would *love* to show you the grounds. They're my absolute favorite. Oh, and Azure! You can get a passport! It'll be such fun!"

Indigo caught my hand under the table. I could feel the pulse of her wrist beneath my fingertips. I waited for her to speak, to shoot down the idea entirely. Her eyes were alert and focused. Overhead, the clouds were released and began to glide across the darkening sky.

Tati stood up from the table, glowing with excitement.

"When do you want to go?" she asked. "You know what, let me make some calls first. This is going to be wonderful! I know it!"

Tati practically skipped back into the House, leaving me and Indigo alone outside.

"Why would we leave?" Indigo said to me, our hands still clasped. Her voice was even. A cold breeze touched my neck. "We're meant to be here. If we leave, the Otherworld might get mad. What if we become Cast-Out Susans?"

Whenever I imagined this fate, I felt a door threatening to close behind me forever. But then I pictured an endless string of frozen summer afternoons, the air brewing so thick and humid I could no longer breathe.

"We're exiles, Indigo," I said. "That means we must've already done something wrong. Maybe we're supposed to learn something out here and bring our knowledge back to the other side."

It had to be true. Or else what would we have to show for the time we were here? I imagined these stories piling up like coins in our hands, bright tithes to the future.

Indigo frowned and sank her teeth into her bottom lip. My mouth felt her ache and I held back a wince.

"We've experienced too little of being mortal," she said, thoughtful now. She raised her eyebrows. "And if we only did what we wanted, maybe we'll be punished even more."

I nodded and grasped her hand tight. "Yes."

Indigo looked up at me. "I will never let us become Cast-Out Susans."

I CAUGHT MY MOTHER IN THE LONE HALF HOUR BEFORE JUPI-
ter came home. When I stepped into the kitchenette, I almost
didn't see her. She was indistinguishable from the brackish walls
and scuffed furniture. Her dull orange sweatshirt matched the
cloth spread over the dining table to hide its stains. Her hair was
the same shade as the scorched cabinets. Jupiter's house had
never been a home at all but a *mouth*—a place that chewed and
swallowed and fed on her so well she couldn't even see how deep
she was buried in its belly.

"Azure?" she said, blinking at me in confusion. "You're home.
Is something wrong?"

I hated the gentle way she said that. When I was little, she
had been a walking flame, but fire requires feeding and either
my mother didn't know how to sustain herself or had stopped
working at it. Over the years she starved and shrank until she
was a matchstick, a short burst that quickly chewed down the
wood and inspired no warmth.

"Azure?" my mother prompted. "Why are you here?"

The way she said it wasn't cruel, only curious. I stopped at
home once a week, but I always took pains not to be noticed. And
she knew that.

"Indigo and Tati—sorry, Miss Hippolyta—want to take me on
a trip overseas." I thrust an official-looking form into her hand.
Tati had given it to me that morning. "You need to sign this so I
can get a passport and go with them. I *can* go, can't I?"

My mother's shoulders dropped. Her brow furrowed. "Azure,
I . . . yes, I want you to go. I want you to see the world. I want that
so badly—" She stopped, gathered herself, turned around, rummaged on the counter for a pen, and quickly signed the form.

I glanced at the clock. Jupiter would be home any moment.
Whatever gentleness I detected in her voice would vanish. I

heard her say my name softly, though I didn't acknowledge it.

"Thanks," I said, taking the form.

I didn't stay once the papers were signed, and my mother didn't stop me. Or maybe she couldn't. Maybe she was too much a part of Jupiter's house that no piece of her could stretch a finger toward me.

IN THE DAYS LEADING UP TO THE TRIP, I BARELY SAW INDIGO, even though I could feel her in the House. Her art, her gift, consumed her. I only saw her step foot outside the Camera Secretum once to whisper something to Mrs. Revand. At dinner, her eyes were glazed over. It didn't matter how much food I ate. I starved until she lifted a fork.

During the day, I read to pass the time. But in the dark, when our knees touched underneath her heavy blankets, I'd tell Indigo how every story we gathered would turn into a bright coin, and when I felt her smile, I'd breathe again. This was as it should be. If I sometimes crept to Tati's study just to touch the pebbled blue edge of my passport—marveling at my name and photo, the blank pages—it meant nothing. If I daydreamed of cobblestones soaked in honeyed light, or the air of some other place . . . it was only the mental cataloguing of future treasures.

The day before we left, Tati caught me in her study with the passport in my hand.

"Sorry—" I said, dropping it back into her bag.

"There's no need to apologize," said Tati, walking over and stroking my hair. "Never apologize for wishing to devour the world whole, child. It makes my heart happy to see you this way. Maybe we'll go on many more adventures after this one. You girls are almost seventeen! It's time to see what's waiting for you out there."

I nodded and leaned against her, breathing in the smell of hot glue and dried roses. As I closed my eyes, a shadow across the room caught my eye. I looked up, but the doorway to Tati's room was empty. I smiled, sure it was the House being playful.

Perhaps it didn't want us to leave.

THE DAY OF OUR TRIP, I DIDN'T SLEEP, DIDN'T BLINK. I COULDN'T remember the last time I had left the island. Mrs. Revand packed us a breakfast for the car ride to Indigo's private charter. I couldn't eat it though. My hands shook as Indigo dressed us for the journey—a white cotton shift for me, a black one for her, matching black and white tulle dress overlays embroidered with flowers.

"Won't this be uncomfortable on the plane?" I asked, plucking at the tulle.

"It won't be a long ride," said Indigo as she tied her hair back. "And you look lovely in it."

It was early, and the sea was molten steel. When I stared out at the water, I thought I saw the scaled tail of a mermaid part the waves. From the landing dock, Tati shepherded us off the ferry and into a sleek black car that smelled of adhesives and sealants and artificial flowers. After an hour in the car, we arrived at the entrance of an airplane hangar, where another sleek machine waited.

"Stay here," said Tati. She patted her bag and smiled at us. Her headscarf was cerulean and matched the scarf draped around the neck of her trench coat. "I'll just give them the documents and we'll be on our way."

I squeezed Indigo's hand, and she smiled back at me.

"It's not what you think, you know," said Indigo, slouching

against me. "Paris is boring. Nothing like here. I've been loads of times when I was little." She wrinkled her nose. "It smells bad too."

I nodded, not quite listening. I was watching Tati rummage through her bag before two men dressed in navy uniforms. A pilot stood beside them, his brow furrowed as he glanced between the car and the plane. Tati's eyes went wide. I couldn't hear what she was saying as she pointed at the bag and the car, then held up her hands and swiftly returned to us. Tati opened the door, a tight smile on her face—

"I'm so sorry, girls," she said quickly. "I know I triple-checked everything last night, but Azure's passport must have fallen out of my bag." Tati shook her head, and a hand of cold closed around my heart. "We'll go back and look for it, okay? Don't worry."

I saw the tight lines around her eyes though. We all climbed in. Indigo yawned and rested her head in my lap. I winced. Her skull was leaden, weighed down by all her power. I worried it might snap my legs. As we drove back to the House, Tati kept up a steady stream of chatter.

"Are you sure you didn't accidentally move your passport?" asked Tati, probing. "I won't be mad. I know how much you liked it. Maybe you took it with you by accident?"

I shook my head. Indigo's head in my lap was so still I wondered if she was breathing. Tati sighed and turned back around in her seat. I touched Indigo's shoulder. She didn't move. I thought maybe she'd fallen asleep, but there was a taut, hyperextended quality to the line of her neck and her grip on my knee was rigid and bloodless. I could not tell whether it was her body she was trying to hold in place or mine.

As the House of Dreams pulled into focus, a lump rose in my chest.

Indigo stirred then, yawning and staring brightly out the window. "Home," she sighed. "Come, Azure. It'll be okay. I promise."

I followed after her, dazed. That time-tethering magic of Indigo's played with my perceptions. The House seemed small enough to fit in my hand. The hydrangeas on the lawn looked as if they were made of sugar paste. The sunlight appeared false, a careless streak from a cheap paintbrush. Tati followed, still clutching her bag.

"I should look upstairs," she said. "We can still make it to the hangar in time—"

"I have something better," said Indigo, grabbing my hand.

Tati and I followed her down the hall, past the kitchen, and into the Room of Secrets. Inside, soft accordion music played from a victrola. Pink bougainvillea was draped around the animal heads and ivy trailed along the bones on the other side of the wall. The table was set with meats and cheeses, pastel-colored macarons and petits fours.

"Voilà," said Indigo, taking a seat. "Way better than anything you'd get in France."

I stared, fixated on the jawbones of a crocodile, propped open with pink blossoms. The air was overly sweet, the cheese beaded with sweat. Beside me, Tati dropped her bag.

"Indigo, what is this?" she asked, breathless.

"I figured if we couldn't go to Paris, then we could bring it here," she said brightly. "See? It's so much better."

I sank into the chair Indigo pulled out for me. The room blurred, turning translucent, and in my delirium, I imagined that I could see the edge of the Otherworld, that it did not melt into fireflies and infinite dusk but stumbled back from the end of Indigo's driveway.

Tati looked stricken. "But how—"

"I asked the ferry captain to send word," said Indigo, looking at me. "I didn't want you to be sad, Azure." Her voice dropped to a whisper. "Don't worry, we will still gather all those stories to offer up like coins. And I promise I won't let us become Cast-Out Susans." She looked up at Tati, and a light entered her eyes. "Come on, Tottlepop. Sit. Eat."

Tati pulled up a chair. She didn't speak, merely stared at the plates. Tati had said she would look for the passport, but if she ever found it, she never told me. The car was sent away, the bags swiftly unpacked, and we did not talk about the trip again.

Chapter Eighteen

THE BRIDEGROOM

Enchantments rely on rules of etiquette. There is a way in which things must be done. If you see an old woman on the road, offer her your lone crust of bread and a sip from your flask. If she thanks you by telling you of a rare treasure in the shadows of the woods, you must listen with your hands over the ears of your curiosity. If she tells you to walk into a cave and there you shall see three dogs with eyes as large as saucers guarding a chest of gold, a chest of silver, and a chest of wood, you should proceed with your eyes fixed on your feet so all you see is the distance closed between yourself and your destiny.

Somewhere inside that cave, the rules of etiquette lose their grip. Your gaze shifts from your feet to this cave of strange wonders. Here, daydreams are pressed between panes of glass, a harp strung with human hair, crystal songbirds blinking obsidian eyes, singing a song of such sorrow that you weep where you stand. Then there are the three dogs with eyes wide as saucers standing before a chest of gold, a chest of silver, and a chest of wood, and though the old woman begged you to touch only the chest of wood, why should you listen to her? Her eyes were rheumy and her hands gnarled, and the chest of wood is far too humble, and you have come this far and surely you deserve more than that for your troubles.

I remembered this ancient etiquette, and I was determined not to forget it, but my knowledge seemed to have abandoned me from the moment we stepped over the threshold into the House of Dreams.

I woke to the moth-winged flutter of Indigo's eyelashes against my pulse, her face hot and sticky from sleep as she molded herself against my chest. It was still dark, our faces inscrutable to each other. Indigo moved my fingers to the fragile velvet of her neck, and in this shared blindness I counted her heartbeats until the sunlight pulled us into two distinct beings.

Indigo was wearing a long-sleeved, ankle-length black velvet dress. Her gloves were gone, and her skin was warm as her fingers brushed mine.

"This will all be over soon," she said, kissing my cheek when we arrived. "Perhaps an hour or so at most. I'll meet you back at the hotel?"

"Sounds good," I said, smiling and watching as she walked down the hall.

In the parlor, the dull chatter of lawyers and the smell of coffee drifted toward the entrance. Indigo had left the front door open, and sunlight pooled across the chestnut floor. Outside, the car was still running, waiting to take me to a library on the mainland, where I told Indigo I'd do some work to pass the time. I waited until she was out of earshot, and then I shut the door and began to climb the grand staircase.

I was loath to speak to Hippolyta again. I didn't want to search for reason in her riddles or end up clutched in her bony grip. But I needed answers if I was to claim my treasure from the House. The night before, Indigo had looked heartbroken. Azure had stolen something from her, and my only source of inquiry was an old woman with a decaying mind who insisted I needed wings to enter the Otherworld.

From the stair's landing, muffled voices came from Hippolyta's room. The hallway was split. Down the right, Hippolyta's red, musty chambers. To my left, an alcove leading to the small spiral staircase and its secret turret. Golden dust motes sifted down the staircase, lending it the look of something rare and hallowed.

I had not noticed before how the walls on my left side were covered in a pink damask. Now it struck me as lurid. Vulgar. The shade was not rose pink or dawn pink but something closer to that cryptic pink between a woman's legs.

I heard Indigo's voice, sultry and taunting, the way she'd look over her shoulder before walking into our bedroom.

"Are you coming or not?" she'd ask.

Are you coming or not? the hallway whispered.

The House was luring me toward Hippolyta's room, warning me away from the side that led to the turret. Indigo had tensed when I pointed it out, and Mrs. Revand had tartly informed me that no one was allowed up there. But if there were answers to be found, I would not find them in Hippolyta's addled mind. I would have to seek them on my own.

Not fifty feet away, I heard the physician speaking in her warm, maternal voice from Hippolyta's room: "No way she'll last the night . . ."

The caretaker, who must have been with her, clucked sadly. I removed my shoes so they would not hear me and made my way to the wrought-iron staircase. It spiraled straight up, broken only by squares of clementine light. Near the top, I smelled the apples-and-honey softness of Indigo's neck.

At the top of the staircase was a large blue door. It appeared antique: eighteenth century if I had to guess. The straight-grained, uneven texture suggested oak. Decorative ironwork adorned the door alongside large, domed studs and smaller nails with two large ring handles at its middle.

This was the entrance to Indigo's childhood bedroom.

When we were first married, I dreamt about what might lie behind this door. Books with creased spines and dog-eared pages, clothes that no longer fit, diary entries filled with looping, girlish handwriting, the names of erstwhile crushes crimping a page from top to bottom. I wanted to see the secret womb that birthed the enigma of my bride, but this place was no womb. It was a wilderness, barred in iron.

I hesitated before it, wondering whether my eyes would betray me.

I have always had problems with my sight. I was barely into my teens when I was saddled with my first pair of thick glasses. And it was at least a year into graduate school before I could afford contact lenses. In those days, I was plagued with the thought that I had not seen something properly. That my ruined eyes—an inheritance, I was told, from my father's side—constantly tricked me.

An old girlfriend from my graduate-school days had told me this was what she loved most about me. We had returned to my apartment after a professor's holiday party. The professor was independently wealthy and kind, though clearly aggrieved by the number of people in his home.

I had been absorbed with the man's library, enchanted by his feast table laden with boughs of pine and holly, roasted meats, and assorted golden pies. The company had turned charming, too, softened by the holiday lights that hung from the banisters and cross-beamed ceilings.

"You didn't notice the professor's wife?" my girlfriend had exclaimed when we returned. She was short, with a wealth of brunette hair and a high-pitched voice that turned to delighted squeaks when I took her to bed. I didn't love her, though I liked her well enough. "That woman was *covered* in bruises. Honestly, her makeup was either a shitty cover-up or a cry for help. She kept flinching when he talked. And didn't you notice how he kept taking her knife from her? Like he thought she was going to run him through with it?"

"No," I said, frowning as I turned over the images I recalled from that evening.

I thought she would scold me for not noticing. Instead, she cupped my face.

"You only see beauty, don't you?" she said. "It's what I love the most about you. You don't see the dark shadows."

The thought had disturbed me at the time. I broke up with her shortly thereafter, but her words have bothered me ever since. She was wrong. I have dedicated my life to careful observation. Yesterday, the House tested my sight and I proved myself. If something was hiding here in Indigo's room, I would see it.

INDIGO'S BEDROOM WAS LARGE AND DIMLY LIT. THE STUBS OF candles in crystal dishes lay scattered about the furniture. The eye-shaped glass window took up the entire far wall. A huff of cold air touched my neck. When I turned, it was only the cooling unit gasping alive.

There was a robe hanging behind the door, embroidered on the sleeves with ivy and jasmine. The bed was stately, Victorian, an imitation of Hippolyta's green canopy in red. Her bookcase held familiar tomes: Grimms' Fairy Tales, the Ramayana, the

Chronicles of Narnia, and *Dune*. There were no photos of her younger self tacked to the walls. No journals, ribbons, movie ticket stubs. No evidence of the ragged threads we trim or tie as time knits us into adults.

Facing Indigo's bed was a large antique standing mirror that leaned against the wall at an angle. On the floor beside it sat a small jar, half the size of my palm. It rattled when I picked it up, and inside I saw a single tooth. I remembered the heavy sphinx paw in our Gallery of Beasts, the bracelet of hair, the letter *A* carved into enamel. An odd tickle started behind my tongue. I cleared my throat, but the sensation persisted.

Near the door was a finely made dresser the color of bone and set with pearl handles. A painting, long faded, stretched across the wood, revealing a pair of birds with iridescent plumage and jewels for eyes. One bird's eye was a ruby. The other's a sapphire. The longer I stared at the painting, the more I recognized it:

A pair of starlings.

Inside the drawers, I found pen caps and bobby pins, ponytail holders, a mirror shard, and the odd sock. But there was something else, too, a little black rectangle. A cassette. I drew it out. The ink had faded to sepia; the writing was slanted, sloppy, and male:

You're my favorite shade of blue. Love, Lyric.

Outside the room came a sound. I shoved the drawer closed and looked around Indigo's bedroom. With my shoes still in my hands, I crouched on the other side of the bed. I knew this sound. It was the unmistakable tread of Indigo's heels clanging on the iron staircase.

I had dreamt about the moment when I would discover her secrets, but I had never considered the nightmare in which I might be caught. Indigo had once told me that she knew she loved me because she was frightened of me. I knew I loved her, too, for when the door opened and her footsteps creaked on the wood, I felt a rush of something acute and exquisite.

Fear.

Chapter Nineteen

AZURE

The first time Indigo kissed me, she drew blood.

"There," she said, leaning back and swiping her thumb across my bottom lip. She sucked on her finger, and I tasted copper in my mouth. "First kiss done. Now whoever comes after has no claim on us."

We were in her bathroom, two stools drawn up to the gilded vanity mirror as we did our makeup for the evening. Outside the windows, autumn embroidered the world with gold and red, and our Otherworld was sweet with woodsmoke and fallen apples.

"It will all be over with soon," Indigo said, her chin jutting out in defiance of some imagined enemy.

According to Indigo, we had less than a year left on this side of the world. For Tati's sake, she had agreed to graduate high school, which we saw as finishing our mortal penance. After graduation, I'd turn eighteen. Indigo said that the moment we both came of age, moonlight would run through our veins and wings would unfurl from our shoulder blades and we would step inside the lands we were always meant to rule. But until then, there were certain mortal experiences we needed to collect.

After the trip we didn't take, Indigo and I divided the summer between our Otherworld and the seashore. In the mornings, we cut out stars and pasted them on our bodies so that by the end of the evening, we could peel off the stickers and see how the sun had baked constellations onto our skin. We watched our classmates hurl themselves against the freezing waves and wondered which of them—if we had to—we might deign to kiss.

We understood that a kiss could be a key. A press of lips could wake the princess from deathlike slumber or shake off the bristling furs of a beast to reveal the prince underneath. But the one who kissed you could also claim you, and since we refused to belong to anyone but ourselves, we entrusted that first and sacred touch only to each other.

At the shore we overheard classmates talking about the warehouse wharfs and the autumn concerts, and decided one of these would be our starting point, the place where we would kiss and be kissed, where we'd press against other limbs and allow the music to shudder through our bones. We'd gather every moment to pay our passage into the Otherworld.

My hand trembled at the thought, and Indigo caught it, smiling.

"It's okay, Azure," she said. "There's nothing to be scared of."

What I felt wasn't fear exactly. I couldn't quite name it. I smacked my lips, thinking of Indigo's kiss. Her mouth had been cold and smooth as a serpent. When she parted my lips with her tongue, I tasted sugar before she bit down, and pain lit up my mind.

Indigo chewed absently at her lower lip. I noticed her teeth worried the same place where she'd bitten me. She rummaged through her drawer. "What color lipstick should we wear? Coral? Red?"

"Red."

Like war paint, I thought.

"Good choice," said Indigo, uncapping the tube.

She swiped glitter onto our eyelids and cheekbones, smudged kohl into the roots of our lashes and added touches of mascara. We combed our hair until it fell in identical black sheets down our backs. That night, we wore matching knee-high boots, lace tights, patent-leather skirts, and blouses that opened at the neck.

As we walked downstairs and headed for the door, I saw Tati in the parlor. She sat with her feet curled under her, combing through skeins of brunette hair that rippled to the ground. Tati had grown quiet since our failed trip overseas. Sometimes, I caught her staring at me. I didn't know what she was looking for in my face. I thought she would look up from her work when we called out our goodbyes, but she kept right on combing the hair.

THE WHARFS SMELLED OF SALT AND CARCASSES. EVEN THOUGH it was too dark to see, I knew the water was shallow and brackish, thick with cigarette butts and bottle caps. Seagulls wheeled overhead, and a crowd—mostly students our age or college kids from the mainland—formed a tattered circle around the pleated aluminum walls of the warehouse. Indigo wrinkled her nose as someone spit on the ground next to us. She folded her arms across her chest and frowned when her eyes landed on the face of a classmate.

"Don't choose anyone we know," she said, under her breath. "Don't choose anyone who would try to keep us." Indigo shuddered. "I hate this place already. Don't you?"

I was spared from answering by the grating metal of the doors creaking open. The crowd surged, and we were carried forward. I had never been around so many people. We had kept ourselves apart for so long that I smiled when the zipper of someone's leather jacket caught on my hair and an elbow dug into my ribs. Whenever anyone looked at me, I felt it like a hand cupping my cheek, and heat pooled in my belly.

I understood why Indigo hated this place—it was crude and inelegant, hot, and loud—but even before we spilled onto the massive poured-concrete dance floor, I could feel the magic there. It was in the slow pulse that gathered the crowd, in the sheen of eyes blackened and primal beneath the broken fluorescent lighting.

Then came the music, and I understood the delicate layers of this magic, too, wrought of the crowd's urgency, daylight stalking the edges of night, the bass trembling up your legs and into your teeth, the slanting light sweeping over our bodies in a benediction. I swayed, transfixed by the radiance of it all. Indigo and I blurred into the mass of people. I felt the bruises forming on my body—the jolts against my spine, knees knocking against mine, liquor splashing my hair—and suddenly I loved the warehouse in a way that made me angry that others knew it existed.

I didn't know the band or the words to the song, but I opened my mouth anyway and they turned succulent on my tongue. I threw back my head and the song caught me around the throat and cast me out past the corrugated metal walls and the dusky wharf waters until I was so vast, I might wrap a whole universe within me.

When the band finished their first set, Indigo caught my hand and I almost recoiled. I stared at her, and for a moment her face seemed alien, unfamiliar. I had forgotten I was not alone.

Indigo clutched me to her, screaming so her voice could be heard: "Come on, I see someone I want to kiss."

I followed Indigo as she moved through the throng and

toward a bar at the back. I was distracted, still caught up in the infinite beat of the music. It had answered something I didn't know I could ask, and when I walked through the crowd, my feet didn't touch the ground.

Indigo approached one of the men who had been on the stage. He had a beautifully carved face and a full mouth that twisted in delight when she spoke to him. I looked away, watching the next band set up before I suddenly tasted cigarette smoke on my tongue. My nose wrinkled and when I turned to Indigo, I saw her arms wrapped around the man, his hands in her hair. When she broke the kiss, she laughed in his face as he leaned forward to catch her.

"Once is enough for us," she said.

The man looked heartbroken. He stared at Indigo with a terrible thirst, and heat traced a sigil in my blood. If Indigo noticed the man's face, she didn't acknowledge it. She grabbed my wrist. "Your turn."

I'd barely taken a step before the man's arms were around me. His mouth, so soft I wanted to gasp, found mine. He parted my lips, just like Indigo had done, but he didn't bite down, only moaned as if somehow weakened by me. After a few moments of this, I drew back, admiring how his eyes were glazed. My teeth sharpened. I had won something, and even though it was too dark to see, I felt my shadow strangle his in the dark.

I leaned forward and kissed him again. I liked losing myself to the kiss. I liked the heat painting my insides. I liked hearing Indigo laughing in the dark.

THE WAREHOUSE BECAME OUR WEEKEND RITUAL. A PLACE where music and men, and sometimes women, left their prints all over us. At the warehouse concerts, Indigo acted as if she were performing penance, and to her that's what it was, a mortal debasing. She kissed with enthusiasm, though she always shuddered in disgust afterward.

"It'll be over soon," she would say, as if comforting me.

I never responded when she said that. The music made me vast, but perhaps it made me weak too. Because every night we spent dancing under those lights didn't feel like penance to me. It felt like a kind of prayer.

And I didn't know what I was praying for exactly.

ONE DAY THAT SUMMER, WE DECIDED TO SWIM IN THE STREAM beside the Otherworld. It was cold, and my body ached from the previous night's party, my lips puffy and bruised. One of the boys I'd kissed—this one dark as night with gold threaded in his braids—had dropped his full mouth to my neck and sucked. I'd almost forgotten until morning, when Indigo rolled over in bed and I saw the circle of broken skin above her collarbone.

I was reluctant to get out of the water. The moment I did, I would have to go home to Jupiter's. I usually went once a week or else my mother would call angrily. Each time I visited, I'd sit through a congealed dinner in the kitchenette, then I would pretend to sleep, but really I'd climb out the window and race back to the House.

Indigo always thought of my return as a game. Every time I snuck past the ogre, I proved to her that I was a fairy-tale princess. She said it was like the tale of Catskins, where the father lusted after his own daughter and tried to trap her in bed.

"He's not my dad," I'd told her.

"That's not what he thinks," laughed Indigo. Jupiter was

nothing but a distant shadow to her, something to be outwitted.

"My brave and fearless Azure," Indigo would say.

But she never asked if I wanted to be those things.

That day when we climbed out of the stream, our clothes were nowhere to be found. Picked up by the wind, perhaps. Or else scurried away by the long-fingered fae who loved us.

"Just take something of mine," said Indigo, shivering.

"You know my mom won't like that."

"You can change when you get there," said Indigo. "She may not even be home. Come on, Catskins, let's go inside or I'll turn to ice and become a snow maiden."

I shivered, too, not from the chill in the air but from that nickname. The sound of it sent tendrils of ice through my veins. Inside, Indigo put me in one of her dresses. I'd never seen her wear it. It was low-necked with long, blue silk sleeves. Even unzipped it hugged my body.

"It looks good on you," said Indigo approvingly. "It doesn't look like that on me."

I glanced into the tall, gilded mirror against her wall and understood what she meant. Although our faces had become similar in the way of a song and its echo, different hands had sculpted our bodies. The years had whittled and stretched Indigo. With me, they had smoothed and rounded. We could wear almost all the same clothes, but the ones we couldn't were distinct.

Indigo moved behind me and reached for the zipper.

"I was thinking of what we need to collect next," she said with a deliberate slowness, as if she had weighed each word on a scale. Her eyes met mine in the mirror. "I think we should have sex."

My face felt suddenly hot when I looked at her. "What?"

"While we're mortal, we should do what begets other mortals, don't you think? It was your idea after all," she said, her voice so casual I could almost mistake the barb beneath. "Maybe it'll be a story we can tell everyone else in the Otherworld when we're done here."

"But with who?"

"With boys," said Indigo with a faint distaste. "Or girls. Whichever you want."

"I'm not sure I *want* to have sex."

"Really?" asked Indigo, zipping up the dress. "I thought you liked kissing."

"Kissing is different."

Indigo sighed. "No, it isn't. It's just more parts touching. Don't worry, I have a plan."

She dusted something invisible from the sleeves before resting her chin on my shoulder. With her hair dripping onto the wood and her bra and panties sheered by the water, she looked like a newly hatched nymph, the love child of an autumn breeze and a rushing stream. Whatever panic had bubbled into my chest melted away, replaced with a truth I'd never doubted: I would always be safe with Indigo.

"I trust you," I said.

Indigo grinned. "Good. Now go do your quest and come back quickly."

I SHOULD NEVER HAVE COME HOME IN THAT DRESS.

When I opened the door, I saw Jupiter sitting on the couch, one hand on his distended belly. The glare of the television turned him fluorescent. Usually, my mother would be in the kitchen or sitting beside him. I didn't see her anywhere.

"I see the princess has decided to grace us with her presence—" he started to say before he looked at me. *Really* looked at me. "Where'd you get a dress like that?"

"Indigo lent it to me," I said quickly. "Is Mom home?"

"Had to make a last-minute grocery run." His voice was oddly flat. "Why don't you sit down?"

"No thanks," I said.

I was breathing too fast. I reached for my magic, the veil I could normally draw up and over me, but Jupiter's focus held me in place.

"I have to change," I said.

Jupiter stretched his fingers. "Looks like you might need help with the zipper."

"I'm okay, thanks."

"It's no problem, princess, come here," he said, standing from the couch.

The air smelled like metal. I couldn't hear the television. *Don't look at me.* I tried, again, to summon the old power born from an even older sacrifice. But Jupiter's attention was too thick, and I couldn't slip away. He came closer—six steps, now four, now two. I wanted the air to disassemble me. I wanted to run. My feet held fast to the ground.

Behind me, the key jangled in the lock. The door creaked. I couldn't see her, but I felt the air gather around the shape of my mother entering the house. Without speaking to either of them, I escaped as fast as I could to my bedroom.

That night, my mother made me stay home. She left her bedroom door open and all night I heard them grunting like beasts until I slipped out the window. This was all I knew of sex, the reminder that the body was meat and stink, and even the divine debased themselves in this. Gods became bulls and swans and wolves, and in this way, they rutted.

FORTUNATELY, BEFORE INDIGO THOUGHT WE SHOULD TRY SEX for ourselves, she said we needed to understand what it meant to lose control. Like the ancient Greeks in their frantic Bacchic rites. I didn't like the idea, but she was insistent.

"If we don't feel it, then what if we end up in exile again?" said Indigo. "Aren't you bored of these bodies?"

We went to the bar room that nobody used and took down the carved crystal decanters full of honey-colored liquid and packed up the slender, velvet-wrapped carafes of Madeira and sherry Manzanilla, and carted all of it to the Otherworld.

"Do we toast to anything?" I asked.

"We can toast to the gods?" Indigo said, pensively swirling her glass the way people did in movies. "I guess . . . that way they know we're ready to see them? All the old rites talk about getting to the point where your soul wants to loosen from your bones, and you're this . . . walking threshold of madness and divinity. That's the only way you can behold the gods."

We drank.

I didn't mind the taste at first. It was a burnt sweetness on the tongue, syrupy too. It was cold outside, and I liked how the drink warmed me.

Indigo poured more. She poured so much the stars spun overhead. I could hear the selkies in the stream laughing at how ridiculous we looked when we danced. We had dressed ourselves from older times so we might look familiar to the old gods. Indigo wove apple blossoms in our hair and tied bedsheets around our bodies. They untied and fell off as the night went on, taking our humanness with them.

Was that what the old stories had meant? To shed what made us human? Would I now grow a mandible? Would the skin on my back slough off and reveal a pair of wet, black wings tightly furled against my spine? All night, I touched my back, my fingers use-lessly searching for a soft bulge of feathers beneath my shoulder blades.

My last sight was of Indigo standing on the roof of our turret. I lay on my back, sides aching from laughter. Indigo's shoulders were shaking, her head bent as she sobbed. The twigs in her hair stood up at odd ends. In the moonlight, she looked horned.

I didn't know who she was speaking to: A god? The moon? There was no difference to us that night.

"You're wrong. It's not supposed to end like that," said Indigo, dragging in a deep breath. "I would never do that. I would never hurt her—"

Something—I could not be sure what—made me start laugh-ing again. I laughed and laughed until eventually the world went dark.

The next day, I woke in Indigo's bed and couldn't speak. We were so tired we couldn't get up for school. I didn't even remem-ber moving from the turret to the House. When Tati checked on us, she snorted. I wanted to be glad for that sound. She had been so silent lately. I couldn't remember the last time she'd laughed. Even so, the pitch of her voice sent a thousand beetles crawling inside my skull and I made myself even smaller under the cov-ers.

"Rough night?" asked Tati. I could hear the grin in her voice.

"Not now," groaned Indigo, curling against me.

Tati walked to the bed and laid her hand on my tangled, twig-scattered hair. I braced myself before finally blinking up at her. I thought she'd yell at us. Instead, I found tears in her eyes. "I'm not mad, sweetheart. You have to grow up sometime, don't you?"

Indigo threw back the sheet and glared at Tati. "I said *not now.*"

Tati removed her hand from my hair as if stung. Her shoulders fell. She turned once in the doorway, and woodenly announced: "I'll have Mrs. Revand send up some aspirin and water."

Once we were alone, I turned to Indigo. My mouth tasted sour, and my tongue was rough. "Who were you talking to last night?"

My vision was still blurry, so it was probably only in my imagination that Indigo's eyes looked, for a moment, ringed white with fear.

"No one," she said. "Nothing."

"But I heard you talking to someone. You were really upset."

"No," said Indigo, her voice cold as she turned from me. "You didn't hear anything because nothing happened. For what it's worth, I think we satisfied that experiment. There's no need to repeat it."

It was the first time she lied to me, and I tried to be angry, but how could I be?

I was lying to her too.

Chapter Twenty

THE BRIDEGROOM

Every fairy tale has blood flecked on its muzzle. Sometimes it's licked up in the second before the story begins—a queen slowly bleeding out onto her birthing bed, a plague having laid waste to a land before "Once upon a time" slouches from the dark. But every so often, one can trace the thick flow of blood as it seeps from the pages.

I have studied it, translated it, and now I was living it. The point at which the too-curious maiden opens the forbidden red door with the littlest key—and the key is important, something always has to bear witness, something has to mark the instant where you have broken the rules and must be made into an example.

But first, always first, a threshold must be crossed. The page must be turned—and it doesn't matter if every bone in your body longs to hold the place before the paper lifts against your will—you cannot go back.

I cannot go back.

From under the bed, I stared at the corner of my reflection in the antique mirror propped against Indigo's bedroom wall. I watched myself draw in quick, shallow breaths. My eyes darted around her room. It was large, though curiously sparse. A decade's worth of dust coated the floor, and in the mirror's reflection I could see the newly blank spaces where my shoes had disturbed its rest.

I had the childish notion that if I couldn't see myself, then no one else could either. My hands were full of treasures—the jar with the one rattling tooth, and the cassette tape—*You're my favorite blue. Love, Lyric.*

My face was half-hidden by the bed skirt as the shuffle of Indigo's shoes hit the wood. I fought a brief, violent impulse to grin or wink at my image in the mirror. That was how I used to play with my brother. If my face was blank, it meant *Don't move.* And if I smiled: *Run.*

The memory of rough, stiff carpet replaced the cold wood beneath me. The ghost of cigarette smoke wove through the dust motes. I was under my parents' bed now, an heirloom made of polished walnut, while my brother breathed heavily next to me. I looked at my hands. They were empty. My fingers appeared bent and blue, their angles wrong.

"Where are you hiding?" Father laughed.

He loved joining in on our hide-and-seek games. Whenever we heard his heavy step on the floor, we nestled together like puppies. My brother and I faced each other. I lowered myself, sticking out my feet. I wanted to be found.

"Aha!" said Father.

I looked at my brother and smiled. *Run.*

Abruptly, I was released from the memory, my father's voice still ringing in my head. Indigo spoke:

"You can't hide forever, can you?"

I had not heard her draw closer. She must have slipped off her shoes. Her light-brown feet were nearly covered by the hem of her black velvet dress.

I waited for her to bend down, twist her neck to peer at me. But she didn't move. Her feet pointed toward the mirror.

Indigo stepped back, turning to the dresser. Through the cut in the bed skirt, I watched her hand drop to her side as she pressed one palm against a painted starling. She opened the drawers one by one. She was looking for something. I glanced at the tape in my hand. *Love, Lyric.*

With a frustrated sigh, she slammed the drawer shut. I could only see the backs of her calves, smooth and bronze, still glossy from the apricot oil I'd rubbed onto her skin last night.

"No one knows," she said. "You belong to me. I own you, body and soul. Even if I see little bits and pieces of you everywhere, Catskins." Indigo sighed and tugged her hair. "I see you in this room and in the shadows, and it makes no sense because I killed you."

Indigo's tone was gentle, lilting. This was her siren's voice. She had used it on me a few months earlier when a fever kept me in bed for days.

"Oh, Catskins," she sang before her voice turned flat. "Why aren't you dead yet?"

Chapter Twenty-One

AZURE

In Indigo's bedroom, I stared at my reflection in her massive silver mirror. It was adorned with acanthus leaves and miniature nymphs. I tried to focus on these details—the half-lidded eyes of a metal satyr, a delicate harp lost in a tangle of gleaming irises—but I couldn't avoid my own gaze. The sight whispered my doubts into life:

What if Indigo is wrong?

What if we aren't a single soul neatly shared between two bodies?

I didn't doubt that we were sisters or even twins from some magical place. When she ached, I wept. When I had nightmares, it was Indigo who screamed for me. But there was also an uneven seam between us where our thoughts stumbled in similarity. I'd traced the raised edge of it for more than a year, struggling to see it in its entirety. That is, until the lights of the warehouse dance floor dragged it into focus. Indigo said she could feel how much I loathed the place . . . but really, I loved it.

Lately, I had started noticing the college announcements pinned to the bulletin board at school. I lingered before them, tracing the names of my senior-year classmates. Indigo and I hadn't applied. There was no point. We would transform soon enough.

Going to college was rare on our island, and so the administration proudly displayed that handful of students on an ancient corkboard decorated with gold paper stars. When no one was looking, I would tap the thumbtacks on all the states they would know: New York, Georgia, New Hampshire. Even sounding them out in my mind felt blasphemous. More damning were the ideas that followed: how the rain might look candied through the windows of a new city, the texture of a breeze winding through unfamiliar streets, the serene embrace of a sea that knew only the hot touch of sultry, sun-drenched days.

Before my mother met Jupiter, she had once told me the women in our family were cursed. She never said what the curse was exactly. Still, I wondered if it had found me and filled my head with these poisonous doubts. I tried to rid myself of them. In Jupiter's house, I poured salt in circles around my feet. I offered my mother's gold bracelet to the water nymphs in the creek. I even begged the Otherworld to cure me. When nothing worked, I told myself it would pass. Come graduation in spring, I would turn eighteen, Indigo would age into her trust, and we would be transformed.

I would become a creature of air.

I had always envisioned it as a moment of extravagant light. But now, when I pictured the gates closing behind us, that wealth of light turned stingy. I realized to accept the hidden half of the world meant denying its counterpart.

It should be an easy choice. What was a world of metal compared to one made of magic? I knew this, and I ached anyway.

These were the thoughts of a Cast-Out Susan.

I would've hidden from the shame forever if the Otherworld

hadn't driven me to confess one day in December.

"I don't see why you won't come with us," said Indigo as we made our way to the wrought-iron gates. "So what if you miss a day or two of school? It's not like it'll matter soon."

For the past few weeks, Tati had been taking Indigo with her into the city. There were forms she had to sign, conferences to sit through. Sometimes I accompanied them.

"Is it because of the city?" asked Indigo, wrinkling her nose. "That much iron. I know. I hate it there too."

It was because of the city. Not because I hated it though. While Indigo waited in her meetings, I would stare out the floor-to-ceiling windows, watch strangers sitting on benches, marveling at the secret intimacy in the space between their bodies. I would count the urgent seconds people spent on a crosswalk, knowing they were needed somewhere else. And as the clock ticked down to when Tati's car appeared, I imagined a circle drawing tighter and tighter within me.

"Yeah," I said. "It's because of the city."

We stood at the gate of our Otherworld. Frost traced a silver finger down the iron curlicues. Behind us, sheaves of ice clung to parts of the stream.

"Ready?" asked Indigo. "Soon it'll be the last time we do this."

My mind snagged on that. The air whose metal scent promised snow now held the tang of blood. I pushed away the thought as we took out our starling keys and the gates swung open—

But this was not our Otherworld.

Winter was supposed to silver it—to hang pearls of ice in the oak branches, sleeve the apple trees in glass, gently curl the ferns like the fists of an infant. Our turret used to glow, promising the warmth of its woodstove, the cashmere blankets neatly tucked into chests of cedar, the samovars waiting to hold tea.

This was something else, like a pocket turned inside out. I stumbled backward.

"What's wrong with it?" I said. "What happened?"

Indigo frowned. "What?"

"Look at it!" I said, pointing. "The tree is all wrong. The turret looks . . . *wrong*."

"I don't see anything," said Indigo, squinting.

I stared at her, my eyes wide. Couldn't she see how dull the light had turned? How stiff the oak tree stood? How ordinary the turret appeared, as if it were nothing more than a pile of rocks? Far off in the distance came the sound of a boat motor running through the water. That sound had never invaded the Otherworld before.

"It doesn't seem different to you?" I asked, and heard the wildness creep into my voice.

Indigo laughed. "No. It's the same, Azure. Nothing's wrong—"

Except for me. *I* was wrong. This was my punishment, I realized. The Otherworld had denied me its magic. I sank to my knees, and Indigo knelt beside me, her hand warm on my shoulder.

"There's something wrong with me," I confessed. I lifted my eyes to hers. "What if I'm the weak one? I can't see the Otherworld anymore. I think it's punishing me. I feel *wrong*, Indigo. I think about things when I shouldn't. Want what I shouldn't have. Sometimes I even wonder if you're wrong about us. What if we're not the same soul? What if I'm different, made wrong, maybe there's some empty space inside me—"

Indigo clapped her hand over my mouth. Her cold palm pressed so hard against my lips, I felt the outline of my teeth. She winced for me, but she didn't move her hand.

"There's nothing wrong with you," she said, her voice fierce and burning. "This is all a test, a way to try to keep us from join-ing together, to keep us as these weak, mortal things." She spat out those last few words before she moved her hand to cup my cheek.

"Don't be scared, Azure," she said, her voice breaking. "All we have to do is wait a little longer and then you'll see for yourself. We'll be linked together, and there won't be any gaps. I promise."

AFTER THAT DAY, INDIGO LEFT FOR A THREE-WEEK TOUR OF HER family's properties in North America.

On the Friday she left, Indigo stood before her mirror comb-ing her hair with long, thoughtful strokes. Whenever she did this, I'd train my eyes on the floor, as if expecting rubies the color of a cut throat to fall from her strands and clatter onto the oak floors. When I raised my chin, our eyes met in the mirror's reflection. Indigo's stare was sharp and assessing, like she'd catalogued all my corners while I wasn't watching.

It made me want to hide.

I'd always thought that Indigo's magic was her flair for won-der, the allure she spun of a girl who lived in a house of magic, who carded jewels from her hair and knew how to braid the moonlight. Now I wondered if it were merely a distraction, the way one could dangle something glittering with one hand while the other moved unseen.

"You'll keep looking for someone, won't you?"

My face heated. Though I kept hoping she'd drop the idea, Indigo was determined that one of us have sex before graduation. She could have had anyone she wanted, but she was ceremo-nial about these things, refusing to waste our time on someone coughed up by mere proximity rather than selected like a pearl from a trove of gems.

We'd already kissed boy after boy and girl after girl during our weekly outings, but we still hadn't found the right one. Even so, with every kiss, part of me grew bolder. I would hold their bodies to me longer, harder, some part of me trying to decipher a language I didn't know how to speak. I would stay awake all night afterward, retracing their contours on my own skin, letting my hands bridge distances I hadn't with anyone else.

"They have to be beautiful," said Indigo, arranging her hair. "And with an aura of something special, like the world has marked them. The light has to treat them differently." Indigo paused to apply a dark shade of lipstick. "Their voice should lure the rusalkas out of the water just to hear them better. And most importantly"—she met my gaze in the mirror—"they cannot linger."

"I know," I said.

TATI GAVE ME THE KEYS TO THE HOUSE OF DREAMS SO I COULD stay overnight while they were traveling. The House was delighted not to be alone, and I was delighted to be alone with the House. The fires crackled like fits of laughter, the rugs remained polite and docile, not a single tassel reaching to catch my ankle. In the evenings, I curled up in the parlor chair and read while the winter wind sang through the glass.

That weekend, I dressed for the wharfs—leather jacket, velvet skirt, Tati's sequined costume tights, black boots. I wore my starling key and hoped that wherever Indigo was, she would hear the music. Without Indigo, I didn't expect anyone to see me. I was only visible when next to her, a shadow revealed by the light cast before it. So I startled when I stepped into the line queueing outside the wharfs and heard someone call out Indigo's name.

I looked over and saw a boy. He was my age and rumpled, with light-brown hair and a wide grin. He wore a red flannel shirt rolled to his elbows and on his wiry, pale forearms I saw the smudges of words written in ballpoint pen.

"Indigo, right?" he asked, strolling toward me.

"You've got the wrong girl," I said, summoning Indigo's wry smile. "I don't know you."

I tried to move past him. He reached out and caught my hand.

"But I do," he said. "I'm sorry I got your name wrong, but I *do* know you." His words tripped in their haste to reach me. "You always come on the weekends with your sister. You're the one who dances. You close your eyes when you like a song. You lick your teeth after a set like you ate the music." He blushed. "I know because I've noticed. I noticed you."

His name, I learned, was Lyric. His too-long arms were covered in song notes, as if all he wished for in life was to be set to music. I studied the elfin point of his chin and the honeyed clumsiness of his smile. This was the most beautiful he would ever be, and he was offering all of it to me.

I'd always wondered why the sailors in the myths can't resist the sirens' call. Why they let themselves drown if only to be close to them. Indigo said the song was so beautiful they couldn't help it, but I think it was more than that. Lyric showed me that a siren's song was about more than music; it was a slant of light, and in its glow, I was drawn into resplendent focus.

"I'm Azure," I said, smiling.

FOR THE NEXT TWO WEEKS, I COMFORTED MYSELF WITH THE knowledge that whatever I felt, Indigo must too. After the night we met, Lyric took me to see a loud action movie and I drank sugary, fizzing soda, my fingers sticky with butter and popcorn, and when he kissed me, he tasted like salt and caramel. His kiss turned me drowsy and frayed, a ribbon held over an open flame.

A few days after that, I went to hear his show and his eyes clasped on mine. *You're my favorite shade of blue,* he sang, and I knew he sang to me. For me. Me, singular. Me, alone. The thought, which had felt so treacherous before, had been gentled, tamed by the coaxing pressure of Lyric's soft mouth and softer kisses.

"I want you, Azure," he whispered one night, and a need awoke within me.

Maybe he shouldn't have said my name. Maybe the sound of it on foreign lips stirred my starling key to life and it flew to warn Indigo while I slept. Maybe that was the reason she returned early, for when I woke the next morning, I felt a shadow pass over me and I blinked to see Indigo standing at the foot of the bed. Her hair was greasy at the roots, the strands frizzed and sticking to a herringbone wool coat two sizes too big for her. She smiled with all her teeth when our eyes met.

"You're home?" I said.

I waited for my heart to sag in relief. Instead, I felt a stab of irritation. I mourned the hours spent alone, or better yet, with Lyric.

"I hated being away from you," said Indigo, drawing her arms around me, burying her warm face in my neck, and turning my irritation into shame. I was a fool. "Let's go to the Otherworld. I can barely breathe when I'm away from it. I know it was difficult for you, too, I could feel it."

But in this, she was wrong, and that truth was a blade cutting straight through my doubts. Indigo had once said that my fears were a test of some kind. What if she was wrong about that too?

Indigo hummed as I trailed after her in the cold. I tried to numb myself to the whip of the icy wind, convinced that if my teeth chattered, it meant that I deserved the pain. At the gated entrance, we took out our keys, and I held my breath as the gate swung open.

My eyes flicked over the stately turret, the harsh lines of the oak branches, the veins of ice and silver along the apple trees. The Otherworld I had known was transformed, but it was no longer wholly unfamiliar.

"It's not destroyed," I said.

If anything, it seemed refocused, reshaped by the light of a truth I had come to understand, the glow of which now revealed pieces I hadn't noticed before—snowdrops glistening like tears, moon-pale winter pansies crowding a boulder, holly berries bright as blood spray. There was a solemnity to the place. Winter had woven a hymn, and I had been too distracted to hear it.

Indigo laughed. "Why would the Otherworld be destroyed?"

"Because . . . because I think you're wrong about us," I said. As each word left my mouth, I felt lighter. "Last time we were here, I thought something was wrong with me for thinking that maybe we're not the same soul. But now I *know* that's true, and the Otherworld hasn't collapsed. It's still here. It's still beautiful."

Indigo did not move. A cloud passed over the sun, leaching the gold from her skin. She looked like a statue carved from granite and when she spoke, her voice came out graveled. "What are you saying, Azure?"

I reached for her hand and tried not to shudder at the cold of her. "Maybe we're exiled fae sisters . . . maybe we're made from the same moonlight, but we don't have to share the same soul, Indigo—"

"Of course we do," she said.

"But you didn't feel it all week, did you?"

"What are you talking about? Feel what?"

"Him," I said, and my hand went to my heart. Indigo's gaze narrowed at the gesture. "Lyric. I met someone who wants *me*."

"Us," Indigo corrected.

I shook my head. "No, Indigo. He noticed *me*. He even wrote a song for me. All week, I've been with him. Did you feel it?"

Indigo was unknowable to me in that moment, and this excited me. Who were we when not cleaved to each other? If the Otherworld was a wonder, imagine what we might discover within ourselves—the raw dreams arranging like constellations at the back of our skulls, satin arteries rushing blood to muscles not yet used. It was heady, this idea that I was not yet articulated into being.

"You're certain he wants you?" she asked.

"Yes," I said. I drew a deep breath, inhaling the perfume of snowdrops, the blood tang of winter, and the promise of crocuses in spring. "I want him too."

Indigo lunged. I nearly raised my arms to do . . . what? I wasn't even sure, but it didn't matter. Her lunge was in fact a lean, and out of nowhere she kissed me on the mouth. Her lips were dry and chilled from the air and the pressure of her lips was brief, harsh.

I made myself smile. "What was that for?"

"For love," she said quietly. "I'd do anything for us, Catskins."

She fell silent for a few moments and then reached out and touched my face. If she saw me flinch at the nickname, it made no difference to her. For her, the name meant that I was something out of a story, and thus to be cherished. It didn't matter that it was a story I hated.

"Why don't you invite Lyric to the House? Show me how much he wants you, and you alone."

As she spoke, I was transfixed by the snowflakes that had begun to line the turrets like the softest velvet. Later, I would realize this was a mistake.

I should have looked at her eyes.

THE DAY I INVITED LYRIC TO THE HOUSE OF DREAMS, THE SKY was the color of a scraped eggshell. I remembered that because it looked odd devoid of all its blue. I took careful pains getting ready that night. Indigo said she had a meeting with Tati in the city, and that I should arrive at ten o'clock. I brushed my hair until it gleamed. I wore a long, black satin dress, a Christmas gift from Tati the year before. The night felt blessed. Even my mother and Jupiter weren't around, so I slipped out unseen.

I thought Lyric would be waiting for me at the gate. When he wasn't, I smiled. Was he inside already? Was he biting his nails and tugging at the front of his hair, or scribbling songs on his arms while he waited?

When I entered the House, I heard cello music and knew Tati was in her studio.

"Indigo?" I called out. "Lyric?"

No one answered.

At that moment, I felt a not-unpleasant heat melt through my body. I looked to the stairs and began to climb. It was hard to breathe, but maybe that was just the flutter of nerves.

At the end of the landing, I saw the black iron stairs that led to Indigo's turret. I heard a different kind of music playing, familiar and yet too soft to discern. Something urgent clambered through my veins, a weight settled against my sternum. Maybe

Indigo had gone to help Tati so she could give us some privacy. As I neared the top of the stairs, a tightness gathered between my legs and I doubled over, gasping at the sudden sharpness.

The door to Indigo's room was half-open. I recognized the music as a song Lyric had recorded with his brother. He had played it for me almost a dozen times.

I opened the door.

There were candles all along the windowsill and in front of Indigo's mirror, and though it wasn't a lot of light, it was still enough to see them. Lyric's hands were in her hair, on her naked waist, and she was moving on top of him, her head thrown back. As she cried out, so did I. I bit my lip so hard I tasted blood, and I knew in that moment so did she.

I watched as they slowly grew aware of my presence. I watched as Lyric's beautiful face crumpled with shock. When Indigo looked at me, her face was blank.

"Azure?" he said, staring at me, stunned, before he looked up at Indigo, still straddled across his waist. "*Fuck.*"

He shoved her off, stumbled from the bed, and reached for his pants crumpled on the floor. "I'm sorry. I came here at eight like you said, but then you didn't show, and Indigo and I had a drink and I swear she started it—"

My face was wet. I was crying. The thought came to me distantly.

I looked past Lyric—still red-faced and mumbling—to Indigo. She rose up on the bed. Her face was lovely and still, but indifferent and blank as a statue.

"Azure, please—" said Lyric, trying to reach for my wrist.

I jerked away from him. "Get out."

"What?" he asked, shocked. "Can't we talk about this? I know I fucked up, but I swear I didn't mean to—"

"You have served your purpose," said Indigo coldly. "Get out. You won't like what happens if you wait."

Lyric scrambled to grab his shoes. One moment he was there; the next, he was gone, and Indigo stood naked before me, bathed in candlelight.

"I know you're hurting, but this is how it had to be. Don't you see? The Otherworld was testing us this whole time, Azure," she said. "He never wanted you, because there's only *us*. I knew you wouldn't believe me, so I needed to prove it to you." She slipped off the bed and came to my side. She smelled like him, of woodchips and sweat. The edges of the room blurred.

"Do you get it now?" Indigo asked. Her voice seemed pulled, stretched, as if it were crossing a vast distance to reach me.

Across the room, the metal nymphs and gray satyrs danced in Indigo's mirror. I looked into it and beheld a candlelit face smiling hopefully. It took me a few moments to realize that it was not my reflection at all, but hers.

Chapter Twenty-Two

THE BRIDEGROOM

I was frozen in a crouch beside Indigo's dusty bed.

Oh, Catskins. Why aren't you dead yet?

The word "dead" did not hang in the air so much as claw through it. But the death I mourned was not Azure's. It was that of my dream—for in that moment, in some distant corner of my heart, I became aware that if there was any spell to be broken, it was the enchantment placed on me. I had married a creature crafted of flowers; an illusion fitted over a woman's shape. But now my eyes must open.

There is always a peculiar distance to fairy tales. They are denuded of urgency, rinsed of true horror even as the words relish in gore. Love is presented to us as something that must be as vast as a horizon and just as unreachable. But as I counted my breaths and hid under the bed, that boundary of the page lifted, and I understood precisely how the maiden in the robber bridegroom tale must have felt. How she had bit down on her tongue to keep from screaming when she realized that she might never escape this house alive.

Indigo's bare feet were ten paces away from me now, still pointed at the mirror. She had always moved gracefully, but this time, her feet made the sucking, slapping sounds of a sea creature as she left the room. This, I thought, was the sound of Melusine's footfall when she curled back her scaled tail and stepped into her bath.

Minutes passed before I finally stood. I returned the bottle holding the tooth and the cassette to their hiding place. What appeared to be blue dye, though I did not know where it had come from, tinted my palms like spreading poison. I wiped uselessly at the dust on my shirt and pants. I thought my hands would shake, but they were still, and the force that moved my body out the door did not belong to me.

Halfway down the stairs, I heard the voices of the physician and nurse rising, the buzz that precedes an emergency. I could hear Indigo from the lower levels of the house, her words indistinct and retreating. She must have gone searching for assistance. I was left alone in the hallway with Hippolyta's door slightly ajar.

Inside, Hippolyta looked entombed in her silks and jewelry of braided hair. Glowing wires crossed her body. Her breathing was shallow, and one hand clutched the oxygen tube attached to her nose.

Hippolyta flinched when I closed the door. Her sightless eyes roved the dark. Sweat glazed her skin and the air smelled unstirred, stamped with the sourness of human waste.

"Who's there?" she asked, neck straining as she pushed herself up.

"Who is Catskins?" I asked, walking toward her bed.

Far outside the room, the voices grew louder. I was aware of each second slipping away from my possession. Hippolyta cracked a smile and licked her lips.

"I told you!" said Hippolyta, speaking to the air. "I told you he would look!" She raised her thin fist, puckered with needles, and thumped her chest. "I can feel the ragged edges of where the secret lived, but it grew tired of me and left . . . so cruel, don't you think? Did you find it? Did you discover what it was I misplaced?"

"Please," I said, straining to keep my voice even. "*Who is Catskins?*"

I could sense the answer, its particles assembling into a haze I could no longer ignore. Indigo's spell on me had begun to slip. But a small, final piece of me was still willing—or needed—to believe there was some misunderstanding.

"It's what Indigo called Azure," said Hippolyta, her voice thready. "Indigo can be so cruel . . . but you already know that, don't you?" Hippolyta said in singsong: "I saw but should not have seen. You should see, but you cannot."

The moment Azure's name was spoken, the House fashioned itself into a hand, reached into my skull, and stirred my memories with one blue finger. Deep within, cramped tight and budlike, lived an image that had been starved of light. Now, it bloomed.

I am nine years old. I am kneeling in the garden outside my parents' house, a plastic bag beside me. It is springtime, and I can smell the charnel sweetness of the flowering Bradford pear trees that line our backyard. I am clawing through the dirt, my fingers closing around a pair of sneakers and the book I'd buried. Treasures I had thought would grow into an athlete and a storyteller, a band of friends for my brother and me to play with. I drop everything except a whistle into a plastic bag and walk across the street. I throw my treasure into the neighbor's trash bin. I do not look back.

Too often the truth of a memory lives not in the mind but in the heart, in the subtle and sacred organization that makes up one's identity. But it is a tender place to reach, and I am wounded by touching it.

The image was true, even if its edges were ragged, poorly defined. I could not piece together what I already knew. Whatever it was, it had been taken from me.

The House was silent once again. It did not care that my heart was broken. We had a bargain, and I still had to honor my part in the deal.

"Where did Azure go?" I asked. "When was the last time she was at the House?"

"Oh, child," said Hippolyta. "Who said she ever left?"

I heard the knives in Indigo's voice. I could see her kneeling in the dirt, pushing mounds of earth and worms over a body whose shape I did not recognize. The room shimmered.

"Where—" I tried to say.

Hippolyta interrupted me. "Shh!" she said. "I already told him!" Her sightless eyes focused somewhere near my face. "The Otherworld kept all from me, and to see you need a key. Indigo wanted a blue-eyed starling and Azure wanted a red, and if I'd never stopped to look then nobody would be dead!"

The Otherworld. That dark turret in the distance.

"Is that where she is? In the Otherworld?" I was close enough to Hippolyta's bedside that I could smell her breath. "How do I get the key to the Otherworld?"

Her body convulsed. She threw back her head and laughed. The machines she was wired to startled alive and began to wail. The door to Hippolyta's room was thrown open. A small knot of doctors, nurses, and attendants stormed inside.

"Step aside, sir—" said a brusque voice.

"No, she needs to tell me more, I—"

A physician shouldered past me. My arm knocked into the bedside table and my hands closed around a bottle of sedatives.

The machines tethered to Hippolyta's veins and lungs screeched.

"Sir, get away, *now*."

I stumbled away, my head ringing. Outside Hippolyta's room, I was met with Indigo's dark silhouette, her smell of apples and honey. A nurse with light skin and pale-green scrubs was speaking to her in hushed tones:

"—not make it through the night, so perhaps you and your husband should stay here to say your goodbyes?" The nurse's smile was efficiently pitiful. "I'll leave you two to talk."

When I looked at Indigo, I could still hear her lilting voice.

Oh, Catskins. Why aren't you dead yet?

And yet my Indigo possessed an inexorable pull, a trick of turning one solid and visible with a single glance. I've never pretended at bravery, and so I let all that was weak within me wish that I'd never heard her say those words. That we could return to who we had been two days ago. If I had any magic, I would've used it for that very purpose.

But I was a mere mortal.

At first, Indigo smiled at the sight of me. Then her gaze dropped to my dusty pants, my shoes. Her eyes flicked to my hair. She looked as if she'd been set into glass. When she smiled, I saw that some of her lipstick had caught on her canines, turning them bloodstained.

"Where have you been wandering, my darling?"

Chapter Twenty-Three

AZURE

You know that feeling of a loose tooth? The way your tongue seeks out the carrion tang of your own mouth, the disgust and wonder that a part of you is breaking down, that one day you will hold a shard of yourself . . . that was what I had become.

As children, Indigo and I learned that teeth were powerful things and the tooth fairy was little more than a common thief.

We were eleven years old, sitting in the kitchens on a bright summer day, eating from a tub of rum raisin ice cream—Tati's favorite flavor—and since it was the only ice cream left in the fridge at the time, it was ours too. Tati had come down from her studio. I rose on my heels to greet her, opened my mouth, and wiggled my loose canine for her.

"I think it's going to come out today!" I said. "And I'm going to leave it under my pillow for the tooth fairy!"

"We've been pulling on it all day," added Indigo.

"The tooth fairy is horrifically cheap," Tati scoffed.

This was not my first loose tooth, but when I'd left the previous ones under my pillow, no one had come for them. No one had wanted them. I looked down now, my face burning. Tati tipped up my chin. I loved how she always smelled of burning things. I wanted to warm myself on her smile.

"Teeth are memory and therefore precious, and worth far more than a dollar," she said, smiling and tapping her incisor. "Did you know that once upon a time, the Vikings used to pay children for their teeth? It was said to bring good luck in battle. Other people burned their baby teeth, hoping it would save them from hardship in life."

Indigo scrunched her face. "Why baby teeth?"

"Because they're your milk teeth," said Tati. "They've documented you before the world could leave its mark, and above all things, they *remember.*"

When Tati said that, my mouth ached in mourning.

"I keep all of Indigo's baby teeth in a jar," said Tati.

"You do?" we said at the same time.

Tati smiled and nodded. "Baby teeth make beautiful art. Queen Victoria wore an emerald thistle tooth pendant fixed with one of her children's teeth. She did the same with a pair of amethyst earrings too. One day, I'll make something for you both."

"Me too?" I'd asked, folding my hands in my lap so I did not look too grasping.

"If you'll let me," said Tati, and the warmth in her voice was like a furnace on my skin.

When my tooth fell out a few days later, I gave it to Tati. She kissed my forehead and made a big show of placing it in a tiny velvet bag, which went into a gold-filigreed box that lived on the highest shelf of her studio. I'd almost forgotten that moment. I wondered if the tooth had kept the recollection all to itself.

THE NIGHT I FOUND INDIGO AND LYRIC TOGETHER, I SCREAMED at her. I locked myself in the bathroom, dragging a duvet off the bed as I went and shoving it into the copper tub. Indigo had bathed an hour earlier, maybe less, and small puddles bled through the blanket. I pictured her soaking in the tub, scrubbing her bronze limbs, rubbing rose oil into her neck while Lyric walked up the stairs. I wondered if our faces blurred together when he was inside her, whether he called her Azure.

In the morning, I stepped out of the copper tub and beheld myself in the mirror. My eyelids were shiny and swollen, my skin cracked from crying. I had forgotten to remove my starling necklace and now clutched it in my hand so tight I could feel the cool edges of its carved wings digging into my palm.

This was not about a boy. This was about theft. The theft of a dream wrought solely for me.

I knew Indigo was on the other side of the door, and I hesitated to open it. I was aware of how little I could call my own. Not a house, not a trust fund, not a Tati. But Lyric had been mine. Or at least, he had wanted to be and that was more than I'd ever had.

For a breath, I was certain we were not the same soul. We were sisters who wandered in the other's dreams and shared magic the way some girls shared clothes. But the previous night had altered me. I was scared that at any instant, my arms would shoot out the windows and my head would snap off the roof and the House would not be able to hold me. I needed space.

I opened the door.

Indigo sat on the floor, naked, her hair hanging all around her. The candles had gone out, leaving uneven pools of wax. She was surrounded by knives: a polished steak knife, a brass letter opener in the shape of a crane, a paring knife, her father's hunting knife. I recognized its ivory hilt. Indigo had once told me her father named it É'leos.

Mercy.

"What are you doing?" I asked.

I stepped toward her. She flinched, shrinking back and drawing her knees to her chest.

"It's over," she said in a small voice. She rocked on her heels. "I tried. You know I tried. But I've failed."

The walls of Indigo's bedroom seemed to bend around her, as if the House were trying to protect her . . . from me.

"You screamed at me for trying to save us," she said, a tear running down her cheek. She lifted her gaze, her black eyes huge and wet. "You want to leave, don't you? You're going to tell me that you need space from me . . . and then you'll never come back. Tell me that isn't what you were going to say? That you need to leave?"

If I had felt gargantuan before, my body pulled back into itself now.

"Indigo . . ." I began.

"Don't," said Indigo. She sounded so frail and delicate, like even moonlight might burn her skin. "I can feel the truth.

"We only needed a little more time and then we would've been reunited, all-powerful. Transformed." She drew in a loud, shuddering breath, biting her trembling lip. "Maybe that was the problem. Maybe we would've been *too* powerful together. Maybe Cast-Out Susan really is happy, and some people can live knowing they'll never be whole."

Indigo ran her finger along the ivory hilt. Winter sunlight spread through the room, and I beheld my fury in all its cold brightness: I had accused Indigo of theft. *Indigo.* The one person who was willing to share everything she had been given. The person who would have given everything to me. Even, I realized as she lifted the knife off the floor, her own life.

"I'm not as strong as you," said Indigo quietly. "I can't stay here like this, like some half thing. Now that I know you're going to leave, what's the point? Maybe next time, we'll get it right. I'm sorry I failed us."

I lunged forward, knocking the blade from her hand and sinking to the ground. I tried to hold her, but she pushed me back, shaking her head.

"You don't want us anymore," said Indigo. "You don't want the Otherworld anymore. You want to be outside. With *him*. With—"

I clamped my hand over her mouth. I trembled in the glare cast by her words. If I left, what would I be? Only a girl orphaned by dreams.

I pictured my mother sitting at the plastic kitchen table, something essential cored out of her and sucked down the mouth of all the carnivorous things that lived in the outside world. That was all that waited for me, and I had almost given in to it.

"I believe you," I said. "I'm sorry. I'll wait, okay? I can be patient. I'm sorry."

Indigo was stiff in my arms, and then, finally, her hand came to rest atop my head.

"I forgive you," she said.

WE WERE GENTLE WITH EACH OTHER IN THE WEEKS THAT FOL-lowed, though my weakness still poisoned me at times. At night, I dreamt of Indigo and Lyric, her knuckles whitening as she gripped the headboard, him thrusting into her. I dreamt of the warehouse clubs and the rancid brine off the wharfs, the delight I felt lifting my sweat-matted hair so the cool air could kiss the back of my neck.

Indigo said there was no point in us returning. She comforted me. She told me that if I was sad—and I grieved the loss of that music like a lost limb—then that was proof of how close I had come to losing it all, and wasn't it good to be reminded of all the brightness that lay ahead?

The Otherworld held little solace for me. The air felt like teeth set on edge. Vines tangled around my ankles. I couldn't feel the warmth of the woodstove in the turret or smell the cinnamon sticks Indigo threw in the fire.

"Don't be sad," said Indigo, petting my hair. "Maybe the Otherworld is a little wounded and that's why it's not letting you in . . . it'll pass. I'm half of you, and I've forgiven you. It'll come around."

But where the Otherworld was cold to me, the House was kind. Often, it lulled me to sleep. I wondered if it was trying to help me pass the days more quickly. It seemed to have the opposite effect on Indigo. Her sleep turned fitful, and she sketched frantically in the Room of Secrets, though I never saw a single paper in her hand.

"It's going to be a wonderful gift," she told me.

I believed her. I wanted nothing more than to be happy again. But somehow, I kept messing it up.

One evening, we were sitting on the rooftop, bundled in blankets. The Otherworld matched us, listless and drowsy, the sort of numb that accompanies being both too cold and too lazy to do much about it. That day in school had been strange. I'd overheard a classmate, a lovely Black girl with a gap-toothed grin whom I used to see at the warehouse, talking about a trip she was planning with her cousin. They were going to pack a single backpack and see as much of the world as they could fit in one summer. She surprised me by turning around in her seat, smiling. Alia was her name.

"What are you going to do after graduation?"

I was grateful when the teacher stepped inside and spared me from answering. I thought of this now, testing the frayed wounds exposed by my weakness. I wanted to *do* something.

Indigo went utterly still beside me. I looked up. She was staring at me, her brows pressed down, her mouth a terse slash. Tears stood in her eyes.

"What's wrong?" I asked.

"You were humming."

"What?"

"You were *humming*," said Indigo, a sob clawing out of her chest. "You were humming one of those stupid songs from the warehouse, and I-I don't understand what I'm doing *wrong*. I thought you understood!"

She stood suddenly, and the paintbrushes she'd been cleaning in her lap clattered to the stone.

"All I want to do is protect you, Azure. All I've done is *love* you, and you won't even try to make things right—"

Around us, the atmosphere of the Otherworld rippled. A low sound, like a whine, gathered. Panic set in. I looked above and saw the sky fragmented through the oak leaves. *Tell me how to fix this*, I begged even as I stood and grabbed Indigo's arm.

She threw off my hand, and I stumbled, my foot rolling on the paintbrush. I heard her gasp and felt her fingers reach for my wrist, but it was too late. My jaw thudded against the stone and blood filled my mouth. I rolled onto my back and when I opened my lips to scream, the air froze on my teeth. I lifted my hand, gingerly touching my lips. A jaggedness met my fingers. Something hit my tongue and I spat. In my hand lay two things tucked into one: a bloodied shard of tooth and, finally, an answer.

I WAS GROGGY FROM SEDATIVES ON THE WAY BACK FROM THE dentist. Outside the car window, the world looked rain-soaked, all the lines of the buildings seeped into the trees. Tati stroked my hair. I glanced at the seat beside me, surprised all over again that Indigo hadn't come with us.

"I need to heal from the pollutants of the outside world," she'd said, her voice clear and cold. "One of us has to keep pure."

I hadn't had time to tell her that I'd found a solution, a means to return to how we'd once been, to remind the Otherworld that I was part of its fabric and finally rid myself of this weakness.

I looked up at Tati. She seemed older these days. Time had stenciled lines around her eyes and bracketed her mouth. She had stopped wearing colorful silk scarves and now only wore plain, cotton wraps around her head.

"Tati, I need our baby teeth back."

Tati laughed. "What did they give you back there, child?"

"I need them back," I repeated.

Tati frowned. "I always thought I'd turn them into something special for you girls, maybe for your twentieth birthdays—"

"There's no point," I said, letting my head rest on the window. "We're going to transform. Indigo's working on our present now." Sleep pulled down my eyelids, loosened my jaw. I knew in that moment that Indigo sat in the Room of Secrets, her hair trailing in pigment. "She's always working on our present."

Tati was quiet. I didn't look at her face. I was too busy watching the trees tangle themselves in the clouds.

"So then why do you need it?" she asked in a careful voice.

"You said teeth hold our memories, who we were before the world touched us," I said. "I need to remember."

"Why would you want to bring back the past, Azure?" she asked. "Little teeth make it quite impossible to consume the world, which is why you are given bigger and better ones. Little teeth mean you're still tender for eating. You don't want that, do you?"

That was exactly what I wanted: not to consume but to be swallowed whole by another realm entirely. I wanted to be tender for eating, for the Otherworld to slurp my measly half soul out of my bones so that it might join with Indigo's forever.

But I'd wandered too far. My teeth ached from the things I'd consumed—concert music, the artificial sweetness of movie-theater lights, a boy's vulnerable moan, the torn edge of a college brochure holding a false autumn.

I needed to forget.

I needed to go back.

As I fell asleep, I thought I felt Tati's hand on my shoulder, her voice threadbare: "*Where is Indigo taking you?*"

WHEN WE RETURNED TO THE HOUSE, TATI LED ME TO HER STU-dio. She patted the walls, and the House gurgled happily. Inside her workspace, her current project was incomplete. A skein of hair lay tugged across her workbench alongside a pair of blue gloves and a bottle of bleach. She bent down, rummaging through her drawers before pulling out the same gold box I remembered.

"You know," said Tati, "change is the great blessing of mortals. Creatures of the Otherworld are always bound by something—moonlight, iron, running water. But the only thing that can act on humans is time. We are not lovely and static. We are ever-changing, vast as seasons. We are *meant* to change. Do you understand, Azure?"

Tati's words reached me warily, like a lynx's paw testing a frozen pond before bounding across it. But I'd seen what hid in the water: my mother's hollow eyes, the static of a television screen, a world empty of apple blossoms.

I understood perfectly.

INDIGO LOVED MY IDEA.

She held the jar of teeth in her fingers and rattled it gently before unscrewing the lid and looking inside. I thought they'd have a smell, an echo of meat and marrow like stale dog treats, but they were scentless. Indigo poured some into her hand. The teeth were the milky color of petrified memory.

"These have so much power," said Indigo. "We'll bury them around the Otherworld, and the memories will go back into the ground and it won't be mad at you anymore. We'll start over."

She traced a circle on the skin beneath my clavicles.

"Like closing all the gaps so nothing can get in," she said softly. "No one will get that close to us again, and if they do, we'll make sure they can never look upon our world."

WE PLANTED THE TEETH ON A FULL MOON, OUR STARLING KEYS dangling from our necks. We dug into the cold earth with our fingers until our nails bore crescents of grime. Over each tooth, we whispered our names and they fell like blue pins, anchoring us to the dirt—

Indigo and Azure.

Indigo and Azure.

Indigo and Azure.

As we spoke our names, our voices climbed in a crescendo, the syllables a spiral of blue. I understood how a pair of words can turn to prayer, plea, or prophecy. I could not tell which one we had become.

All I knew was that together we were greater than ourselves. Together we were boundless, oceanic. Together, we commanded the heft of a planet.

We were impossible to outrun.

IN THE WEEKS THAT FOLLOWED, A DIFFERENT MAGIC TOOK root in me. Our Otherworld no longer snarled with winter thunderstorms, the vines did not grasp at my ankles, and the winter pansies blinked back to life. These were the days where I was able to ignore the siren song of the outside world. I knew that if I stayed here long enough then that restless, loose-tooth discomfort would settle on its own.

One evening, Tati found us in the parlor, lying on our bellies, stringing together a long rope of marigolds and carnations to make a canopy of springtime for our bed. I kept pricking my hand, which made Indigo wince in pain.

"Indigo," said Tati, appearing in the doorway. She had drawn her wrap tightly around her shoulders. I'd never heard her voice sound like that—urgent and low, simmering. "I need to speak with you."

Tati clutched a crumpled piece of paper in her fist. In the seconds before Indigo turned around, I was struck by how startlingly pretty she was: lissome and golden, her skin glazed by the firelight and so delicate-looking you could scratch her with a thought.

And then she turned.

All that softness resolved to stone. I could see a choice glitter in her eyes. Of what, I didn't know.

"I'll just be a second," said Indigo.

I watched her dust the rose petals from her long, white night-gown before they left me alone by the fire. I turned onto my back and continued weaving flowers into a garland. The floor was warm, and my stomach was full of Mrs. Revand's homemade pasta. All around me, the world was opulent with warmth and the frail satin of petals, and soon, my eyes closed.

But not for long.

A scream woke me, loud and deep. Ancient. I sat up, flowers falling from my face. The fire had gone out, and a cold, silver haze hung over the parlor.

"Tati?" I called. "Indigo?"

I ran down the hall and felt the House panic and vibrate, the halls lengthening as if it wished to put some distance between itself and the awful sound. I stopped at the base of the stairs. On the landing, a creature writhed and squirmed. The moonlight striped across it, revealing the hump of a hip, the elbow bend of a pale, outflung arm. I crept up the stairs and saw a black veil pulled over the figure's face. One bony hand stretched out while the other clawed at its face—

"Help."

The House recognized the voice and threw light over the body. Tati, I realized, and my fear melted away. The veil was nothing more than her headscarf come undone. An acrid, am-moniac smell filled my nose. Tati moaned, slowly tugging at the black cloth on her face. I reached out for her. At my touch, she scuttled back like an animal. I didn't like that I flinched from her.

"It's me," I said.

The cloth molded to her face as she sucked in her breath. In, out, in, out. Like she didn't quite believe me.

"I saw it all wrong," she said, her voice shattered and high-pitched.

"Where's Indigo?" I asked. My eyes searched the empty hallways. I thought I caught a flash of white near Tati's room. When I blinked, it was gone.

Tati whimpered as the long, black cloth slid to the floor. I saw bits of bone, skin engorged and purple, hanks of hair flopping across the exposed musculature of a cheek. Tati's once-brown eyes were now milky, roving in red sockets. She opened her mouth, but this time I screamed for her.

And the House screamed with me.

Chapter Twenty-Four

THE BRIDEGROOM

This is why fairy tales are dangerous: their words sneak into your veins and travel into the chambers of your heart, where they whisper of your exceptionalism. They say: *Ah, but remember the boy who walked into the woods and came out a king? Oh, but what of the girl who was kicked and slept in ashes? Remember the man who was only kind and so life bent around the shape of his smile?*

But we are not exceptional.

When Indigo caught me outside Hippolyta's room, I thought of all the wives who preceded the famous Scheherazade, the many women who wed a bloodthirsty sultan known to kill his brides. Here is how the fairy tale leaves you disfigured. You think death will not touch you as it did the others. You lie down in that blood-soaked bed and forget the noose will caress your neck by dawn. You look your wife in the eye knowing full well that she is a stranger to you, knowing that by now she must have guessed you have rummaged through her secrets, but when she lays her hand on your cheek, you turn your face so that you might kiss her palm.

Where have you been wandering, my darling?

Behind me, the machines in Hippolyta's room continued to

scream. Indigo's smile did not waver.

"I got lost."

Indigo closed her lips over her teeth, though the grin remained.

"Well, it's a good thing you weren't hurt," she said. Her hand left my cheek and solemnly searched my face—my eyelashes, the angle of my jaw, the knobs of my knuckles that she used to kiss in the afternoons. I was being committed to memory.

The density Indigo had once placed in my existence was dissolving. I could feel myself ceasing to matter to her, my own skin flickering translucent, her eyes hardly registering my gaze.

"I would hate for something to happen to you, my love," she said.

I was beginning to understand that it was dangerous not to matter to Indigo Maxwell-Casteñada—and tucked behind my fear was the humiliating realization that I cared for her more than she did for me.

"I believe you," I lied.

We were silent for a moment as I braced for her questions. I had told her I would be at a library on the mainland, and yet here I was. But Indigo did not ask. Perhaps she did not see the point.

"My aunt has one last request," she said. "She would like us to eat under this roof while it is still hers. We will have a feast to honor her life in the formal dining room."

I noticed she did not use its proper name—Camera Secretum.

There was a flash, there and gone, in her gaze. Like hunger. Or sorrow. I couldn't tell.

"A last meal, a final farewell," she said, and her fingers skimmed my hand.

When Indigo touched me, I was reminded of all the times she had put her fingers to my pulse or kept vigil over me in the night. I could not always see her in the dark, but whatever form she took—maiden or monstrous—had not mattered to me then.

Now at her touch, I became aware of two things: The first was that whatever she had done to Azure, she meant to do to me. I was sure that when she spoke of a final farewell, it was not meant for Hippolyta. Thus, there were only a handful of hours left for me to uphold my end of the bargain.

The second realization was that I did not know who or what Indigo was, and yet I loved her anyway.

Perhaps this marks the place in the story where I should have raced down the stairs and out of the House of Dreams. But like all the fair-of-face fools before me, I did not. Sometimes you are lured not by the promise of safety but the safety of knowing that here lies a sure thing.

Here is a path, and on it you may find riches and wonders and certain death. You will never have to return to the other side where riches are scant and wonders are stingy. There, death is hidden, but here, death wears a face that you love. Here, you can be certain that death loves you, too, in its own fashion.

I smiled at Indigo. "Name a time."

AFTER, INDIGO PROMISED TO SEND FOR MY SUIT AND TOLD ME she needed to make some calls.

"I'll see you soon," she said, and kissed me.

It was indecorous and fierce, and when she pulled back, there was an air of finality in her gaze.

Now I knew why all those Grecian youths threw back their shoulders before they faced down the Minotaur in a labyrinth. This was the ultimate test. To see whether the dream of yourself aligned with your destiny.

If it turned out you were as mundane as you feared, then at least the epiphany would be brief.

Mrs. Revand led me past the foyer preemptively lined with calla lilies and condolence flowers, past the buzzing, sour-smelling parlor where a half dozen solicitors left coffee rings on antique wood and past the entrance to the wine cellar, where a cook, I assumed, examined a dusty bottle of wine with an assistant. There were people here, but they left no impression.

All I sensed was Indigo. My Indigo, inexorable and unknowable as fate. With every step, I was certain that's what she was—an ending culled from the milk of stars long before I ever dared to draw breath.

Eventually, Mrs. Revand opened the door to a guest room covered in faded wallpaper, with nothing but slits in the wall to serve as windows. The air smelled neglected and powdery. The beds were stripped, the mattresses stained. An en suite bathroom boasted a bronze tub shaped like a halved egg.

"I'm so sorry," Mrs. Revand said. "If I had more notice, I could have had the rooms properly aired out, but Miss Indigo said you only need them for changing. I'll have the master guest suite ready for your stay tonight."

My eye was drawn to a side table between the two beds. It had golden pin legs and a deep green marble circle. Three corvid skulls sat atop it alongside a glass vase holding dried flowers and raven feathers.

"You'll never leave, you know," said Mrs. Revand, smiling. "I can tell the House likes you. And when the House likes someone, it keeps them forever."

"Did the House like Azure?"

"Oh yes," said Mrs. Revand, fluffing an errant pillow. "It loved her even more than Indigo, though I'll never tell her that. Indigo was born to this grandeur. But the House *chose* Azure."

"And did the House keep her forever?" I asked.

Is she sleeping under the floor in a plastic bag? Is she in its hearth, in a thousand pieces?

Mrs. Revand laughed. "Oh, I don't know about that. I've never looked too closely. The House loves me, too, you know, so I never stay overnight. It might get ideas."

She patted the footboard of the bed as if it were an unruly dog and, with a final, gentle smile, closed the door behind her.

I was left alone with the shadows and the dwindling hours. I considered what I had been told. Hippolyta said the girls had a key to the Otherworld. I could just as easily try to climb its gate, but what if the key opened something else? What if it held a message?

"Where would she have hidden it?"

My eye kept returning to the corvid skulls, their gaping ovals and yellowing ridges. The longer I looked, the more certain I was of where the keys might be hidden. I thought of Indigo's second favorite place, the walls lined with the blank faces of creatures who could say nothing of what they'd seen. The Room of Secrets.

Light dappled across my feet as if in answer. Only Indigo knew for sure, and though she kept her secrets close, there was one thing I knew she could not resist: a game.

The House seemed to purr in response and then the room disappeared. I could not tell if it was trying to reward me. If so, its kindness and cruelty wore the same face.

Look close, it insisted. *Look now.*

Another truth: folded up so tightly it lengthened and took shape in blips and blurs.

It was the day before my brother and I entered the cedar armoire to look for Faerie.

It was autumn, and the world was gold and woodsmoke. Mother had not made dinner, and my brother and I pretended we were pirates on a long sea voyage forced to quell the grumbles in our bellies with saltines. I told him they were precious hardtack. I lingered in that memory and conjured what I knew. Mother was sweet and playful; she must have been distracted or too busy pretending to be a deep-sea leviathan stalking us from behind the couches to make dinner.

No, said the House of Dreams. *Look again.*

Mother was slumped over the kitchen table, a lit cigarette smoldering to ash in a teacup. She screamed at us when we woke her. She was the leviathan in the deep, that which had to be maneuvered around.

Father came home early. My brother and I were laughing because he had sneezed like an elephant. Our father wanted to join in on our fun. He was pretending to be another pirate. He ran at us. *"What's so funny?"* he boomed. High, golden laughter, deer-black eyes, legs twisting—

Look again, said the House.

I was on the floor. A knee was on my chest. My brother cried and began to cough, his face paling. My mother rose from the table, annoyed, grabbed my brother's inhaler from inside one of the dark-brown cabinets. She threw it at his feet. She did not look at me as she retreated into the dark.

"Why are you laughing at me?" said my father. *"You think it's funny that I work all day to put food on the table—"*

We were only play wrestling, a lion and its cub, our foyer a vast Serengeti—

No, said the House.

I opened my eyes. A wall of a thousand thorns surrounded the secret inside me. The thin gauze I stretched over my childhood ripped, and in the holes, I saw what I had not forgotten but willfully misplaced. I knew why we had to run.

But where did he run to?

One might think this knowledge would lay waste to me. But I had years of practice when it came to avoiding what I knew, and so I held it away from me, to feel at a later time. A time that, if I did not play this game correctly, might never come to pass.

Chapter Twenty-Five

AZURE

In the days following Tati's injury, I struggled to process the truth of it, to call it an "accident," though it never sat right in my heart. I would find myself repeating everything the doctors had said—she worked late in the night, she was getting older, she was confused.

She must have slipped and fallen in her studio and a bottle of bleach fell into her eyes and blinded her. She must have hit her head for that skull fracture. She must have, for now she was concussed, so confused, and she would never be the same.

Indigo had a few weeks left before she officially aged into her trust, but she took over the household responsibilities when Tati returned from the hospital. For the first week, there was no silence to be found. Workers moved through the House, rearranging furniture, cushioning all the edges. Tati's workshop was sealed, her inventory emptied, her commissions delivered in whatever state she had left them.

In the mornings, Indigo and I would go to Tati's bedroom. We would slide braided bracelets around her wrists and hang woven blond and brunette pendants from her neck. We wrapped her in memory and hoped that she would return.

I was never sure if it made a difference though. Tati seemed almost comatose during our visits. One day, while Indigo ran to the kitchens to fetch her a bowl of lukewarm broth, I watched Tati's face closely. Her eyelids were closed tight. Indigo and I used to do that when we were pretending to be asleep.

"Tati?" I whispered, placing a hand on her wrist. "Are you awake?"

She looked different now. The stark lights leached the cinnamon warmth from her skin. Her body was too slender, hollowed out by the loss of her sight and her mind. Her shorn head was bandaged and stippled with age spots that I'd never realized were underneath those beautiful headscarves. I ran my fingers over the velvet nap of her scalp, wondering if I might feel the hard outline of the secret she kept in her skull. Tati's last words had carved a space out of me, and in that new darkness, something I could not bring myself to look at bloomed—*I saw it all wrong*.

I wasn't sure what I'd seen that night. I caught a flash of Indigo's white nightdress in the hallway after I found Tati, but that couldn't be right. The moment I'd screamed, Indigo appeared at the base of the stairs. She was wearing black. I had been out of it before I found Tati, dreaming, and sleeping in a pile of petals. I must have been confused.

"Tati." I leaned in close and whispered. "What did you see?"

Her eyes opened. My face was only a few inches away from hers. Tati's lips smacked wetly. Her milky eyes landed on nothing. And then, she opened her mouth and screamed.

Mrs. Revand threw open the doors, rushed inside. Indigo stood outside the threshold, her face curiously blank.

"Give her time," said Mrs. Revand as she reached for a syringe and grabbed Tati's thrashing arm.

"I saw nothing!" Tati bellowed. "I don't want to see!"

"Shhh, Miss Hippolyta, there's nothing to see," murmured Mrs. Revand. She glanced at me over her shoulder. "You girls go play. I'll take care of this."

I met Indigo outside the door. I could feel the House's worry—the floorboards vibrated, tapestries slipped off their hooks, the walls sagged. I rubbed my palm along the banister and tried to soothe it.

Beside me, Indigo was quiet. We hadn't been alone in a while. At night, Indigo fell into an exhausted, dreamless sleep and in the morning, solicitors and agents clamored for her attention. We hadn't been back to school in the two weeks since the accident, and though arrangements had been made so my grades wouldn't suffer, those two weeks melted into one long, terrible night without the rhythm of schoolwork. Even my mother did not try to summon me home. When she heard about Tati's misfortune, she had only closed her eyes.

Take all the time you need with her, she'd said.

I'd always thought I'd feel relieved—victorious, even—the day I saw guilt in my mother's eyes, but when it finally happened, all I felt was exhaustion. *How did we come to this?* I wanted to ask her from where we stood on opposite ends of the dingy kitchenette. But Tati, the one who had kissed my scraped knees since I was ten years old, needed me, and so I left.

"It's Tati's fault, you know," said Indigo as she brewed us cups of hibiscus tea.

I was the one who had found Tati screaming and scratching at her face. I didn't see any signs of fault. Only pain.

"You heard her," said Indigo, glancing upstairs, like she could see through the kitchen ceiling and into Tati's bedroom. "She saw something she shouldn't. Maybe she tried to get into the Other-world when we weren't there, and the fae punished her. Divine things don't like to be exposed like that. She's lucky it wasn't a goddess who could send packs of wild dogs after her or a god hurling thunderbolts." Indigo shivered, and only then did the cold in her voice thaw. "But that's how you can tell the Otherworld loves us. They kept her alive for us when they should've done so much worse."

Indigo loved Tati. She wept when we went to the hospital. She tested every tea and broth in the morning to make sure it wasn't too hot, and when we left Tati's room, Indigo always kissed her on the cheek. I knew she didn't mourn like others did. Even when her own parents died, she told me she hardly wept.

"The sacred world has its own calculus," she said.

There was no reason for me to look closely at the set of her mouth or the angle of her shoulders. Still, I did.

"Where were you when Tati got hurt?"

Indigo frowned. "Why?"

"I never had a chance to ask you," I said carefully. My eyes must have given me away though. Indigo was wearing the same black linen shift from the night of Tati's accident and I stared at it now, certain that she had worn something else earlier in the evening.

"I thought you were wearing a white dress that night," I said.

"Oh, that," said Indigo, plucking at the cloth. "I'd gotten some paint on my white nightgown, so I was changing in the laundry room when I heard you scream."

I nodded. I wanted that dark space inside me to disappear . . . but I'd looked in the laundry room and I'd found no sign of the white dress.

"Let's go to the Otherworld," said Indigo, grabbing my hand. "I want to start planning my birthday."

SPRING HAD BEGUN TO TRACE A WARM FINGER ALONG THE branches of the thundercloud plum and empress trees, though the apple blossom buds were still pressed tight as pursed mouths. Around the great oak, the daffodils remained hard and green. And deep in my chest, in the place where I wanted to believe Indigo most, an icy knot of doubt refused to thaw.

I tried to ignore it, even though I could feel it growing, unspooling threads of frost that haunted every movement. Maybe I had let it get out of control. Maybe it had entwined with my veins, and that's how I found myself a few days before Indigo's birthday, alone, and inside her bedroom.

The House had been lulled to sleep by afternoon fires in the parlor. Indigo was taking a meeting in the Camera Secretum, and Mrs. Revand was bathing Tati with the nurse they'd hired. I was supposed to be catching up on schoolwork. Instead, I ran my hands along Indigo's dresser. I wasn't even sure what I was looking for, all I knew was that there was something she didn't wish me to see.

In the first drawer, I found silk camisoles and black panties, hair ties scrunched to one side, and Tati's favorite polka-dotted headscarf, which Indigo had once complained about Tati wearing too often. The second drawer smelled sickly sweet, like overripened fruit. There was nothing inside except Indigo's blank canvas papers and the neat cedar boxes that held her pastels.

At the back of the drawer lay something crumpled. I picked it up. It had an odd smell, like mushrooms. I unfolded it carefully.

It was a torn corner of canvas paper bearing Indigo's precise, slanting handwriting—

all of glass

I turned it over.

But that was it. I crumpled it back up and tossed it inside the second drawer. The third drawer was darker, deeper. I plunged my hands to the back, seeking out the feel of cloth only for something sharp to slide across my palm. I winced as I drew out a dull blue razor.

It was so ordinary . . . the kind you bought at grocery stores. I picked it up and saw bits of hair caught in its teeth. I knew it wasn't mine. My razor was pink and lived in the toiletry bag where I kept all my things.

Indigo had mocked me for shaving my legs. She called it a slippery mortal habit, one that we shouldn't indulge because we were of the fae and their skin was marble smooth or else made of polished bark from the tender hearts of willow trees. She said she never bothered, and her legs were smooth, polished, and bronze.

"If you believed me, then you wouldn't have to do any of that," she liked to say.

I used to let these words shame me, but here was her slippery mortal habit, tucked inside a drawer so no one could see. I ran my thumb along the razor's teeth. My hand ached, but not where I felt the cut.

I stared at the razor for so long I almost didn't hear the footsteps approaching on the stairs until it was too late. I dropped it in the drawer and closed it, my heart pounding.

What would happen if I showed it to her? If I demanded to know whether she had as many mortal habits as I did?

I braced myself. The door opened. Mrs. Revand was breathless, wisps of gray hair snuck out to frame her face.

"Azure," she said. "Your mother called. You're needed at home. Immediately."

THE WHOLE WALK THERE I WAS TERRIFIED OF JUPITER'S SHADOW

greeting me at the front door, but Jupiter, as it turned out, had left. His mother was sick. Of all the things that shocked me, it was that Jupiter had been young once. He hadn't slid wetly out of some crevice in the world. He had been birthed. Fed.

Maybe even loved.

"Will you . . . will you stay?" my mother asked, her voice small and tender. "Just for the night? Please? You know I don't sleep well alone."

She was sitting at the dining table when I arrived, her hands twisting in her lap. A hair clip barely held back her curls. I could hear her the bruise in her voice, and it stole my balance.

"Okay," I said.

I didn't want to, but I remembered when we'd camped out in the living room, the blankets strung over the chairs like tents. We would lie in piles of pillows and watch movies together. I had never slept so well. Not even in the House of Dreams.

"When's he coming back?" I asked.

"He'll be gone for at least two months," my mother said. "After that, we'll see where he goes."

I stayed the night, and my sleep was sweet and dreamless. When I woke, my mother had breakfast waiting—eggs, burnt toast, watery coffee. I didn't want to sit at that table, so I picked up my plate and brought it to my bedroom. After she left for her Saturday shift, I walked around the house, marveling at how the quiet fell around me like snow. Indigo would be with the lawyers well into the evening, and the day felt like a treasure stumbled upon.

I walked through the woods, where the air sparkled on my skin, and along the highway, down to the gas station where Lyric had once bought cigarettes. It was sad, and kind of embarrassing, to think of him now. Not because of what I felt but because of what I didn't feel. I thought he had a power not even Indigo possessed. I thought he had translated my every cell to flame. I thought I was his air. I thought no one, surely, knew what this was like, that the marvel of us proved we couldn't possibly be *just* human. A piece of me grieved that I was wrong, but another part—one with lengthening teeth and huge, wet eyes—was profoundly relieved. Giddy, even.

Because if I could be wrong about something that had felt so sure and so vast, then what else could I be wrong about?

INDIGO'S EIGHTEENTH BIRTHDAY WAS A SMALL AFFAIR. WE went to the Otherworld, carting our rugs and pillows, blankets, and candles. Indigo took a small wagon with her, all bundled up in ropes. I figured they were different tea supplies than the ones we always kept in the turret, but when she untied the ropes, my eyes widened.

Inside was a handful of priceless heirlooms, pieces of Casteñada conquest that I had only ever seen from the other side of the glass cabinets that held them—pink and blue imperial porcelain from the Ming dynasty; a necklace of Colombian emeralds, each pendant fat as an egg; a glass panel of coins from the ancient kingdom of Pontus; and a beautiful jade bowl that Tati had won in an auction last year.

I loved that bowl. It was rumored to have once been used by Mongolian khans who prized jade for its ability to neutralize poisons. I'd been too scared to touch it when Tati had brought it out to show us. Now I watched as Indigo arranged flowers in the vase, hung the emeralds around her neck, propped the coins against the teapot, and poured raspberries and cream into the bowl's jade hollow, mixing them with a finger before popping a sweetened berry into her mouth.

It was a hopelessly decadent display of treasure, and where it might've once made me delight in her casualness, now the tea turned to acid in my belly. It meant nothing to her, when to the world outside every artifact was a piece of some grand, infinite story . . . and here she was wearing it around her neck like a charm.

"What?" asked Indigo, holding out the bowl. "Want one?"

I shook my head.

Indigo shrugged, relaxed against one of the pillows. "Now that I'm officially the adult, I can take care of us both and you won't have to go back to Jupiter and his hovel."

Indigo and I often laughed about Jupiter's house. Now that he wasn't in it, though, I thought only of my mother wiping down the counters, heating two noodle cups, stepping carefully as she brought them to the couch. I thought of the self-conscious way she arranged flowers picked by the roadside on the table. We didn't have a vase, so we used an old liquor bottle with the label peeled off. It wasn't the vintage crystal Indigo used, but it still caught the light.

"I have to go back to her," I said before amending my words: "I mean, *them*."

Indigo wrinkled her nose. "Why?"

Even I didn't know the reason. I fumbled for one Indigo might accept.

"Because she can curse us," I said. "You always said the women who gave birth to us had to possess some magic. If I make her mad before graduation, she might ruin things."

Indigo held my gaze over the rim of her teacup and then she nodded.

"Fine," she said. "At least it will all be done soon. Then we'll be transformed, and we won't even remember their names."

THE NEXT MORNING, I RETURNED TO MY MOTHER'S HOUSE. Without Jupiter, the place seemed a little wider, the gray carpet cleaner, the light brighter. It was almost . . . friendly. My mother sat at the dented square dining table, feet propped up on the gingham seat cover of a chair. This time, I spoke first:

"You used to say we were cursed."

My mother blinked at me. "I know."

"How?" I asked. "Why?"

My mother looked at me with a steely tenderness I'd forgotten she could summon. Once, that look had meant she'd hold off the night for me if I asked. That old ache to throw myself into her arms wrenched through me, and the force of it made me sway. I hadn't felt that impulse in so long I'd forgotten how to guard myself from feeling it anymore.

Silently, my mother stood and walked the short distance to the kitchen. She reached into a cabinet by the stove, shoving things aside, standing on her tiptoes, until she had pried something loose. It was an envelope, which she set down on the table and slid toward me. Neither of us sat.

"The curse is that we get trapped easily," she said, still not looking at me. "Our illusions weave roses around us, and when we try to escape, we are met with thorns. I see that now. I see that as someone who, even if I can't open the lock, at least knows it's there." She nodded at the envelope. "I've been saving this for you for years. I know I haven't done many things well, but I never forgot the curse. I don't want you to be trapped. Like me."

My mother's fingers trembled on the table.

"I don't want you to get trapped by things you thought were

there and weren't . . . or by someone who says they're the only one who can love you."

I opened the envelope. Inside was an index card with the name and address of a bank, a routing and account number. Another folded slip of paper showed the balance in the account, which was under my name. It would not be a lot of money to Indigo, but it was a fortune to me.

"When I turned eighteen, I moved in with my boyfriend and never spoke to my parents again," she said with a faint laugh. She sank into the chair. Her sweater slipped off her shoulder. She looked so bony, like she'd been worn down to a gristle of a woman.

"Soon, you'll be eighteen and you won't have to live under my roof. You're barely here anyway." Her mouth twisted, and I braced myself for a kick that never came. "But whatever you do, I want it to be on your own terms. You could use the money for college if you wanted. Or travel? What will you do after graduation?"

I will grow wings and become a queen, I thought. But I said nothing. Part of me believed I kept quiet because it was a sacred destiny that only Indigo and I knew about, another part knew I stayed silent out of doubt and shame. Shame that when I tried to say those words, they no longer sat easily on my tongue. What had once tasted true had gone slanted.

Or maybe I didn't want that to be the truth anymore.

I clutched my mother's envelope to my chest. Her gaze was a painful invitation. I couldn't bring myself to answer it directly, so I reached for the chair beside her, and for the first time in ages, I sat down.

A WEEK LATER, I FOUND TATI ALONE IN HER BEDROOM. LUCIDITY

came to her in short spells those days. She stiffened when she heard me enter. She sniffed the air, and goose bumps trailed along my skin. Tati always said that she could tell who we were on scent alone because Indigo smelled of apples, and I of honeysuckle.

"Does Indigo know you're here?"

"I told her I wanted to read."

Tati smiled. "But you did not say that you wanted to read to *me.*"

Tati was working her own enchantments on me, that quiet coaxing, nearly undetectable, like hair slipping loose from a braid. Tati was right. I hadn't told Indigo that I was going to read to her. She didn't like it when I was alone with Tati.

"Come," said Tati, rasping.

She gestured me closer, and I obeyed. I could smell the food dropped onto her dressing gown, unnoticed by the nurse and now pungent. Tati parted her lips. Her breath was medicinal sweetness laid over the rot.

Tati reached out, her hand patting up my arm. I bent down, thinking she wished to whisper in my ear. She stroked my cheek once, and then grabbed me around the neck, pulling me close.

"My eyes may be useless, but we both know that I am not the one who is blind," said Tati in a fierce whisper. "Open your eyes."

Chapter Twenty-Six

THE BRIDEGROOM

Once, I gave Indigo my heart.

It was our first Valentine's Day together. I knew she abhorred the holiday, and I had nothing to offer that she couldn't already buy herself ten times over. But on that morning, I slid into bed beside her with a plush rabbit toy in my hand.

"I have something for you," I said. "A present. A gift inspired by Koschei himself."

Indigo's eyes flew open. She saw the toy rabbit and the corner of her mouth lifted. "And who is Koschei? The rabbit?"

I pulled her to me. She was sleep-mussed, her bronze skin like newly pressed satin. "No. He was a sorcerer who could not be killed. He separated himself from his very soul which he hid in a duck, in a sheep, in a tree."

Indigo didn't look at me. She traced circles on my chest. "Nested souls and nested secrets."

"Precisely."

She reached for the rabbit. "Is your soul my present?"

"Alas, only my mortal heart. But I've hidden it in a rose, in an egg, in a box, in a rabbit," I announced.

Indigo found the seam in the toy rabbit and prized it open. I cried out and clutched my chest, and she laughed. Inside was a box, and inside that an eggshell, and inside that a packet of Indigo Rose tomato seeds.

Not long before she had told me she sometimes dreamt of a garden where things grew bright and nourishing. I thought she would be delighted. Instead, her fingers shook. Before I could ask whether she liked the gift or not, she drew me to her, and the packet of seeds fell to the floor.

She never planted them, and now I knew she had lied that day. Indigo had always known how Koschei had separated his soul from his body and drawn out his death as if it were a pin holding cloth in place. She knew because she had done the same thing.

Inside the Room of Secrets, I smoothed down my tie, glanced at the gold-and-crystal clock that stood beside a dead, snarling black bear. The clock read fifteen minutes before dinner. I waited for Indigo. This would be the last time I waited for her.

The staff had left once dinner was prepared, and the House was empty. Normally, the cook informed me, they would have stayed to clear up after the meal, but considering it was a final feast in honor of the nearly deceased, Indigo had told her the dishes could wait for morning. I pictured Hippolyta in her great bed. I wondered if she could still see the blinking lights of the machines surrounding her. I hoped she mistook them for stars.

While I waited for my wife, I surveyed the Room of Secrets. It appeared restrained. The shadows neatly pinned beneath the preserved faces of roe bucks and oryxes, hares and bison. Opposite the shadows, candlelight lacquered the femurs, fangs, and bleached mandibles.

On the table lay a final feast—a haunch of roasted venison stewed in its juices, flanked with plums and sour cherries.

Blue-veined and moon-white rinds of cheese stood in towers beside bowls of fruit. Several glass decanters of garnet-red and honey-pale wines sweated beads of quartz.

Soon, Indigo and I would play our final game.

What happens next? I wanted to ask the House, but it was silent, so silent that it hid Indigo's footsteps on the carpet until she was almost directly in front of me.

"Is it wrong that death gives me such an appetite?" she asked.

"No," I said. "I'm starving."

This was the truth. I was starving to be at an end of something.

"How are you?" I asked, and immediately regretted the empty platitude.

Indigo raised an eyebrow and spared me an imperious glance. She wore a black, feathered gown with a high, funereal neck. It looked less like a dress and more like a pair of great wings folded against her body. Her hair was shiny, pulled away from her face. If she was crying as her aunt died, there was no evidence on her smoothly arranged features.

"I am tired," she said.

We beheld each other. I didn't know Indigo, and yet I loved her in spite of this. Or perhaps because of it. In the unknown of our marriage, I became known to myself and that was an incarnation of love too.

For the first half hour, we ate in near silence. She hardly looked up from her plate. Indigo was not focused on her meal so much as she was avoiding being the focus of something else.

Behind her, a stag's face swiveled in our direction. The shadows of its antlers were vast and oddly mobile, as if poured onto the walls in thick, black syrup. The room had come alive. It was time.

I wiped my hands and leaned forward. "I figured that tonight you would be in need of a distraction. I thought we could play a game."

"A game?" asked Indigo, looking up from her plate. Her voice was careful, strained by her eagerness. I was reminded, anew, of how Indigo moved through the world with the infinite precision of one who knows that she can break it with a well-placed heel. "What kind of game?"

"Your favorite kind," I said. "One with a story and a bit of a sacrifice, where the key to winning is nothing but restraint."

Indigo's face stayed blank. "What are the rules?"

"I will tell you a fairy tale, and you must listen. No sound can escape your lips. No emotion can ghost across your face."

Something playful touched the corner of her mouth. We have played games like this our whole marriage. Games of touch where a sigh was punished with a kiss, and even the loser delighted in defeat. Indigo was always better at those games. I was always hungry to touch her, too eager to lose.

"And if I do?" she asked.

"If you do, then you must tell me where you keep your secrets."

She could walk away. She could refuse me. But instead, she sat still and held my gaze. She twisted her wedding ring, a plain band of iron.

"You lied," she said mildly. "You told me you could live without knowing. You made a vow."

"It was not a lie," I said. "And it was a vow I intended to keep to a woman, not a bride made of flowers, no matter how lovely I find her."

No matter how much I have come to love you.

I could tell the barb landed by the sudden tightness around Indigo's mouth. She didn't flinch though. She nodded with an air of reluctant approval. We had made a world for ourselves, and even as I set out to destroy it, I would honor its rules.

"Then let's play your game, husband," she said, reaching for her wineglass. "Begin your tale."

Indigo steeled herself. The feathers at her neck fluttered even though there was no wind. She had warned me that knowing her secrets would destroy us, and so I fashioned my words into a knife and began:

"Once upon a time, a king promised his dying wife that he would not marry unless it was to a woman who equaled her in beauty. As time passed, the only one who fit that description was his own daughter."

The Room of Secrets still loved Indigo. It threw protective shadows on her face, revealing only the shuddering of her feathers. It was like the first time I beheld her in that Paris apartment, when she looked like a woman assembled from squares of light. Indigo drank from her glass of wine. I continued.

"Desperate to hold off her father's advances, the princess requested three dresses. One as golden as the sun, another as silver as the moon, and the third as shimmering as the stars. And last, of course, a mantle made from every feather and pelt of all the birds and animals in the kingdom," I said. "The night before her wedding, she donned her mantle of every fur, covered her hair and face in soot for she longed to be invisible, and ran away until she found shelter in the palace of another king. The young king pitied her miserable appearance and agreed to give her work. And since she had no name, she was called Allerleirauh."

The wineglass trembled in Indigo's grip. We had been dancing around what we both knew, careful not to step too close to the edges, but with my next words, I would reveal my hand:

"Or, depending on the tale, her name was Catskins."

Chapter Twenty-Seven

AZURE

I wanted to believe Tati had cursed me.

With little over a month left until we transformed into our new selves, that dark space within me had grown. Every now and then, I looked over its edge and beheld all the things I'd dropped into it—the envelope and bank account information from my mother, the college brochure I hid under the lumpy mattress in Jupiter's house, the way I had come to hate the taste of tea.

I knew what Indigo would say. This was the behavior of a Cast-Out Susan, and it must be stopped. I didn't want to stand on the other side of a door full of light knowing it was locked to me forever. I was almost scared to enter the Otherworld with her—terrified that it would set me aflame if I stepped over the threshold—and so I was relieved when Indigo announced that we must not enter anymore.

We had just returned from school. The House was quiet, which meant Tati was asleep, pulled under by the strong sedatives she kept at her bedside. Now that Indigo ran the House, it seemed emptier. She had retained only half the staff, and there were no more fresh flowers in vases. The creamy tapered candles that Tati so loved were no longer lit for dinner, and inside the crystal bowls of the parlors, no one had replaced the brightly wrapped truffles.

"Otherworld?" I asked, looking down the hall when Indigo caught my hand.

"Not today."

That day, Indigo had outfitted us in magic—black turtleneck dresses with long, silver-sequined shawls that caught the light when we moved. She'd rubbed glitter onto our eyelids and the crescent of our cheekbones. At school, it had looked foolish. We glinted under the fluorescent lights and my hair caught in the sequins. But in the House of Dreams, she looked like a seer and I could feel the air shift around us when she spoke, as if accounting for the weight of prophecy:

"We should give it time to prepare itself for us," she said.

A COUPLE HOURS LATER, I GATHERED MY THINGS INTO MY BACK-pack to spend the night at my mother's house. Indigo leaned against the wall. Her expression was lost in the shadows cast by the parlor's fireplace.

"You seem excited to go back there, Catskins," she said.

"I'm not," I said, bristling at the nickname.

"It's cold out," said Indigo, rising from the settee and making her way to the coatrack. She pulled out one of Tati's silvery mink coats. "Here, take it."

"I'll be fine," I said.

"You know, if you wore that coat then you'd really be like Catskins," she said.

That nickname was a well-placed blade, yet when I looked at Indigo, I saw no malice.

"You know I don't want to be anything like Catskins."

She blinked at me, too sleepy-eyed to glare properly. "I don't know why. It proves that you're something out of a fairy tale. Which, I guess, makes Jupiter something out of a fairy tale too."

Even though I hadn't seen him in weeks, his name conjured an oily memory. The last time I saw him I had dropped a fork while cleaning up after a mandatory dinner in my mother's presence. When I reached to grab it, I felt him pressed against my back.

"Sorry, princess," he'd said, each word clinging wetly to the back of my neck. "Bumped right into you." His hands snaked to my hips. His voice creeped to a place where I did not want it felt. "You're such a clumsy little thing."

I'd confessed all these things to Indigo not long after we dropped our teeth into the ground. We were in her bed and my pain lay between us and I was shaking from the effort it took to pull it out of me. I wanted Indigo to hold this with me, but she didn't understand.

"So what if he wants to fuck you?" she asked, laughing. "Kings and gods have unnatural lust for their daughters all the time. Maybe he's cursed. Or maybe a love arrow went astray. Or maybe your mom is secretly dying, and she told him he could only be with someone who rivaled her in beauty and that's you."

I'd started crying after that, and Indigo, confused, had pulled me to her and wiped the tears into my hair until we fell asleep. Maybe she thought I was crying over Jupiter. I wasn't. I was crying because magic was not fair. She and I could share the same soul, but not the same pain.

I wished that I could grab her hand and plunge it into the dark spaces between my bones. What lived there would bite at her fingers and maybe then she'd know the weight of my mother's hands in my hair for the last time or the peppercorn cologne

Jupiter sprayed onto his chest.

But nothing could bite Indigo.

Indigo shrugged and hung Tati's fur coat back on the rack.

"I just don't get it," she said, pursing her mouth. "If you hate him so much, then why go home? He's going to be there. Waiting for you."

But that's where she was wrong.

"You know why," I said, not looking at her directly. "I made a promise to my mom, and I don't want to break it . . . not when we're so close."

Indigo sighed, nodding. "Be here tomorrow at sunset."

"I will," I said.

My lies wriggled on my tongue, flirting with the tops of my teeth. I blew her a kiss, shut the door behind me, and clamped my lips together. I told myself that my lies were a penance, a way of keeping this darkness to myself until I understood what to do with it. That I had come to enjoy the time with my mother was another thing I dropped into that yawning space within me.

The whole time I walked home, I imagined entering the Otherworld. I pictured the turret iced over, thick snow on the ground, the apple branches snapped off from the cold, and Indigo howling that I alone had killed it.

Tomorrow would be a reckoning, and I was not ready.

BY THE TIME I REACHED MY MOTHER'S HOUSE, THE SKY WAS BE-ginning to darken. I found my mother sitting at the dining table. Over the past month and a half, she had changed. Her hair was washed, curled neatly around her shoulders. There was color in her clothes and cheeks, and her eyes held a new brightness. She welcomed me with a smile before quickly putting it away. This warmth between us was new and it spooked easily.

"I wasn't sure you were coming here today," she said, careful not to say the word "home" because we both knew this had not been one for me.

I shrugged, waiting.

Slowly, she slid something across the table. Her car keys. She looked up at me through her lashes. "You ready to go?"

"Yeah," I said, and when I smiled, I let it linger on my face.

HERE WAS SOMETHING INDIGO DIDN'T KNOW ABOUT ME, SOME-thing I didn't even know about myself until my mother asked if I wanted to learn:

I liked driving.

I liked putting distance between myself and the world. I liked the way the asphalt rumbled beneath me, the stubborn yield of the gear shifts, the way I could sip the perfume of honeysuckles through a rolled-down window. When the stars blurred overhead or the sunshine lanced through the windshield, I turned winged and sleek, a creature climbing through the sky beholden to no place on earth.

"You're a fast learner," my mother had said after my first les-son. She let out a breath that might have been a laugh held tight in her chest. "Next time I'm going to have to bring a helmet, won't I?"

We spoke around what we wanted, and in this, I'd heard an-other question—*Can we do this again?*

So we did.

Our island wasn't big, but the roads were long and empty, yawning past bridges that had fallen into creeks, snaking be-tween spruces and firs tall as giants and outlining hidden coves that clung to secret beaches I'd never seen before.

Driving made everything seem large and within reach, and when I sank into my mother's rusty sedan and heard the engine roar and felt the afternoon warm the back of my arms, I imagined I was the one pulling the sun across the horizon. Because with every drive, the world I did not know was illuminated.

My mother climbed into the seat beside me and for the rest of the evening I guided us down the winding roads. My mother didn't say much during these drives, but the air rushing through the windows reassembled the space between us, rubbing out the edges so it didn't hurt to sit so close.

When I sat in the car that day, I pulled the night alongside me. And in that shadow, my mother spoke:

"Not long left until graduation," she said, then added, "and your birthday." I could hear her mouth crinkle in a shy smile.

I heard her question between the things she said aloud: *Have you thought about what you will do? Whether you'll take the money I've saved for you and go elsewhere?*

"I know," I said.

And I knew she heard my answer: *I don't know yet.*

"There's still time," she said quietly.

When we got back to the house, I tried giving her the keys, but she folded them in my hand.

"I've got a friend picking me up for the Saturday shift tomorrow," she said. "Why don't you take the car for the afternoon?"

"Am I allowed to do that?" I asked, my eyes wide even as I felt a pang. My mother had a friend, a friend she laughed with, shared food with—when did that happen?

She shrugged. "I won't tell if you won't."

EARLY THE NEXT MORNING, I SAT ALONE IN THE CAR. THE DAY was a road, and it belonged to me. Indigo wouldn't be expecting me until sunset so we could say our goodbye to the Otherworld before we said hello to our new lives.

I was reckless that day. I went to the gas station and bought candy, which Indigo expressly forbade. If we ate sweets, we had honeycomb dipped in chocolate and wrapped in gold leaf, or thick Mexican hot chocolate in blue porcelain cups. Indigo loved beautiful things, but nothing was more tempting to me than the bright packet of little red candies. They smelled like plastic and cinnamon, tasted of the exotic. I got goose bumps as I ate them in the parking lot, fingers splayed against my mouth to keep from losing a single one.

Afterward, I went back inside and bought a bottle of pop and more of the candies. I drove to the movies and snuck into the theater. I walked through a store and tried on sunglasses, imagined a place where I might need them. I recognized people from school and flashed them smiles, which they awkwardly returned. I ate a hot cinnamon bun, drank a smoothie, bought vending-machine chips, and played in an arcade with the quarters I had left before slouching back into the car, glutted on all that I'd consumed. I was vast, a horizon folded into a human, and lost in that vastness, I nearly forgot the hour.

I didn't have time to shower or change before I went to the House of Dreams. My treachery was a scent, the buttered popcorn clinging to my hair, the smell of cinnamon on my breath. Indigo was waiting for me outside the gates, wrapped in the sable fur coat she'd offered me the day before.

"You're almost late," she said, tugging on her starling necklace.

"Sorry," I mumbled.

Indigo sniffed the air. In the half-light, I couldn't see the whites of her eyes. She licked her lips and held out her hand.

"Time for us to say goodbye," she said.

Hand in hand, we walked to the Otherworld. With every step, the food in my stomach congealed. I thought I'd be thrown out for good, met with a wall of air, but with every step my starling necklace fluttered against my bare skin—warm, breathing. Before long, it was my hand on the gate, our keys turning in the locks, the gates swinging open, and the smell of apple blossoms embracing us.

"It's perfect," Indigo sighed.

It was perfect. And here I was, untouched. The Otherworld had beheld me in all my grime and sin, and still loved me.

"Oh," I said, my soul sagging in relief.

"I know," said Indigo, wrapping her arms around me. "But we'll be back soon."

I didn't answer. I was lost in the embrace of something greater. The moment I crossed the threshold, the Otherworld reached for me. The oak groaned and the willow stretched its limbs, the lilies nodded in acknowledgment, and the blossoms sang on the apple trees. I had been prepared to be orphaned by this world. Instead, it welcomed me, and in that second I understood the movement of holy things.

Hallowed ground was not always a fixed, physical place. Some sacred spaces were indivisible, the taking of them an endless communion that ate of your flesh, drank of your blood, and its grisly alchemy fused itself to the very skin of your soul so that no matter where you were, you would never be without it.

Indigo and I were the Otherworld, and the Otherworld was us, and for as long as we lived, it would live too.

I had known the Otherworld would lay me bare, and it did.

It plucked out every piece I'd hidden in that dark space, fanned them out like so many cards—the smell of asphalt, the edge of a college brochure, the roads spread out like veins carrying the pulse of vastness—and it asked me this:

If the Otherworld would always be there, then why must we disappear into it so soon?

THE QUESTION BURROWED NEW SPACE INSIDE ME, AND INDIGO could smell it on my skin. In the weeks that followed, she turned dreamy. She looped wire around my shoulders, hung gossamer gowns from them as if we were sampling wings. In the mornings, she'd gather dew and hand it to me in little quartz glasses so I might be purified. She'd muse about all the things we would do with our power.

"When we're in the Otherworld, maybe we can restore Tati's sight," she'd say. "Poor, silly Tottlepop."

Two weeks before my birthday, I woke to a pressure on my chest.

"Wake up, Catskins," whispered Indigo. "Look what happened."

I rose up on my elbows, wincing at the pinch in my scalp. I lifted one hand, ran my palm down the dozens of braids that had been looped and knotted around the bars of Indigo's headboard.

"Elf knots," said Indigo, giggling. "They must have done it in the night. I told you to keep a bowl of cream and blood outside! But you must have forgotten. They're so good about climbing around unnoticed. They must have knelt on your pillow, braiding every strand with their little brown fingers as punishment. Did you feel anything?"

"No," I said.

But that was a lie.

I had felt Indigo braiding each strand, looping it around the metal bars of her headboard. I felt her gently brush the hair from my face, the weight of the bed shift as she rose to her knees and lowered herself slowly onto my body. I felt the scratch of her bare legs, prickled from her last shave even though she still hid her razor.

"I wouldn't worry too much," said Indigo lightly. "In a few weeks we'll be one of them."

I closed my eyes, imagining what that would look like. I saw our days melting together from the sunlit hours beneath the apple blossoms. Indigo braiding violets into my hair. The Otherworld slowly sipping away our mortal flaws until our bones were rendered to glass and our black hair resolved into shadows, our teeth grown animal-sharp, and our human lives turned to woodsmoke—a flimsy echo of a fire that had already died.

INDIGO WATCHED ME FROM HER BED AS I DRESSED FOR MY mother's house.

"Ugh," she said, flopping back into the pillows. "You must hate it."

I dragged a brush down my long black hair. It hung to my waist now, and I'd begun to hate how it was always in my face, how I kept rolling over it in the night.

"Yeah," I said, staring at my hair. "I hate it."

The House of Dreams grew agitated when I left. The staircase lengthened; the halls darkened. It knew I was eager to leave.

"Shhh," I soothed, rubbing its walls. They prickled beneath my palm.

I held my breath as I walked to the front door only to hear a sound behind me.

"You've got your eyes open now, don't you, child," said a voice.

I whirled around, but there was no one there. I looked up. Tati was leaning over the stair railing. I wasn't used to seeing her awake this early. Her sedatives were powerful and often kept her in bed for days at a time.

Tati's blind eyes were fixed in a direction where I wasn't. Mrs. Revand had bound her hair in a polka-dotted silk scarf, and her nightgown was buttoned wrong, revealing the coarse, wrinkled brown of her chest and part of her breast. I didn't answer as I reached for the front door and ran out into the early spring sunshine.

Tati was right. My eyes were open, and with every day, I grew more frustrated. My powers of invisibility had faltered. More and more, I stood in stark relief against the world. Even my shadow had thickened. I wanted to say that it was Tati's fault. She'd told me to open my eyes, and maybe the more I beheld the world outside the House of Dreams, the more the world beheld me.

. . . and I liked it.

I thought maybe I could wait for the right answer to come, but my hand was forced.

That day, I went to my mother's house. She was not sitting at the dining table with the car keys in her hand and a plate of snacks for us. Instead, she stood in the doorway, her shoulders narrowed, tugging at her hair. Her clothes hung off her.

"He's coming back," she said without looking up at me.

I was glad she didn't say his name. The air between us was frail as glass, and we had taken such pains not to let it break. I couldn't speak around it anymore:

"What do you want?"

My mother looked at me, bewildered. When was the last time

someone had asked her this? She blinked a couple times, then swallowed hard.

"I want to sell the house. I want to"—my mother gathered herself—"I want to leave *him*. I can do it now. I know it. If you don't want to see me again, I'll understand . . . but if you want me, Azure . . ." She held my gaze: "If you want me, I can stay. We can . . . we can try again."

My mother's words filled me with light. I knew my answer. I smiled, and she smiled back, and I was Helios in his chariot, pulling the sun behind me so today could become a tomorrow.

But I'd forgotten about the other story. The one of Phaethon, the son of the sun, who yoked his father's fiery steeds and crashed into constellations, scorching the Earth until he was thrown from his blazing path by Zeus hurling a lightning bolt at his head.

Perhaps Phaethon didn't know that bolt of brightness would be his death.

Perhaps he couldn't tell all that splendid illumination apart.

Chapter Twenty-Eight

THE BRIDEGROOM

My story was nearly over.

The words of closure rose through me like a hymn. The light shifted. The food had cooled, and Indigo's face was monstrous in its stillness.

"Eventually the king discovered that the beautiful woman he had seen at the ball was none other than the serving girl who wore a coat of many furs," I said. "When she tried to escape, he tugged off her coat, revealing the shimmering dress of starlight that she had worn only the night before. Overjoyed, the king and Catskins married the same day and she lived happily ever—"

Across from me, Indigo swayed. Her eyes slitted. Until that moment, her composure was like glass heated slowly, betraying nothing more than a wrinkled translucence. She had always been good at this game. She had always known how to hide her feelings. But those final words hit her like a gust of ice.

She swiped her plate and wineglass off the dining table and onto the floor.

Happily ever after.

The words shattered with the porcelain plates.

Who can say for certain what happened in those private

nights after a fairy tale? Whether the princess turned from her new husband in bed and longed for her coat of camouflage? Whether the king, having satisfied his pursuit, now allowed his eyes to wander to a girl in the village?

Of all the things fairy tales demanded I should believe—dogs with eyes as big as saucers, maidens felled by spindles, queens who do not remove red-hot iron shoes and dance in them until they die—this is the only thing that stretches credulity. That happiness demands so little to stay. That it will curl willingly between two bodies every night, wrap 'round their children's brows and take root in a kingdom's earth whose peasants would thresh joy in the autumn and pickle smiles in winter and, come spring, watch it all bloom anew.

"You have the tale all wrong," said Indigo, rising.

I leaned back. "And you have lost the game."

She was breathing hard. She flashed her teeth at me. Her feathered gown billowed around her. "Quite right, my love. And what was the wager? That I should tell you where I keep my secrets? What good is that going to do when I'm done with you?"

I reached for my wine and sipped. "Humor me."

Indigo skulked, feathered and beastlike. She was a creature of the Otherworld through and through, and though I knew she meant to hurt me, she would honor her word first. Even monsters were bound by the rules of their world.

"Well, let's see," said Indigo, tapping her lip. Her eyes darted around the room. Her face settled into a jagged, determined grin. "I hid my secrets inside an egg, inside a box, inside a beast the opposite of foresight."

Now, her hand went to some secret fold in her feathered pocket. Behind her, the baboon skull grinned. The bleached crocodile skull unhinged its jaw.

"I told you not to pry," she said, stepping toward me.

Still, I did not move.

"I *begged* you not to," she said, and for a moment, the wounded tinge to her voice was a noose that looped around my heart. "But now you—"

Indigo swayed, grabbing the edge of the table. She missed. A candelabra crashed to the floor, the candles spitting wax and droplets of fire. Indigo heaved. Her body hunched over, and the black feathers of her gown lifted and fell before she raised her gaze to mine.

"The wine," she said, her voice thready. "You put something in the wine."

"No, my love, I put something in *your* wine."

Indigo listed to one side, and I shot out of my chair, catching her before she fell. Her head tipped back, throat bared. Sweat sheened across her brow as a metal object clattered to the floor.

I looked over Indigo's shoulder and saw the reason I had crushed three of Hippolyta's pills into her wine. A curved hunting knife had slipped out of her pocket. It looked crude, like a misshapen letter. On the walls behind us, the animals and their bones shuddered.

Indigo clutched me. Her mouth looked greasy with animal fat, her eyes were full of tears, and I felt my heart break. Her voice was small, like that of a cornered child.

"Was our life so terrible that you had to destroy it?"

"I'm not trying to destroy anything," I said. "I'm merely trying to survive you."

Indigo clawed weakly at the front of my blazer before her eyes fluttered shut.

I lowered her gently to the ground, far away from the bits of glass where she might hurt herself when she woke up. I stood over her. My flower wife, my sly blue sky. I had not fully registered, until that moment, that I was destined to lose something that night. The House had gambled on whether it would be my life, my love, or my memory.

I faced the wall of animal heads. The oryx and wildcat leered. The alpine goats smirked with their square pupils. The chamois and musk oxen looked bored. And the roe deer peered through her lashes.

I hid my secrets inside an egg, inside a box, inside a beast the opposite of foresight.

The opposite of foresight was hindsight. I smiled as the riddle became clear. A hind sight. A hind was nothing more than a female red deer, and there was one in this room.

I grabbed the hunting knife and went to the deer mounted behind me. I sank the knife below her whiskered chin and tugged. Dust puffed into the air and dried rose petals fell to the ground. My blade hit something solid. A little golden box.

Inside, a ripped bus ticket. The name of the ticket holder had been torn off and dark-brown spots marred the paper. I pushed the paper aside to what lay underneath. There, on a square of red velvet, was a rusted starling key on a golden chain.

Chapter Twenty-Nine

AZURE

You can know a person in totality—as they are revealed in the angle of light hitting your eyes, in a poem of photons and particles, in the particular wavelengths adjusted to your height, the contours of your nostrils, the private landscape of your synapses. Your mind makes a map of them and even barefoot and blindfolded, this terrain becomes a truth.

And it is a truth.

But only at an angle.

A WEEK BEFORE MY BIRTHDAY, I DECIDED TO TELL INDIGO MY decision. I wasn't ready to join the Otherworld just yet, and I wasn't going to be a Cast-Out Susan either. The Otherworld had told me as much, and its beauty was a promise: it would never abandon me.

I'd been trying to tell Indigo ever since I accepted my mother's offer, but each time I straightened my shoulders and practiced what I would say, my resolve deflated, punctured by the iron gates of the House of Dreams. Each time, I hesitated. One afternoon, Tati had a screaming fit and slapped Indigo across the face so hard she'd wept for half an hour. Another time, Indigo was in a dark mood, having thrown all her paints onto the lawn because something about our "gift" had gone wrong.

But today was different.

Today, I missed Indigo.

A couple days ago she rang me at my mother's house, explaining that some work being completed on the grounds would make it too noisy for the two of us. I'd been happy to stay back—relieved, also, that she hadn't asked to come to my mother's—and it was only now when I stood outside the House of Dreams that I realized how much I had missed my friend.

For the first time in what felt like eons, I missed our tea parties on the turret, the way she'd hang jewels in my hair and let me lie in her lap and read me stories where clever men caught seal wives and kingdoms grew on the other side of a grandfather clock.

I missed the easy wonder that came with living with Indigo. When I tried on her pigeon's-blood ruby earrings, I could see where they had come from, the outline of spired palaces crouched in mist and lavish green mountains. When I slept on a pillowcase of raw silk, I dreamt of colorful tents and horse musk, the dusty roads that bore its name.

In my mother's house, there was none of that. There were trips to the library, documents to be faxed, research over the cost of college programs, and the endless fine print of applications. On this side of the world, there were no pigeon's-blood rubies and raw silk pillows, no gilded books beside a chest of drawers bought from the palace of a guillotined viscount.

The difference was clear: in the Otherworld I would want for nothing, whereas in this world there was nothing I couldn't want.

Even so, the moment I stepped into the House of Dreams,

I felt like crying. My mother had begun to look at apartments for us on the mainland. They were dingy, cramped rooms with no chandeliers, no medieval tapestries hanging from polished wooden walls, no magic soaked into the floorboards.

I froze at the threshold, sagging against the door. The House pitied me.

Don't be sad, it said. *I will wait.*

The House wrapped up the Sunday-afternoon light in sleepy carelessness and hung diamonds and dust motes in the air. It pulled close the fragrance of gardenias and lilies and threaded a sweet, delicate humming sound from upstairs around my neck. I knew that humming sound. It was a sign that Tati was awake and lucid. Perhaps even happy.

Indigo stepped out of the parlor and laughed to see me clutching the doorframe. "Why are you standing like that? Come in!"

She was dressed in a long emerald satin robe with nothing but a T-shirt and boxers underneath. Her hair was tangled and crimped from braids she must have worn earlier. Her skin shone, and I felt overwhelmed by her beauty.

All this time, I had been thinking of what it would be like when I left, all the things I would do and places I would see. Part of me must have assumed Indigo would come, too, but the longer I looked at her, the more I realized this was all of her I could ever take with me—the curvature of her smile, an abundance of dust motes, this echo of honeysuckle.

So often we had dreamt the same thing that I'd imagined they slipped between our skulls, passed back and forth like breaths. But how far and fast could a dream run from one mind to the next? What if ours got lost over the sea between us?

"Azure?" asked Indigo, her eyebrows rising. "Are you all right?"

I threw my arms around Indigo. "I missed you."

She stiffened, then relaxed. Her fingers carded through my hair. She smelled so sweet, apples on the edge of ripeness.

"It's painful for me too," she said.

That day was like our earliest adventures. It began to rain shortly after, and the House offered up all its treasures for our amusement. We had tea by the fire, stacked our cups atop small towers of precious books with painted, cracking spines. Indigo had found another of her mother's jewelry boxes, so we sleeved our arms in pearls and ate cake with our fingers. We were so light that I almost didn't feel the starling key hanging from my neck. I imagined it had flown off and would return to my breast when I grew drowsy. It was only when the rain stopped and the sky outside turned the color of damsons that I remembered I had something to tell her.

I was leaning against one of the brocade couches and Indigo lay in my lap, braiding our hair together.

"This was a perfect day," I said.

"All the days will be perfect soon," said Indigo, tilting her chin up to grin at me. "We'll be forever whole, like a full moon."

I held that image in my mind. Even the moon existed in phases—crescents that waned and waxed and sometimes vanished entirely. If it was always full, then there would be nothing to dream about.

"Not yet," I said.

Indigo sat up, and I flinched from the tension in my scalp as our braided-together hair pulled too tight. "What do you mean?"

Now that the first words came, the rest quickly followed.

"I'm not . . . I'm not ready to be in the Otherworld. I'm not ready to transform," I said. "I want to be part of it, with you, of course, but not yet. The last time we saw the Otherworld I *felt* that it wasn't mad at me for wanting this. That it would transform me when I'm ready and I'm not, Indigo." The way she'd braided our hair forced my chin down, and so when I looked up at her I felt mulish and bowed. "I feel . . . unfinished."

"Unfinished," she repeated. She paused for a few seconds. "So then, what will you do?"

"Well, me and my mom—" I started to say before Indigo laughed sharply.

"I'm sorry, you think spending time with the woman who didn't even want you in the same room as her will make you feel 'finished'?" asked Indigo. "What has she *ever* done for you?"

In the shadow of that sentence, I glimpsed the real words: *Look at what I have done for you.* And there was nothing I could say but the truth.

"She's different now," I said. "Or at least, she wants to be."

I couldn't keep the hope from my voice, and Indigo smelled it on me like a shark sensing blood. Her eyes narrowed. I pulled back, and our braid loosened.

"What does that mean?"

"She's changed," I said. "She wants us to move together to the mainland, where she'll get a new job and I can work and apply to schools next year. She even wants to get rid of Jupiter." I almost laughed, picturing him oozing through the doorway only to be cast out. "I won't be Catskins anymore."

I thought Indigo would smile. I thought she'd at least understand that much. She frowned. "That's not how the story is supposed to go."

I unwound my hair from hers, and only then could I meet her at eye level. "Maybe mine is different."

Indigo stared at me. Her eyes flicked over my mouth, my nose, my scalp. As if she were studying a counterfeit.

"And that's what you want?" she asked. "Something . . . different. Just like a Cast-Out—"

"Stop," I said. It was the first time I'd ever used a steely tone on her, and Indigo flinched. "That's not what I am, and that's not what I'll be. I know that."

I thought of Susan Pevensie, grown old, her lipstick smearing outside the lines of her mouth. Who was to say she didn't stretch her neck from side to side, hang up her nylon stockings in her closet, press her palm to the back of her wardrobe, and say: "Now I'll go"? Who was to say she didn't know exactly where the lantern in the snow waited for her? What if every time she opened a closet, she saw a path lit by fireflies and merely chose to reach for her scarf instead of that secret doorknob?

"Everything will change," whispered Indigo.

"That doesn't have to be a bad thing," I said, and reached for her hand. "I love you."

I wished I could show her my daydreams and spread them out on a table like so many cards. *Here, there's me wandering through a marketplace where people speak in a language that smells of rosewater and spices. Look, there's us, picking apple blossoms while we talk about our adventures. And again, we are holding hands. Now our teacups tremble and Time nips at our heels. Turn the card—*

Us.

We are two blues, the neat seam of dusk and dawn.

We share a sky, if not a soul, and yet we are cut of the same shades.

INDIGO NEVER WEPT OR YELLED. IF ANYTHING, SHE SEEMED RE-signed. For the next week, I still spent some nights at the House of Dreams. Indigo remained distant though. More and more, her arms were covered in paint splotches. At night, she clutched her starling key so tightly that I could feel my own necklace cinching around my throat like a noose. Sometimes when I woke up, I couldn't breathe. And when I'd turn over in bed, she would be staring at me, and I'd wonder how long she'd watched me trying to pull the air into my lungs.

A FEW NIGHTS BEFORE GRADUATION, THE DOORBELL RANG.

I was packing to spend the night at Indigo's. I knew she was mad at me, but we continued as we'd always done. In the past, I would have been worried, but these days I was blinded by happiness.

That night, my mother was working through the evening. She wouldn't be home until the next morning, when Jupiter's plane landed, and she told me she would end things with him that same hour. I didn't want to be in the house when he was there. I wanted to return when I knew he would never step foot in it again.

When the doorbell rang, I thought it was a delivery, until Indigo stepped across the threshold. In all these years, she'd never once come over. A few times when we were little, I had begged her to stay with me so I wouldn't have to be alone in Jupiter's house, but she'd refused. *I just can't*, she'd insisted, shaking her shining head. After a while, I'd stopped asking. I'd even forgotten all about it until she stood before me. I'd never wanted to be there, so why should she? But then I saw her expression, and anger—immaculate and sharp as lightning—hit me.

When she stepped inside, the cheap lightbulbs showed the crimp of her mouth and the slight crinkle of her brow. It revealed her *disappointment*.

Indigo liked imagining that I lived in a stone cottage with sloped walls, with a lonely fireplace and a mat of cinders where I made my bed. She had wanted Jupiter to be an ogre, for my mother to be slim and transparent with her frailties. She had wanted a story, and the truth would have spoiled it.

"What are you doing here?" I asked, my voice harsher than I intended.

Indigo looked at me, confused. She smoothed down her chiffon gown and her silvery mink coat, tucked her hair shyly behind her ear. Maybe in the House, she would have looked lovely and intriguing. But here, she looked ridiculous.

Whatever fury I had felt quickly curdled. I saw the disappointment in her eyes, but there was longing there too. For me.

"I, um, I thought we could walk home together and celebrate all the new things ahead."

She held up a bottle of Champagne and two flutes. The Champagne had already been opened, and even from where I was I could smell it: like nectarines and rain-washed stone.

"But we don't drink?" I said.

"This is a special occasion, silly," said Indigo, grinning. "We're crossing a threshold. Soon, you'll be the age of a Cast-Out Susan." This last sentence, a barb. She winked. "I'm joking. We're trying something new, right? I think that's worthy of a toast."

Indigo poured some of the Champagne into her flute, then mine. The last time Indigo and I had gotten drunk, I remembered her standing on the turret, her shoulders shaking as she screamed at a silhouette draped in smoke and moonlight. I looked at her, she grinned, and the movement eased my hesitation.

When I blinked, I saw those daydream cards spread out before me—our hands interlinked, our lives taking root and yet always tethered. I saw my mother and me picking out new carpet.

I saw the willow branches quiver, heard the Otherworld sigh. I touched my glass to hers and threw it back.

I remembered looking at Indigo through the prism of the Champagne flute. She was not drinking. She wavered; her face warped through the glass like a scream birthed into human shape. A white sediment filmed the bubbles and Indigo whispered:

"I told you I'd always keep you safe."

I did not remember what happened after that.

Chapter Thirty

THE BRIDEGROOM

I was coming to the end of something. It hemmed me in the way a sunset traced a brutal red line around the day, drawing it to a close. I found my way to the Otherworld in the dark with a flashlight in hand. In my other, the rusted starling key hummed and fluttered.

I walked down the stone steps, past the linden trees, through a long path overgrown with ivy and rhododendrons until I came to a small stream that fed into the waters nearby. On the opposite bank rose a high stone wall. I shined my flashlight on the stones, and the light caught on an ornate gate. At the center was a lock that looked like a birdcage.

The stream was narrow but surprisingly deep. When I climbed out the other side, my pants were sopping wet. I bit down on the flashlight as I slid the key into the locked gate. The light caught on the jewel in the starling's eye. Dirt and dust glommed the stone. I wanted to look closer, but right then the gate swung open, and I was pulled into another world entirely.

I had always imagined that the Otherworld longed to stay hidden, that it was only ingenuity or innocence that forced the doors open from one world to the next. If the doors opened easily, then whatever waited on the other side had not lured you there for delight but for devouring.

Indigo and Azure's Otherworld was none of these things. It was lonely, a place obsessed with its own emptiness. When I stepped past the gate, the land stirred miserably awake in the same way a neglected animal can be at once dulled to hope and driven by instinct to lift its head at the sound of approaching feet.

Perhaps this Otherworld had long ago been the devouring kind, like a witch's cottage hidden in a deep, dark wood. Once, it had been made of gingerbread walls and sugar pane windows with a panting, red-bellied oven at its core and a cleverly hidden cage for children just behind the curtains. But the witch had abandoned it, and the house had lost its appetite. Now it was simply looking for someone who might occasionally tend its hearth and sing within its walls.

There was a large oak tree with a tarp-covered table beside its trunk. At the center loomed a tall stone turret covered in ivy and wild roses. Off to its side wobbled a crumbling staircase whose steps vanished in midair. Behind that, a row of dead trees. I could smell the ghosts of apple blossoms in the air. A lonely wind combed through the branches, and the Otherworld released a low sigh of disappointment.

I was not who it had expected.

Or wanted.

I cast my flashlight over the ground. Perhaps these grounds had once been well maintained, but they'd reverted to wilderness over time. As I walked, I sank up to my ankles in dead leaves.

Here and there, the beam of the flashlight picked out memories—a yellowed ribbon, a vial of glitter, rotting satin slippers. I moved closer to the turret.

A pair of staffs twined with plastic ivy lay on the ground,

their juncture marked through with an iron stake so that they'd kept their shape even after all these years. *X* marked the spot. Like treasure on a map.

A prickling crawled up my spine. I pointed my flashlight to the end of the staff and followed it in a straight line toward the black tarp covering the table. The wind rippled the fabric, and the light bounced off a corner of glass and metal. It was not a table at all but a kind of glass box.

I moved closer, my eyes slowly adjusting to the glare of my flashlight refracted through the glass. When I blinked, I thought I had glimpsed something gray and mottled. Its shape was vague, rounded, like an unfortunate rabbit had gotten trapped inside.

The wind lifted the corner of the tarp, pulling it back like a smile reveals teeth. My flashlight roamed over the inside of the box. Only, it was not a glass box. It was a casket.

And inside it lay a body.

Chapter Thirty-One

AZURE

When Indigo and I were young, we dreamt about transforming into other animals. We tried on pairs of wings, threw spotted pelts over our bodies, held our breath underwater for as long as we could. We stayed in the water until the pads of our fingers crinkled, as if they were on the verge of peeling back and revealing new, opaline extremities. We knew we could manage it, but in the end, we decided against it. We didn't know for certain whether our human thoughts would remain in animal form, and we didn't want to risk getting trapped.

It was a mercy, I thought, that maybe those maidens never truly knew what was happening when they were altered. That if they must be cursed or robbed or raped, then at least they didn't have to remember everything. Maybe that's why the swan maiden's midnight lament sounded so sweet. It didn't hold the memory of loss, but the knowledge of the memory's absence. Maybe that's why the selkies breached gray waters, always swimming close to the ruddy-cheeked fishermen before darting away and staring at them from the rocks. They didn't remember what it was like to be a clumsy, fragile-skinned girl lying still beneath a panting stranger. All that remained was the animal instinct:

Don't get caught.

When I opened my eyes, I was not in my room. I was not in my bed. I was not in my skin.

I pushed myself up on my elbows and a musty fur pelt slipped off my bare shoulders. It was the silvery mink Indigo had been wearing when she came over. The same one, I dimly remembered, that she once insisted on giving to me.

So you can really be like Catskins, she'd said.

Cool air grazed my skin.

I wasn't wearing clothes.

My heartbeat was animal quick. I wondered if this was how the enchanted maidens felt when they looked down to see a pile of feathers at their feet or seal skin pooling around their ankles. Did their mouths taste of fish roe from their last meal? Did their bodies feel like mine felt right then, as if it had been conquered by a land that had not bothered to learn its native language?

My senses were slow to return. The edges of my mind blurred, and it took me a full minute to realize I was lying in my mother and Jupiter's bed. The sheets were rumpled where yesterday they had been made. A smell of sweat and ammonia hung in the air, and my stomach heaved. Ten feet away, the door was ajar, and on the hallway floor, I could see three shadows.

"—didn't do anything," said a voice.

The voice was smoky and wheedling. It belonged to Jupiter. Next to it, a great heaving and sobbing, the efforts of someone trying to be turned inside out by the force of her cries. I knew that cry. It was my mother. Then, clear and silver, came a different voice:

"It's been going on for almost a year. I tried to get her to stop, but you know how stubborn she is," said Indigo. "I was worried last night when she didn't show up at my house . . . and that's when I found them."

"Honey, that's not true. Nothing happened—"

I touched my thigh, the instep of my foot, the veins of my wrist. My body was mute. I was in the dark.

Later, Indigo would assure me that nothing happened. She would fill in the missing details with clinical recitation: the sedatives in my Champagne took effect, my clothes were stripped, the bed was mussed, my limbs were arranged in the fur coat. Jupiter had come home in the early hours, and when I did not answer his calls, he stood by the bed and watched me.

"He only touched himself," said Indigo sweetly, as if this would make me feel safer now that I knew. "Not you. I would never let anything happen to you, Azure. I told you I'd keep you safe, and I have."

Indigo knew this for certain because she had stayed behind the door the whole time, a Polaroid camera in her hand. She knew my mother's jealousy and thought the pictures would prove to her that I was not worth the effort of changing her life. But the photos turned out to be unnecessary.

My mother had never needed evidence.

"Honey, *wait*—" said Jupiter.

I cried out for her to wait, too, but my mother had been right about us. We were cursed and we were trapped. She by the nightmare of love. And I by the reality of it.

My memories of that night were a black puddle, flexible in their horror for they had nothing to cling to—and this was the real curse of transforming. Not the body you were returned to, but the memories you were stripped of, the new caverns in your thoughts shaped by nights that had been thieved from your life.

A few days later, Indigo would offer to show the pictures to me, thinking that seeing them would cure my silence. I threw them into the fire without looking, hoped that burning them would give me back the memories I'd lost. But whoever or whatever watched me—dark-eyed gods or horned faeries, silent stars or simply the wind—didn't accept my sacrifice. When Indigo saw what I'd done, she chided me.

You should've looked.

THE LAST TIME I SAW MY MOTHER SHE WAS SITTING INSIDE JUPIter's scuffed, gray sedan applying lipstick. For the last hour, I had been standing, near-hidden, behind the scraggly pines that grew opposite the road. I'd watched him drag their suitcases, throw them into the broken trunk that needed rope to stay shut. I'd watched him turn off the lights, take in the mail and the newspaper, whistling the whole time. I'd watched him slide into the front seat before he patted his shirt pocket, mumbled something to my mother, and loped back into the house.

He had left his car keys on the front seat.

I could open the door and sit on the smoke-stained leather. I could fit my hands to the steering wheel, adjust the mirrors, toss out the furry pink dice Jupiter hung from the rearview mirror, and drive us off into the morning fog. I knew I could. After all, my mother had taught me. But that wasn't enough. I wanted her to *ask*.

I approached the window right as my mother blotted her lipstick. When she saw me, she shuddered and closed her eyes. Her shoulders shook as she dropped her face into her hands.

In the reflection of the glass, I looked watery, translucent, a phantom. And as I watched her sob, I understood that was what she wished me to be: a ghost.

In the distance, the handle of Jupiter's front door turned. I could have waited. I could have shaken the car and forced her to speak to me. But in the end, I turned back to the woods.

I chose not to haunt her.

THE HOUSE OF DREAMS WHIMPERED WHEN I WALKED. I DID NOT speak to anyone. I knew my role. I crawled into bed beside Indigo. I wore the clothes she laid out for me. I walked in her shadow. Curiously, it was Indigo who was the most understanding of my silence.

"You're in shock," she'd say, patting my back sympathetically. "That's understandable. You were yanked from one realm to the next, Azure. When you're ready to come back, tell me. And if you want anything—*anything*—I will make it real for you."

There were only a few weeks to go until our graduation, both from school and the mortal world altogether. A single month until my half soul was stirred into the apple-scented pollen of the Otherworld. Indigo refused to let us enter until we were ready, and I missed it.

When we were together, she tended to me with gentle fingers and soothing words. She combed my long black hair and braided it with golden thread. She fed me small cakes and spread herbs and cheeses on crackers and held them warily to my mouth as if I were a beast newly tamed.

Even though we couldn't go to the Otherworld, I visited it every night in my sleep. It was winter within its walls of stone and when the snow fell, it sounded like a poem spoken in glass. Snowflakes ornamented my hair like seed pearls. Past the threshold, the turret appeared frozen. Beside it, the oak tree creaked, and the Otherworld spoke in a language heard only in dreams—

We are sorry, child. We did not mean to love you so well.

This was a truth I hadn't understood until now.

You see, nothing good can come from being loved by old gods. Their love of mortals turns them neglectful and petty. When they move on, they lay waste in their path—cicada wings and bear paw prints, sacs of spider silk, echoes and anemone, the limbs of lovers now rendered to stars.

I WAS NOTHING BUT SHADOW. I EXISTED IN THE AFTERTHOUGHT of resplendence. I was a moving spot of cold. I was a home for ghosts.

I might have stayed that way forever had it not been for the envelope I received in the middle of class one day. It was like a sly gust of air from another land. Indigo had excused herself to go to the restroom when it was handed to me by a pale-skinned, pimpled hall monitor. I recognized it the moment I touched it, the worn edges, the blocky, blue script spelling out my name. My heart raced as I opened it. I knew my mother, but still I found myself wishing for the impossible. Instead, I found hope.

The words "for escaping traps" were hastily scrawled on the slip of paper with the bank account she had opened in my name. There was a small scratched-out splotch beside it, the size of a dime. I stared at that splotch, wondering what had been beneath it. A heart? The letter *M*? This, of all things, was the most fitting goodbye from my mother. An ugly celebration of a space that might've held something other than a dark blot.

The dream I'd held—my mother and me on the ferry, the dingy apartment, the space between us closing on the couch until I might rest my head on her shoulder—was gone forever. But that was not the whole of my dream. I also dreamt of a new city falling open to my touch. I dreamt of horizons.

I would not let one version of my dream trap me.

Slowly, I began to plan.

FOR OUR FINAL MORTAL EXPERIENCE, INDIGO WANTED A GRAND graduation party. It was to be a costumed gala, and our whole school was invited. Indigo threw herself into the preparations and on the morning of the celebration, she was too busy to notice when I went to see Tati on my own.

I was lucky Tati was having one of her lucid phases. I stepped into her room and found her crocheting in the dark. A blanket that looked like a pierced and bleeding sunset puddled from the top of the bed and onto the floor. She lifted her head, sniffed at the air.

"Azure," she said, relaxing when she caught my scent. "What is it, child?"

This wasn't my first time alone with Tati. She'd found me in the parlor the first week my belongings were moved into the House of Dreams, and I understood my mother was never coming back. Tati had reached out, her fingertips lightly touching my eyelids.

"You did not open them fast enough," she'd said, her voice thick with grief.

Now I walked to Tati's bedside. My long braid of hair swung against my hip as I moved. I took her hand and placed it on my hair.

"Like a cold winter night," said Tati, smiling a moment before she frowned. I think she had guessed what I meant to do with it, and disapproval slashed her mouth into a grim line. "No."

"Cut it, Tati," I said. "I need to make a sacrifice."

THERE WAS ALWAYS A REVEL IN FAIRY TALES. GRAND SPECTA-cles held for kings and queens, golden tables aching beneath the weight of glossy plums and dripping meats, hunting dogs panting in the halls, pearls crushed underfoot, tender secrets newly hatched and kept warm—for now—in the fat cheeks of lovestruck girls. At its heart, a true revel was nothing more than a gorgeous held breath, a moment where Fate herself pivots on a frail ankle, and destinies snap shut or burst forth when her heel hits the wood. Revels existed to mark thresholds, to coax change. Revels were for endings or beginnings, and tonight I prayed for both.

I would hold my breath and take Indigo's hand. A few strands of my shorn hair lay in a little locket that I planned to drop into the ground as a sacrifice. I'd offer a part of myself as barter for safe passage. Maybe the House wouldn't mourn my loss this way, for part of me would always be here. Then, I would slip through the sea of guests and vanish. I would end us, and in doing so, we would begin anew. Without me, the Otherworld's hold over Indigo would loosen. She would see that we did not need each other's light to exist, that we could be whole unto ourselves.

We could be free.

The House of Dreams did not like my plan though. It whimpered and whined the day I bought my bus ticket and hid it in the Room of Secrets. It did not matter how many times I stroked the stair banister and promised to return.

I chose our costumes from the depths of Tati's closet, two skies hanging on velvet hangers—one was rich cerulean and silver, lace siphoned off the sea, the other was damson dark and smoky, all the edges of dusk cast into silk. I fashioned us a pair of thyrsus staffs, like the ones once borne aloft by Bacchic maenads. I crowned our spears with pinecones and wrapped them round with ribbons and ivy. We wore no jewelry, but we dusted our arms and chests with pulverized pearls. Indigo spritzed herself with perfume. Normally, I didn't wear any, but tonight I opened my hand for the slender glass vial and satin atomizer, wrapping myself in the thick scent of green apples. I tied back the long, curling hair that hung over my breasts with a bone-colored ribbon. The hair was not mine, but Indigo couldn't tell.

I remembered how she stared at me, her eyes so full of love and her voice so tender I almost lost all desire to leave.

"You're happy," she said.

"Of course I am," I said. I wanted to make her smile, so I added: "I'm with you."

Her eyes shone.

Before I went to the party, I visited Tati one last time. I heard her singing before I entered, a shrill tune, mixed with humming and growls. She sniffed the air when I stepped inside, her back straightened against her pillows.

"I have kept your secret safe," she said, rocking back and forth.

And then she began to sing. "*I can smell the sweet meat and the gold trail of fat from the tender lamb . . . I remember what I should not have seen . . . the honey drip and the clasped hands and the shroud of oak.*"

"Tati," I tried again, my chest tightening. "I want you to know that I love you."

All I wanted was to hold her, to lay my cheek against her bony shoulder. She had loved us, and she had fallen on that love as if it were a blade. Abruptly, Tati stopped singing.

Behind me, I heard Indigo coming up the stairs. For all that she spoke of the fae and lightness, she had a heavy, mortal tread. I had already backed away, halfway through the door with my hand on the knob when Tati's head snapped up. Though she was blind, I felt the connection of her gaze as she rasped—

"You should have run faster."

I couldn't tell her that there was no need for her to worry, that already I was vanishing from the House. I closed the door behind me moments before Indigo saw me. Through the wood, I heard Tati sigh:

"I am too late."

GUESTS POURED INTO THE GARDENS OF THE HOUSE OF DREAMS. There hadn't been a party on the premises since Indigo's sixteenth birthday, and curiosity more than anything coaxed our island to answer the invitation.

The gardens were strung with lights. Huge pillars like temple ruins squatted before the linden trees. Marble tables were laden with ice sculptures and small white cakes, pyramids of apples and towers of Champagne formed a glittering wall between the gardens and our Otherworld. At the center, the dance floors looked like a grand reflecting pool and the strobe lights and music tangled with the rhododendrons and lilacs.

I could not say how many people were there. I could feel the air slendered by their bodies, and that was all they were to us, assembled matter that parted when Indigo and I moved through them.

This was my last gift to her. Tonight, we were the god of revels. We raised our thyrsi and touched madness to the stars. A holy mania glazed our classmates' eyes, loosened their mouths with raw wonder, painted their spines in primal hues as they hurled themselves against the music. As the revels stripped off veils and sharpened the light, I finally understood why magic loved us so well. We had it all wrong. It was never about who we were, but what we were—

Young.

Downy-feathered, soft-skinned, milk-teethed young. Un-marked and limpid, so clear-eyed that where adults saw bitterness and shadows, we saw a language that might still be translated into light. We were so young that even our bones still grew, still dreamt, still performed miracles in the daylight. We could fall and not break. We could alchemize music, make it physical, let it touch our unsettled souls. Our youth was so powerful it could not possibly last, or it would consume us whole.

That's why magic kissed our bruises, coddled our hearts, and then sent us on our way. Magic hoped we would carry its echo out into the world, for we were never meant to stay here.

This truth broke my heart, even as I understood it. After all, wonder begets wonder, and to play within its borders forever meant never finding out how far we might truly go on our own. I was caught in the teeth of this truth when Indigo touched my hand.

"I have a present for you," she said. "I've been working on it for ages."

I looked up and realized that we had walked away from the revels and now stood at the stone path. I was ready for this and all that would come later. My bus was leaving soon, my tickets were waiting for me. Around my neck, my ruby-eyed starling key flashed. I felt the softest of brass flutters, as if it wished to take flight.

I followed Indigo into the dark, into the Otherworld, into the realm we had once ruled. I followed her into the shadows of the apple blossoms and the great oak tree, and up the turret where we had spent so many sunlit hours. On the roof, she held out a great floodlight, which illuminated the gnarled trunk and roots of the oak tree. When I beheld what Indigo had planned, I understood Tati's warning.

I FOLLOWED INDIGO INTO THE OTHERWORLD THAT NIGHT.

I did not come out.

Chapter Thirty-Two

THE BRIDEGROOM

I stared at the body in the glass casket.

Disgust and horror reached me, but only on the heels of something far worse, a cold and viscous sense of disappointment. I was, though it repulsed me, annoyed at the sight of the corpse. For that's all it was: a body that had festered in the dark.

I had hoped the body would be beautiful, preserved like some princess in a fairy tale. That she might be lily-necked, with a torrent of black hair, the hard swell of an apple breaking the line of her throat. But what lay within the casket was ugly. It took a full minute for pity to find me.

Strands of black hair clung to the skull. What may have once been a lushly shaped mouth was now a slash of brown. The mottled, threadbare hands clutched a starling key, the twin of the one in my hand. Yellowed bones peered through a rotted dress.

"You must be Azure," I said. "I have heard a great deal about you."

The Otherworld moaned.

I drew away the rest of the clumsily nailed tarp. The scene had been disguised only in the thinnest sense of the word, and I could not help but marvel at Indigo's confidence. She knew that she could not be touched and had not even tried to conceal what she'd done.

"Did you pry into her secrets too?"

I touched the gilt edges of the casket, and the earth underfoot quivered. In my head, another petal of memory peeled back.

This was what the House had promised me. Should I find Azure, then I would know where my brother went. I would know how to follow him. I closed my eyes and reached into the image—

I see a small, wooden casket that smells of pine. I see a tiny plot of artificial grass. I watch my mother from the shadows of the staircase as she takes down the photos, throws away clothes in black trash bags, declares we will never speak of him again.

He's dead. My brother is dead.

I strained my thoughts, wanting some other image to correct me, some memory of having glimpsed his face in the depths of another closet. But this was the only truth. I should have been re-lieved, and yet incompletion haunted me. There was something else here, something that demanded witnessing.

A loud, banging sound made me jerk my hand from the cas-ket. "Get away from her."

I swung my flashlight in the direction of the voice. Indigo was less than ten feet from me. Her speech was slurred. She wa-vered on the spot, still fighting off the effects of the sedative. Tears streamed down her face and a gun trembled in her grip.

I raised my hands slowly.

The flashlight skimmed over her feathered form. She was more beast than beauty. Her eyes were wild and round. She had the look of a creature cornered. She gulped down huge breaths and the feathers of her dress rose and fell like a second skin.

I almost spoke, then snapped my mouth shut at the instinct to tell her a story. It was a Filipino tale of a sky maiden with a winged dress who often bathed with her sisters in a clear pool only to be spied upon by a huntsman. The huntsman stole the sky maiden's dress, and, unable to fly home, she became his wife.

I ached. Even if I ripped the feathered dress off Indigo's skin and hid it in the loose boards of an attic ceiling, I could not keep her. And I did not know what it meant that I had beheld her true form, glimpsed the blood spatter on her muzzle and teeth, and still felt a thread stretched between us.

Was this how Bluebeard's wives felt when he placed his hands around their necks? Did their smile go slack when they realized not who he was, but who *they* were? Mere humans who were exceptionally suited to sacrifice?

"Indigo—"

"Get *away*."

She aimed the gun, flicked off the safety. I leapt aside only to slip in the wet leaves. I crashed into the glass casket. The flashlight fell from my hands, rolling across the glass pane and illuminating the husks of insect shells, the curled, yellow finger bones clasping the starling key that lay on Azure's sunken chest.

I pushed myself up.

"Don't move," she said.

My hands were splayed on the glass. I looked down, staring at the starling key on the corpse. Above me, the wind screamed in the oak. "Is this really what you want, Indigo?"

"Stop speaking."

"This isn't you."

Indigo laughed. "You don't know me."

But her voice broke.

"I thought you—" She stopped. "It doesn't matter. Not anymore."

I was not scared of death, but in those final moments, I felt cheated. I had found Azure, and yet my own memory remained incomplete. I was missing something.

The light slanted across the corpse, catching on the starling necklace. It was still bright, the jewel in its eye shining. Somewhere in the House of Dreams, Tati lay dying, but her singsong voice slipped from her bones and found me here—

Indigo wanted a blue-eyed starling and Azure wanted a red, and if I'd never stopped to look then nobody would be dead.

The starling key on the corpse's chest beheld me with a blue eye.

I lifted my hands off the glass pane.

"What are you doing? I said *don't move*—"

I looked into the face of my wife.

"Azure," I said.

Her arms dropped a fraction.

"Azure, I see you."

Chapter Thirty-Three

AZURE

You never forget the moment when beauty turns to horror.

And at first, all I saw was beauty: the coffin made of glass and silver, its joints a calligraphy of ivy scrollwork and starlings. It was the sort of thing that might be used to display a saint. I could see it in the future, the white quilting within stained and yellow with bodily seepage, the bones untethering from tendons, falling in the cracks between satin and glass. The glass casket would hold it all together.

Forever.

"What is this?"

"My gift," said Indigo, touching my cheek. "This is where we belong, Azure. This is how we leave the mortal world for good. And then we'll be in the Otherworld forever."

My ears were ringing. I had dreamt, for years, that Indigo knew something I didn't. That when she said we would be transformed, she did not mean . . . like *this*.

Indigo stepped toward me. She was as vast as the sky, starstrewn and infinite, her black hair dissolving into the night. Indigo held out the ivory hilt of her father's hunting knife. É'leos. *Mercy.*

Indigo thought the glass casket was her greatest gift. But to me, her greatest gift had been the belief that I might be so much more than what I was. Because of her, I believed I was someone who deserved things, someone for whom destiny itself had fashioned a cozy, star-lined pocket. The sight of the hunting knife cut through all of that.

Around us, the Otherworld wept. The sky trembled with lightning. In the distance, the shrieking laughter of the guests and the harsh flapping of the tents barely registered. The Otherworld's tears were hot on my face.

"What have we done to each other, Indigo?"

I rarely cried. But now, great heaving sobs ripped out of my chest. I wept for the girl we had called Puck. I wept for the boy I wanted to love. I wept for my mother, for Tati, and myself. I wept, the most, for Indigo, for she was lost, and I could not save her from the dark.

"Don't you see?" she said, smiling. "No one will kiss us awake when we fall asleep. We'll be untouched, forever, folded into the roots. We'll have toadstools in our arteries and ant nests in our mouths. We'll sprout roses in our eyes, and we'll be knitted together, and I will never leave you, and you will never leave me—"

She lunged.

The sudden jerk of her body startled me. I had forgotten how fast she could move. When we raced as kids, she always won. The blade blurred in her hand.

I stepped.

I thought of the revels, of Fate pivoting on her ankle, her heel not yet connecting to the wooden floor. Indigo's heel skidded on a rain puddle, flinging her against the stone of the turret. Her gasp was childlike, startled. She arched over the stone, hair streaming behind her, the open mouth of the glass casket far below. The blade clattered to the wood and the rain hit the metal, and I ran to her because I loved her.

I would always love her. Even when she hurt me. Even when she held a blade to my throat. Perhaps especially so, for no one else had ever bothered.

I offered my hand, but Indigo didn't take it. I tried to stop her, but she reached, instead, for the hair that was not mine. She meant to take me over the edge with her so we might fall together, but at that moment, Fate's heel slammed down. The Otherworld's grief was a bellow of thunder as Indigo fell, the false hair I'd taken from Tati streaming from her grasp.

She made no sound, and so I screamed for us both. I screamed until I heard the thud of her skull, and after that I was mute. I held still. I squeezed my eyes shut and opened them again, doing it over and over as if they could reveal another reality, but I was locked in this place.

Cold rain sluiced down the back of my neck. I was exposed now, the chopped edges of my hair clumped together in the rain.

"Hair is memory," Tati had said. "That is a lot of sacrifice, and for what, child? What do you hope to gain by losing all that life?"

I had been quiet. I thought of Indigo and me playing by the pool, hunting for rusalkas in the creek, packing suitcases for the Otherworld and wondering how we would carry Tati's heavy silver samovar across the ends of the world.

"Freedom."

RAIN FILLED INDIGO'S MOUTH. HER EYES WERE OPEN AND STARing. Her hair a spill of ink, pleated around the edge of the gilded casket that had broken her fall. Her body was already half inside. I knew she would not like any sign of sloppiness, and I refused to leave her like this.

Indigo was heavy as I slid her down and arranged the blood-matted hair around her shoulders. I tried to scatter the rose petals on her body, but they were rain crinkled and stuck to my skin, so I wiped my palms down her dress. I folded her hands and closed her eyes, and when I drew back, the small tithing pouch that held the cut strands of my hair was nowhere to be found. The air smelled of Indigo, of apples and salt, and it clung to me.

When all was done, I watched the rain throw diamonds on the glass casket, and then I left. I stumbled on where to go without Indigo. I had wanted an end to us, but I had not wanted this to be the end.

At the gate of the Otherworld, I took off my starling key and locked it behind me. For a while, I stood there, my hand on the iron knob.

I did not understand. I could see, as if through a smoked pane of glass, the things I had yet to feel—the anger that she had left me when I was supposed to have done the leaving, the nauseous shame of my relief that she would never find the backpack and pair of sneakers I had hidden under the basement stairs, the ache that split my heart knowing we would never curl into each other as we read a book, me holding the spine, her turning the pages, a dream of hot chocolate and cakes taking shape at the back of our heads.

I stared through the iron bars at the oak tree, the turret, the sky. The Otherworld had watched and wept and done nothing.

"I thought you loved us," I said, my voice breaking. "Or maybe I just don't understand your love."

A mournful wind shook the trees.

You will.

I DIDN'T KNOW, YET, WHERE I WAS GOING.

I was driven only to be where the Otherworld was not, and so I didn't notice that the revels had finished. I was dimly aware of the absence of guests, the tipped-over tents. Occasionally, glass crunched beneath my feet. A song whose words I didn't know played to a threadbare audience who were either too drunk to move or friends of the immobile and intoxicated.

"Indigo! Hey!"

My stomach pinched. I turned around and saw Alia. She had always been friendly to me, not like some of the other girls who were fake nice and then talked about me and Indigo behind our backs. Alia was moving to New York for film school and to-night she looked like she'd raided the school's stage department. She wore horns in her hair, glitter on her dark arms. When she walked toward me, I kept expecting her to realize I wasn't Indigo. But her eyes remained bright. "Just wanted to thank you for an amazing party! Kinda wish it hadn't taken until the end of senior year to get an invite . . . um, where's Azure?"

I blinked at her. "What?"

"Did she go home already?" asked Alia, rising on tiptoes to look behind me.

I stared at her, confused. Alia's friends called her up ahead. Two of them had their arms around a boy with his head lolled back. Together, they made slow progress toward the exit.

"He doesn't look so good," said Alia, laughing a little. "Any-way, thanks again!"

She turned and fled back toward her friends. I watched her. I almost said: *I am Azure.* But my own name, even in thought, tasted like acid.

A FAINT BUZZING SETTLED INTO MY SKULL AS I ENTERED THE House of Dreams. The House was silent. Even the clocks had stopped. For the first time, the House was mute and distant. I could feel it holding itself apart from me and yet still watching, the way a cat inspects a stranger in its midst.

Wrongness slanted through me. The hairs on the back of my neck prickled as I went up the stairs. Alia's gaze had been so *certain.*

As I climbed the stairs, I reached for all the moments Tati had told me she loved me. They lived in a secret chamber in my bones, and now, before her closed bedroom door, I felt them begin to dissolve. Each time she'd let her hand rest on my scalp, drape her arm around my shoulder, let me breathe the scorched scent of her skin. In a few moments, she would recognize me, and she would smile, and I would confess and watch that smile wither. I'd watch her mouth slouch open, hear her voice unhinge into an animal howl that would last until the police cars came and the flashlights caught on Indigo's teeth and metal circles would clamp down on my wrists.

I opened the door. "Tati?"

She was sitting up in her bed, staring into nothingness. Her eyes were ruined, but her focus sharpened when I entered. She was lucid, and I might've fallen to my knees to have this one last conscious moment of her knowing me, loving me, persist a minute longer. Tati sniffed the air, a muscle in her cheek twitched in distaste.

"I can smell your sins on you, child," she said. "What have you done?"

I went to her, knelt by her bed, and bowed my head. My voice trembled. "Tati, I need to tell you something. It happened when we went to the Otherworld."

Tati shrank against her pillows, her fists balling the covers. She began to shake, and even though her hand lay inches from mine, I didn't touch her. I didn't want to see her revulsion. "There is a heart that has ceased to sing."

"It was an accident, I swear—"

Tears rolled down Tati's brown skin. She sobbed for almost a whole minute before clutching her blankets and nodding. "An accident," she said hoarsely. "I believe you, child. I know you didn't mean to. You couldn't have known, could you? You never meant to do anything wrong."

Tati turned her palm faceup. I couldn't speak. I used to remember my mother on the sidewalks offering me her hand like that. Offering herself to be a living link, that which would mark me and say I belonged to someone. I grabbed Tati's hand, pressed my face into it, and I wept. She sighed, her other hand stroking my head.

"That poor child," said Tati. "She didn't deserve that. I loved her, too, you know, but you are my own and I will always keep you safe."

I cried harder, disgusted by my delight more than my relief. I sometimes dreamt of what would happen if Indigo left and I was Tati's only choice to love. I dreamt of the way she would let me sag against her body, the way the years would pass before she quietly confessed: *I would've chosen you from the start.*

"I will keep your secrets, Indigo," said Tati. "I will keep your secrets until they poison me, but you have to leave. Now. Azure wanted to run away, so that's what we'll tell the world." Tati licked her lips, nodding to herself. "No one will look for her, but you must never come back here. Never. To be honest, child, I am glad for my blindness for I don't know how I could bear to look at you again."

I raised my head slowly. I tried, once more, to say my name, but it was stuck fast. I took a breath and all I smelled were apples. All I smelled was *her*.

"I'm—" I tried. "I am—"

"I know you're sorry," she said. "I am too."

I became grossly aware of all the mechanical parts that let me stand and leave that room—every muscle lifting my bones, every synapse flaring to life, every spurt of blood dancing through my heart's chambers. I was a machine at the mercy of bodily parts no one would recognize as my own.

I slid against Tati's closed door and pulled my knees to my chest. The buzzing in my skull grew louder, and, finally, I understood the Otherworld's love. It had tried to give me and Indigo what we most desired. I closed my eyes, remembering Indigo's frantic, wide-eyed gaze. *I will never leave you and you will never leave me.*

Slowly, I held my hands up to my face. I couldn't remember if they'd always looked like this—etched and pale, the fingers small, not quite stubbed and not quite slender—or whether they were secretly Indigo's. Had she been fitted over me like a shroud? Was that what had made me so deserving of forgiveness, of love?

I didn't know back then how this question would come to haunt me. How I would wonder whether being denied myself was the greatest kindness the world could have shown me because then, and only then, might I hold some semblance of love.

Alone in the hallway, I touched the ends of my hair. I had bartered its length and all its memories for freedom, but I had been careless in the wording. I was left with everything and nothing. I was free and forever trapped. I was a multitude of blues.

I was many things, but I was not Azure, and perhaps I never would be again.

Chapter Thirty-Four

THE BRIDEGROOM

The breaking of a spell is nothing more than a dislocation of light. What could not be seen before can now be glimpsed in a wealth of radiance. The moment I uttered my wife's true name, I looked through the sudden glow of that broken spell and saw my brother.

He was holding my right hand. My left hand was sprained from when father stepped on my wrist. Before us, the doors of the cedar armoire lay open. The winter coats stood wary and dark as December trees.

We were going to escape forever.

I waited until midnight and carried my brother down the stairs. I told him to pick out his favorite sweets, to pack his best toys and to wrap them in an old kitchen towel. He was quiet, grinning at our new game. He was too young to remember yesterday. He had not been hit, only grabbed by the scruff of his neck like a kitten and hoisted into the air before being dropped. When that happened, he'd looked to me, and I made myself laugh, and this told him there was no reason to cry.

"Go inside," I said, pointing into the dark of the armoire. "I'll find you and we'll go to Faerie. We'll spend every day outside."

He threw his pudgy arms around my waist, and I held him back: "We'll always be together."

When he was safely in the dark, I went to gather my own things. But halfway up the stairs, the light flickered on. I was caught.

Father dragged me back down the stairs. My knees slammed on each step. He shouted. I saw his arm raised and then I saw nothing.

I drifted asleep. I dreamt of snow. Downstairs, in the sweet cedar lull of the armoire, my brother fumbled for air and did not find it. His inhaler had been in my backpack, and lay mute beside me while he waited for me, his face turning blue. That night, I dreamt that when I opened my eyes, we would be running together under trees that grew moons and beneath a sky rippled with rainbows. But when I opened my eyes, he was gone, and I had been left behind.

"GO."

A ragged voice. I looked up and beheld Indigo. *Azure.* A split being. The gun dangled from her hand.

"Go now before I change my mind," she said wearily. "Run."

I stumbled through the leaves as the Otherworld released me. I limped to the gate, but I could go no farther. I was a mended limb, unfamiliar to this new distribution of memory, and could not remember how I once walked through the world. I stared out the gate, heard the rush of water, the soft tread of a pack of tomorrows moving through the gloaming to find me. I would not survive on my own.

Once, I had let someone I loved go into the dark without me. I did not know if I could survive that again. And so, against the instruction of a thousand stories, I turned my head and looked back.

IN THE END, A FAIRY TALE IS NOTHING MORE THAN A SENSE OF hope. Hope lures and tricks. It tempts with shining thrones, exquisite nectars, and loving arms. It whispers to us that we are extraordinary. Exempt. Thus lured, we follow its path. Sometimes we are led to riches. Other times, we are led astray. But this hope never hides its shape, and for its honesty we reach for it and pull its sweet and stinking furs up to our chins, for to live without it means living without magic.

I held this truth in my bones as I limped back to the woman who was still my wife. She did not disappear. She did not dissolve when I touched her shoulder and offered my hand.

She startled, still kneeling in the dark with death in her lap. Her feathers were soaked. Even from where I stood, I caught the scent of her, washed true by the rain. Honeysuckles.

"You came back."

I nodded.

"Why?"

There were a dozen reasons, none of which I could easily articulate. I was thinking of her pulse beneath my fingertips and my brother's small feet vanishing into the armoire. Of the artless way the body had been covered, the plea therein a hope not simply to be discovered but punished. I wondered at the way she had devised to be hurt. Perhaps she thought she deserved it. Just as I had expected her to leave me for the simple reason that I could not fathom a world in which I was not worth being left.

"It's not you that I wish to leave behind."

When I looked at her, I saw all the people we had been to each other. Beast, maiden, lover, god: a thousand iterations. I held out my hand farther.

It was dim all around us, but we could clearly see the only future left to us. A wilderness without walls, a place where pointed silences and unanswered questions could not survive. We shrank to behold this future so nakedly, but we did not run. I watched as she took my hand, her grip slippery.

Slowly, silently, we made our way out of the dark.

Chapter Thirty-Five

AZURE

My husband finds me on the porch of the House of Dreams and hands me a cup of tea. He's brought a candelabra and the light flickers weakly on the handsome planes of his face as he sets it on the ground between us.

I take him in—the way his tall frame stoops through doors, the gold of his hair, the ink smudges on those slender, scholarly hands. His hand twitches on his leg, and I am both surprised and relieved he wants to touch me.

When we touch, I am my most honest with him. When we move together, I try to show him the truth of myself. He loves *her*, but when I step into the role of a dozen different women, I imagine these are the moments when he can see through all the costumes.

"Azure," he says, and I try not to flinch.

I let myself meet his gaze and I cannot breathe. When he looks at me, the light in his eyes is soft. And it is for me.

For a long time, I've been waiting for judgment. For some god to hurl a lightning bolt at me or strike me dead. I wonder now if I've been looking for gods in all the wrong places. There is a bruised recognition in his gaze and that—this singular truth that

I am not alone—expands the universe in a way that faith never has.

"Azure," he says again, and I can tell that he is testing out this name's shape against his teeth. "Tell me your story."

Azure. It has been years since that was my name. Years since I remembered how to answer to it. I tried to say the name aloud to Tati, but there was nothing left of her in that body.

My husband reaches for my hand. Our wedding rings touch. I have never before considered what it means to have a good marriage. I thought it was finding intriguing and attractive company. But maybe it is about finding someone whose heart is like a mirror, whose love can make you stand the sight of yourself.

I look into his eyes, aware that we are starting down a path I had not envisioned. I don't know where it ends, but I know this is not the first time we will sit like this, with our hands intertwined, the space between us aching to be remade by every confession we have folded within the dark of ourselves.

I take a deep breath, and I speak:

"The first thing you have to understand is that I loved her."

EPILOGUE

Long ago, there lived a king and queen in a house of dreams, and there they quietly tended to their ghosts and knew all the shadows by name. The house was vast. Sometimes the king or queen got lost. When that happened, they would hold each other's hands and say—

It was once upon a time.

That was all it was. A prayer and a promise in one. A single page composed of the past.

Eventually, what was *once* softened to a palimpsest of lost words and snowfall, starlings and sparrow wings and blue ink. In this way, the king and queen crafted a tale of their own.

In the end, they lived.

ACKNOWLEDGMENTS

Thank you to my editor, Jessica Williams, whose brilliance and precision unearthed what this book wanted to be. To Julia Elliott, whose enthusiasm and sharp insight made this editorial process intensely rewarding. Thank you to my agent, Thao Le, who gave this story a home here, and Andrea Cavallaro, who gave this story a home abroad. To Sarah Simpson-Weiss, thank you for wrangling hours so I can write tales.

Thank you to Brittani Hilles, D.J. Desmyter, and everyone at the William Morrow publicity, sales, audio, and marketing teams who helped guide this story into the light, gave it new form, and delivered it into the hands of readers. Thank you to Amy R. for the thoughtful sensitivity read.

This book came together at a time when I needed friends and family most. To Niv, Bismah, McKenzie, Cara-Joy, Cali, Nirvi, and Marta—your friendship is a treasure. To Renee, Lemon, JJ, Jen Cervantes, Katie Webber, Evie Dunmore, Shannon Chakraborty, Sabaa Tahir, Ayana Gray, Lyra Selene, Sanjena Sathian, Stephanie Garber, and Holly Black—I would be lost without your wisdom, kindness, feedback, and friendship. To Ali, Kaitlin, MeiLin, Hailey, Natasha, and Katie, thanks for indulging my nonsense and keeping me grounded.

To my family, you know who you are. Your love and support is a light. And last, to Aman, without whom this story would not exist. Your love lets me look into mirrors and smile.

ABOUT THE AUTHOR

ROSHANI CHOKSHI is the award-winning author of the *New York Times* bestselling series the Star-Touched Queen, the Gilded Wolves, and *Aru Shah and the End of Time*, which *Time* magazine named one of the Top 100 Fantasy Books of All Time. She lives in Atlanta, Georgia. This is her adult debut.